Under Ground

By Linda Shenton Matchett

To

The 127 certified female war correspondents during WWII

who risked life and limb to get the story

Chapter One

At the familiar whistle of a V1 bomb, Ruth Brown dove under her bed, praying this was not her day to die. Seconds later, the explosion tore away half the house, exposing the tiny room she shared with her best friend, Varis Gladstone, to the cold, damp dawn. A second hit, and the bed collapsed on top of her. Stunned, she lay under the debris. Bits of glass, wood, and plaster rained down upon the mattress and floor. Her ears rang, and dust filled her throat.

"Ruth!" Varis's voice came from a distance.

Ruth coughed and gagged.

"Where are you? Ruth!" Footsteps thundered toward her then the sweet release of pressure when the mattress was lifted away. Varis shoved the wooden bed slats aside and leaned close. "Can you hear me? Are you all right? I thought I'd lost you." Tears streamed down her face.

Ruth eased herself to a sitting position, wincing at the pain that peppered her body.

Varis draped an arm around her shoulder. "Can you stand? We should evacuate the house. It could fall at any moment."

"I think so." Ruth climbed to her feet and took an inventory of her injuries. Nothing seemed to be broken. She shivered and turned to her closet. "Let me get a jacket. Then I need to find my typewriter."

Varis frowned and shook her head. "We need to leave *now.*"

"It will just take a few minutes. We'll be fine. The bomb was a probably a one off, some Jerry who got lost on his way home hadn't used all his armament."

"I'm not worried about more bombs. The house could collapse." Varis's trembling voice was scratchy, from dust or screaming Ruth didn't know.

Ruth had done some screaming herself. Even after living six months in London and experiencing the explosion in Ireland, she couldn't get used to the horror of a falling bomb with its high-pitched, ear-splitting whistle and the tearing sound it made as it rushed toward them from the sky. The ground shook and shuddered with the impact, followed by the crash of masonry as houses and buildings toppled. The pervasive smell of gas mingled with the ash from crackling fires.

Shaking the memories from her mind, she rose. They picked their way through the ruins and out the front door that sagged on its hinges. "I thought I could keep you safe if we lived outside the city, Varis."

"I knew the dangers when I chose to come to England." With a crooked grin, she gestured to the broken plaster, boards, and debris shrouding their belongings. "Besides, who else would help you sort through this mess to find your precious Smith Corona?"

UNDER GROUND 2

"No one but you, that's for sure."

"We need to collect our clothes, too. This outfit is about done."

"Mine, too." Ruth stuck a finger through the gaping tear in her trousers. With smudges, stains, and holes, her blouse had fared no better.

"First, help me move the sofa. I think your typewriter was on the table next to it."

The pair climbed over a massive oak tree that lay on its side, scorched and half buried by the fallen chimney.

Ruth stood at one end of the couch. "On three."

Varis gripped her end and nodded.

"One...two...three!"

They rolled the couch onto its side flinging dust into the air. Ruth's machine sat on the ground intact with a sheet of paper still in the roller. Ruth giggled at the sight, and Varis soon joined her. Laughing uncontrollably, their merriment quickly turned to sobs. Tears cut rivulets through the ochre-colored dirt on their faces as they clung to each other and wept. Minutes passed, and their cries abated to whimpers and then the occasional hiccupped sigh.

Ruth spoke first. "This is awful. I don't know what I'd do without you, Varis."

"You'd do fine, but thanks for saying that. I feel the same about you. I thank God every day for our friendship." She gave a tremulous smile. "Even if you did drag me over here to get bombed out."

"At least your first month here was relatively uneventful."

Varis's eyes danced. "If you call finding my way to work and back with no street signs in blackout conditions, learning the difference between a shilling and a pound, and creating meals out of canned foods uneventful."

"I do! Now, let's see what else we can salvage."

Varis nodded. "All right, but let's be quick about it." She turned to sort through a pile of rubble next to the couch, and Ruth tackled the pieces of their broken dresser searching for undergarments and socks for each of them. While she worked, she could hear Varis praying for the families affected by the bomb. Ruth had been so intent on the destruction of her own place she hadn't given a thought to anyone else. She loved how Varis spoke to God as if He were sitting right next to her. Ruth hadn't always thought that way. She had blamed her sister Jane's death on Him. Blamed Pearl Harbor and a host of other evils on Him as well.

But that had changed thanks to her brother. He had shown her that life was about choices, many of which were outside God's plans. Jane made choices that resulted in her getting killed. Chip helped Ruth see God's hand in their lives despite the pain of losing their sister. He had also helped her find Jane's murderer. It had been a bittersweet discovery. Jane was still dead, but at least they knew who had done it and why.

Ruth took a deep breath. Her fingertips were raw, and her back ached from moving dozens of bricks and countless pieces of wood scattered on top of their belongings. Weary to the bone, she leaned against the wall still standing.

With a crack, the plaster gave way. Arms flailing, Ruth reached out for something, anything, to hold on to prevent her from falling. Enveloped in fabric as she fell into a closet full of clothes and fought to breathe. Blindly, her fingers scrabbled for and then caught the first garment she could reach, but the item slid off its hanger, and she landed with a thud under a pile of blouses, skirts, and trousers. She coughed, and her ribs sharply protested. Bruised and aching, she shifted to take the weight off her hip. The floorboards snapped, and she plunged into a dank hole.

"Ruth! Ruth! Are you all right? Where are you?"

"I'm down here. Under the floor." Something jabbed her in the back. "Ouch. Bring a flashlight. I need to see how to get out of here."

A murky ray of light cut through the darkness. Ruth screamed and leapt to her feet, brushing away the cobwebs that clung to her and a large human skeleton lying in pieces on the dirt. Several articles of clothing from the closet above were in a lump beside it. She shuddered and looked at Varis who goggled at the pile of bones. "Who could it be?"

"Whoever it is has been down here a long time. Only his shoes are left." With a shaking hand, Varis pointed to the skeleton's legs that disappeared into the tops of crumbling, black leather boots.

Ruth grit her teeth, rubbed her arms, and finished clearing away the sticky fibers. Her reporter's curiosity surfaced, and she reached toward Varis. "Let me see the light. Maybe there's something down here that will tell us who he is."

Eyes wide, Varis leaned into the opening and handed Ruth the flashlight. "Be careful."

Sweeping the beam back and forth, Ruth searched the dim recesses. Seeing nothing, she turned her gaze to the body. Its arms were flung out to the side as if he, too, had fallen backward into the hole. The right arm was splintered where she had landed. Legs splayed, the boots lay on their sides. They looked like her brother's military issue, so she crouched down for a closer inspection. The laces were gone and the soles worn down, but they were definitely army boots. Two small pieces of paper stuck out the top.

She pulled out the scraps, trying to avoid touching either the bones or the leather. Photographs. A quick glance showed identical prints of four men in uniform.

"You there!"

The crunch of footsteps approaching. Varis whirled toward the voice, Ruth stuffed one of the pictures in her pocket and dropped the other next to the body.

Varis stood, and Ruth scrambled out of the hole. An Air Raid Precaution warden scowled at them.

"What are you doing?"

Hands on her hips, Ruth returned the look. "We're searching for our personal effects after the bombing. I fell through the floor!"

The man's face changed to one of concern. "Are you hurt?"

"I'm fine, but you'll need to call the police. There's a skeleton down there."

"What?"

"See for yourself."

He peered over the edge, and his eyes bulged. "Well, I'll be. Been there a while, hasn't he?" The warden motioned them away. "Wait over there. I'll take care of this." He walked toward the call box across the street.

Ruth muttered to Varis. "I found a photo. Wait till you see it. Too bad I didn't have more time. Who knows what else we'd find?"

"I know that look, Ruth. This is a matter for the police. They don't need your help."

"Who said anything about helping the police? I'm a journalist, Varis, and there's some kind of story here."

Chapter Two

Detective Inspector Trevor Gelson stepped out of the police car at the bomb scene and buttoned his camel-colored trench coat against the damp wind. Sergeant Sean Phillips climbed out behind him as a uniformed officer clambered toward them over the wreckage, bricks, and shattered plaster shifting and snapping under his feet.

The man snapped a salute. "Sirs! Follow me. The victim is over here."

Trevor trailed the bobby, his eyes absorbing the devastation. Most of the house still remained. It appeared as if a giant knife had sliced off a portion, leaving the rest intact. Where rooms once stood, twisted wood lay on top of crumpled furniture. Clothing was strewn throughout, and shards of glass glittered in the emerging sunshine. The murmur of the crowd drifted toward him. Held back by a pair of ARP workers, the throng craned their necks to catch a glimpse of the activity. Two women stood near a tilted letter box speaking with one of his men. The taller of the pair gestured as she spoke, hands punctuating her words. He glanced at the sergeant and nodded toward the women. "Phillips, see what you can find out."

"Yes, sir."

Arriving at the splintered hole in the floor, he peered inside. A yellowed skeleton stared back at him. Trevor lowered himself into the opening, "Don't you worry about a thing. I'll find who did this to you." Drawing out his notebook, he began to catalog the scene.

A thin layer of plaster dust covered the moist soil under his shoes. Several pieces of rumpled women's clothing lay next to the skeleton who had several broken bones. The injuries must have happened during the bombing from the looks of the jagged white edges. The straw-colored skull was misshapen. He leaned closer to study the spiderweb of cracks along the left temple. Whoever this was had been dead—or almost—when he'd been dumped into the small cavity. Decayed bits of dark green cloth clung to the bones, and the poor soul's boots were still on his feet. Trevor cast his gaze about and spied a yellowed scrap of paper nearby. He plucked it from the ground and held it toward the light streaming from above.

Hmm. A photograph of four men in uniform—doughboys, if his guess was right. Arms draped across each other's shoulders, they mugged for the camera. They stood before the mouth of a cave, packages and crates scattered throughout the scene. In the background, a small statue graced the top of one of the boxes. A hill sprinkled with scrub brush rose up behind the cavern. Two trees with weeping leaf-filled branches towered over the men on either side. The front end of a jeep peeked into the edge of the picture. Trevor sighed. The photo could have been taken anywhere.

He turned the image over and brushed away the dirt that clung to the back. Faded writing appeared. Trevor squinted at the scrawl, shifting the photo back and forth to capture the light. No good. He could only pick out a letter here and there. He'd check it later. Tucking it into his notebook, he sifted through the skirts and blouses to see if anything was hidden underneath, then he perused the rest of the area. Nothing. Reaching up, he hoisted himself to the floor above.

The police photographer waited to memorialize the scene on film, and the medical officer loitered close by. They moved past him and scrambled into the hole. Trevor walked toward Phillips, who was still interviewing the women. He smiled and briefly lifted his brown fedora when they looked toward him.

Trevor stopped for a moment as his gaze rested on the willowy brunette. Even in her disheveled state, she was a striking woman. Her pleated trousers were torn and muddy, her tailored blouse wrinkled and stained. A riot of shoulder-length curls surrounded her smooth oval face, and deep chocolate-colored eyes sparkled against her fair complexion. Her petite friend looked childlike in comparison. He schooled his features and bowed slightly.

"Good afternoon. I'm Detective Inspector Trevor Gelson."

"I'm Ruth Brown. This is my friend Varis Gladstone."

"You're Americans?"

She nodded. "I'm here with the Associated Press. Varis works at the embassy."

"Awfully young for that, aren't you?"

Miss Brown drew herself up and squared her shoulders. "Not really. Are you here to investigate us or the murder of that poor man?"

"How do you know it's a murder?"

"Most people don't bury their dead in the floor."

"Quite right." He cleared his throat and continued, "You're the one who found him?"

"Yes. I fell through the floor on top of…it…him. That's why he looks a little mangled." She gave a small shiver.

He searched her face for a moment. "I know you've been speaking with my sergeant, but would you be kind enough to answer a few more questions?"

"Of course. Will we be allowed to continue searching for our personal items?"

"Not today. This is a crime scene now."

"But…"

Trevor held up a hand. "However, we will do our best to collect what we need in the next day or two. Then if the ARP says you may return…"

Miss Gladstone laid a hand on Miss Brown's arm and smiled at Trevor. "That will be fine, Detective Inspector Gelson. We appreciate your efforts."

Miss Brown's mouth set in a thin line. "What else would you like to know?"

Pencil poised over his pad, Trevor asked, "Did you see anything unusual?"

"Other than the skeleton?"

He looked up to see her grinning at him, eyes twinkling. He gave her a wry smile in return. "Yes, other than the skeleton."

"There was a photo." She swiped at her arms. "And lots of spiderwebs."

"We found the picture. Anything else?"

She shook her head. "I wasn't down there very long before the warden came by."

"How long have you been in England?"

"Six months. I got here just before Eisenhower."

"What do you think of our fair country?"

"I love it."

"Even in its dilapidated condition?"

"Especially so. That's why I invited my friend Varis to join me. I knew she'd love it, too. The people have been so warm. The hills and forests are lovely, and the sense of history simply envelopes me."

"An Anglophile, Miss Brown?"

She shrugged and scraped windblown strands from her face. When she did so, he caught a faint floral scent.

"What sorts of stories do you cover for the wire service?"

"My job is to put a face on this war for our readers in the US. Even after Pearl Harbor, many folks don't understand why we're in Europe.

They expect us to fight the war against the Japs. They need to see we're all in this together."

"Very commendable." He scrutinized her face. She seemed to be holding back. "Are you sure there isn't anything else you're forgetting to tell me?"

"Such as?"

"Anything you would have seen or heard."

"No, nothing. I leaned against the wall, and the next thing I knew, I was falling backward through it. Then the floor gave way, and I landed on top of him. I saw the photo, then the warden came by."

Trevor handed her a small card. "If you think of anything else, please contact me. The warden can help you get in touch with the housing officer. Once you're settled, let me know how I may reach you."

"You're very kind. Varis has connections through the embassy. Someone there can help us find a place. And you can always reach me through her."

"Good day." He touched the brim of his hat before turning away. She's leaving something out. She'd met his eyes when she spoke, but there was more to what happened than she let on. He'd bet a week's wages. Maybe he didn't believe her because she was a reporter. They couldn't be trusted. Always trying to find a story and protect their sources. She was probably no different. Too bad. She was an attractive woman. And intelligent, too. He smiled at the thought. Bah! Who was he kidding? An

American reporter. The two of them had about as much in common as a flea and an elephant.

He waved away the thoughts and made his way over the uneven ground to the hole.

The medical officer emerged from below and brushed the dirt from his jacket. He looked up as Trevor drew near.

"Trevor, how goes it?"

"You tell me, Christopher."

"This could be an interesting one. I'll know more once I do the post mortem, but it's most certainly a male, and I'd say he probably wasn't over twenty-five or thirty years old. Did you see the cracks on the skull? That's probably how the poor bloke died. But like I said, I'll know more later."

"How much later?"

"Two or three days."

"I don't suppose you could rush it."

Christopher peered over dark horn-rimmed glasses perched on the end of his nose. "Some of us do actually celebrate the holidays, Trevor. You should try it."

"How long has he been there?"

"Avoiding the subject, eh? Fine. Hard to say for sure but maybe twenty years." He wagged his finger. "Now stop trying to get my report before I finish my investigation." He glanced toward the women. "Surely you have more questions for those lovely ladies. Or some villains to hunt down."

Trevor looked at Miss Brown and her friend picking their way through the debris before meandering away. "I'm quite finished with the ladies, and I can't begin my hunt till I get your report."

Christopher snorted a laugh. "Don't get sullen with me, *Detective Inspector* Gelson. It doesn't become you, and we've been at this together for too long for me to fall prey to your attempts to manipulate me. Go spend time with your father."

"Thanks for the advice *Doctor* Ledger."

The doctor clapped Trevor on the back before reaching down to collect his black leather bag. He snatched the glasses from his face and dropped them into his front jacket pocket. He waved his hand and climbed into his vehicle. "Happy Christmas, Trevor. Give my best to your dad."

Trevor shook his head. The holidays only served as a roadblock to getting on with the case. Except for those businesses producing for the war, most others would be closed or short staffed. He surveyed the scene. Some of the men were packing it in, and the crowd was beginning to disperse.

Now would be a good time to start knocking on doors to see if anyone had lived here since the last war. Where to start? He glanced across the street. A curtain fell back into place in the house huddled between piles of rubble. "I know exactly where to start."

Chapter Three

Ruth sat up in the bed and stretched her arms over her head. She leaned over and opened the blackout curtain. Another dreary day greeted her. The problem with being on an island in the middle of an ocean was all the mist and fog that constantly rolled in.

She looked at Varis in the other bed and smiled. Balled up under the covers, Varis's face was hidden under her thick mane of hair. She snored softly.

Muted voices and footsteps could be heard from elsewhere in the house. Varis had called one of her friends from the embassy, and the woman immediately offered to put them up. She and her husband, who was also on the diplomatic staff, had three children they sent back to the States when the war began.

Varis pawed the hair away from her face and sighed heavily. She met Ruth's eyes with a groggy smile.

Ruth waggled her fingers. "Merry Christmas, sleepyhead."

"Merry Christmas." Varis untangled herself and pulled the blankets up to her chin. "Is everyone else awake?"

"I heard noise from downstairs. We should join them, but I was enjoying the quiet." She cocked her head. "What will your family be doing today?"

Varis grinned. "It will be utter mayhem. My brothers try to act nonchalant, but they're always awake before dawn, and they make just enough noise to disturb the rest of us. Once they've torn through the packages, Mother will cook a huge breakfast of ham, eggs, pancakes, and biscuits. Makes my mouth water thinking about it."

"Sounds delicious."

"What about your folks?"

"My parents probably spent the night at Chip's place, so they could be there when the twins wake up. They'll spoil them rotten with too many gifts, then Mother will help Fran in the kitchen. It's usually a big plate of cinnamon rolls and fresh bread, but I don't know about this year. I've lost track of what they're rationing at home. Can they still get flour?"

"I'm not sure."

Lost in memories of past Christmases, they sat, wordless. Moments later, a knock on the door broke the silence.

"Merry Christmas, girls. I know you're awake. We heard your voices."

"Merry Christmas, Louise. We'll be right down."

They quickly took turns in the bathroom and soon descended into the dining room. An earthy scent emanated from the pine boughs Louise had draped across the mantel and on top of the sideboard. Scarlet ribbons were woven through the branches, and a Hummel nativity set was nestled among the greenery. An ivory-colored tablecloth covered the table, on top of which a trio of burgundy pillar candles clustered amid some greens.

Ruth pointed to the empty manger. "Where is baby Jesus? Did he get broken?"

Louise's husband, Rick, held up the minute figure. "We always wait until Christmas morning to add Him to the crèche. Would you like the honor?"

Ruth hesitated. "Are you sure?"

He nodded. "We would love for you to do it."

She took the porcelain statue from him and tenderly placed it into the tiny manger. Her heart swelled at the vision of the sleeping infant. She stroked the smooth surface of its face. "This is an exquisite set. Where did you get it?"

Louise picked up one of the shepherds. "In Germany. Rick's first post was at the American embassy in Berlin. The purchase was a real splurge, since we were scraping to get by on his starting wages. But it was before the boys were born, so we went without a few things to put money aside each week. We bought a piece at a time. It took quite a while, but we've never regretted it." She returned the piece into place and smiled at the group. "Gifts or breakfast?"

Rick rubbed his stomach. "Breakfast. I'm starving."

Louise laughed. "You're always hungry. But I agree. Let's eat first. How about if you slice the bread and make the toast?" She turned to Ruth and Varis. "Can you two set the table while I make quick work of the eggs?"

Several minutes later, the group sat in front of a steaming platter of fluffy scrambled eggs and lightly browned bread. They joined hands, and Rick asked the blessing.

"Thank You, Father, for Your generosity and grace. Thank You for keeping us safe during this terrible time of war." His voice broke. "We miss our loved ones but know You are watching over them. Help us in our daily walk to live only for You. Thank You for the food You have provided. We don't take it for granted. We love You. In the name of Your precious Son, Jesus, amen."

Rick reached for Varis's plate. "The egg dish is heavy. Why don't I serve everyone?"

"That's very kind. Thank you."

"My pleasure." He distributed the food, and they began to eat. Music from the radio drifted in from the living room and mixed with the sound of silverware on the china plates.

After several minutes, Rick laid down his fork and leaned back with a sigh. "Delicious as usual, Louise. I'm going to live."

She gave him a playful pat on the arm. "Like there was any risk of you dying of starvation. You never miss a meal."

"Not if I can help it." He turned to Ruth and Varis. "How about you, ladies? Did you get enough?"

Varis sighed. "Plenty."

Ruth downed the last of her water then dabbed her mouth with her napkin. "It was marvelous. Thank you."

Rick smiled. "Excellent. Let's adjourn to the living room, shall we?"

Varis picked up her plate and reached for Ruth's. "What about the dishes?"

He shooed them away and stacked the plates. "I've got this covered. You go relax, and I'll join you in a jiffy."

They wandered into the cozy parlor and sank into the overstuffed chairs.

Ruth looked over her shoulder at Rick then back at Louise. "You're so lucky, Louise. Not too many men are willing to help in the kitchen."

Louise laughed. "Luck has nothing to do with it, my friends. It took a lot of hard work. And the Lord."

"What do you mean?"

"The first ten years of our marriage were different. Rick grew up with his mother doing all the household chores. His father would come home and read the paper or work in his office. He was very remote with his family. So that's how Rick behaved. I tried to get him to pitch in, and he'd sometimes help if asked, but it was a constant battle."

Ruth cocked her head. "What changed?"

"I was out walking one night, and I passed a church. The doors were open, and the music was captivating. It drew me inside. The building was jammed with people, but the folks in the last pew shifted to make room for me, so I stayed. The singing went on for a long time." She sighed. "It was wonderful. Then it was time for the sermon. The preacher stood and began to speak. I was mesmerized. Everyone else must have been, too, because you could hear a pin drop. He spoke with such passion about Jesus—not like those preachers who scowl and shout and pound the pulpit—but with excitement. His face glowed, and his eyes shone. After the service I asked how I could become a Christian. I came home and told Rick about it. He was skeptical. Said he was a good man and didn't need church, but if I wanted to go he wouldn't stop me. I was so disappointed. I wanted him to join me."

Rick entered the room and stood behind Louise with his hand on her shoulder. "I was stubborn back then. But I watched Louise and could see a difference in her. It intrigued me. She was gracious and loving when we married, but after she became a Christian, there was more depth to her. She was so content. Anyway, Christmas came, and she asked me to accompany her to church. She said I didn't have to give her any other gifts that year. Sounded easy enough, so I went."

His Adam's apple bobbled as he swallowed. "The man laid it out so simply. He made me realize there was a huge hole in my life. I could hardly wait to become a Christian. It changed my whole life. I couldn't get enough of reading the Bible. Then I discovered the fifth chapter of Ephesians that talked about how husbands were to love their wives, enough to give up their lives for them. The pastor helped me see it also meant figuratively and on a daily basis. Putting her first. I've been helping around the house ever since. The best part is that it gives us more time together."

Ruth grinned. "Marriage might not be so bad if I could find a man like you, Rick."

"Louise will tell you it's not always roses, Ruth, but we work hard at getting it right." He chuckled. "Marriage is not for the faint of heart."

The group laughed, and Varis said, "Thanks for telling us about coming to faith. It's quite a story."

He rubbed his hands. "You're welcome. But enough seriousness. It's time for the goods. I'll be St. Nicholas." He moved to the brightly decorated stack of boxes. Everyone had done something different to compensate for the lack of wrapping paper. Louise used fabric, and Rick painted pictures directly onto the boxes. Ruth and Varis covered theirs with pages torn from old magazines.

Rick announced each name and distributed the presents with a flourish. They took turns opening the presents, and everyone "oohed" and "aahed."

Louise sighed. "I hope the children received our gifts. I sent them home in August."

Varis rose and hugged her. "You must miss them very much."

"We do, but it's much safer for them to be in the States. It was a terribly difficult decision, but we felt that's what the Lord wanted us to do."

Rick squeezed her hand. "We'll try to get a line through later today."

She gave him a shaky smile. "I didn't mean to put a damper on Christmas."

"Maybe this will pick you up. I've saved the best for last." He reached behind his chair and drew out a small brown paper bag. He wiggled his eyebrows up and down and made a show of digging into the bottom of the sack as if it were quite deep.

Louise wiped the tears from her face. "This had better be good after all the showmanship."

"I think you'll be pleased." He pulled out an orange with a flourish.

Varis clapped her hands. "Rick, it's beautiful!"

"I can't remember the last time I've seen an orange," Ruth said.

"There's more where that came from." He tossed the fruit to his wife and pulled out two more that he passed to Ruth and Varis before withdrawing the last one for himself.

"Where did you get them?"

Rick winked. "I have my sources."

"They must have been quite dear."

"Actually, they didn't cost a thing. They were shipped over by the Red Cross for embassy families."

Ruth held the fragrant, dimpled rind to her nose and took a deep breath. "I can't decide whether to eat it immediately, or save it and savor the anticipation."

Louise nodded. "I know what you mean. How about if we do a bit of both? If we share two now, we can save the others for later or another day."

Rick smacked his lips together. "Excellent idea. And while we eat, Ruth can tell us what's going on with that skeleton of hers."

"There's not much to tell."

He leaned toward her. "Maybe not now, but you're not one to let something like this alone. Am I right?"

Ruth face heated. "Am I that easy to read?"

"No, but you're a top-notch reporter, and this could be intriguing. What are your plans to dig out the story?" He gave a wry grin. "No pun intended."

They all groaned, and Ruth opened her purse to retrieve the yellowed photograph. She passed it to Rick. "My first job will be to find out the identity of these men. One of them has to be the dead man."

"You think so?" He handed the picture to Louise.

"It's a strong possibility. If not, there's got to be some connection. Why were there two copies of the same picture? Why were they tucked into his boot? Was he hiding them?" Ruth took the worn picture from Louise and flipped it over. "There are names on the back. Not very readable, but maybe with a magnifying glass or a microscope I could pick out the letters on the back and get a better view of what's on the front." She shrugged. "That's my plan, anyway."

Varis pointed to the photo. "It's a murder inquiry, not a story. It's bad enough you took this from the crime scene. You need to leave the investigation to the professionals."

"Who said anything about getting involved in the investigation? I just want to know who the guy is."

"Uh-huh."

Rick sat back and crossed his legs. "Varis is right. You probably shouldn't have taken the photo. Will you give it back?"

"Of course. But I want to examine it first. DI Gelson already has a copy." She warmed at the thought of seeing the handsome detective to return the photo then waved away the thought. "I wonder where I can get a microscope."

Rick stood and walked to the sideboard. He pulled the top drawer out and dug through the contents that rattled and banged as he pushed them back and forth. "Ah-ha! Here it is." He held up a battered magnifying glass. "Will this be of any use?"

Chapter Four

Trevor looked at the wooden clock on the mantle. Striking four o'clock, its somber tones joined the rain thrumming against the window. Rain was expected this time of year, but a white Christmas would have been a nice change. He hovered over the teapot waiting for the tea to steep. The dreary morning drizzle had escalated into an angry, shrieking storm, and the chill seeped through his sweater to his bones.

Bones. Skeleton. Even though it was Boxing Day tomorrow, he would contact Christopher to see if the man could be nudged into starting his autopsy. Trevor fingered the photo in his pocket. After tea, he'd study it.

Insistent knocking penetrated his thoughts. Who would be out on this dreadful afternoon? He turned from the table to see his father open the door to a drenched Mrs. Cookson, the elderly widow next door. Buttoned into a bright yellow slicker, she clutched a cloth-wrapped bundle. His father stepped back, and she scurried inside. Rivers of water coursed down the coat onto the floor.

"It's a fright, isn't it?" She held out the fragrant lump, and Trevor moved forward to take it. She shook herself out of the dripping coat and draped it on the hall tree. Her wizened face creased into a broad smile as she rubbed her hands together. Although well over eighty, the sprightly woman volunteered at the Red Cross, held a weekly Bible study for young mothers, and recently joined the WVS. Even the ATS knew better than to turn her down.

She had the squeaky voice of a child. "Fresh scones. I've been saving my sugar for the occasion. We deserve something special for the holiday, don't we, William?" She sniffed the air. "Is the tea ready?"

"It is indeed." His father held his arm toward the diminutive woman who nodded her thanks and tucked her hand into the crook of his elbow. They made their way to the sitting room where she perched on the edge of the worn, blue brocade couch.

Trevor went back to the kitchen, added the still-warm scones to the tray that held the teapot and a stack of Royal Doulton plates, and carried it into the parlor. He placed it next to the cups already on the claw-foot table and lowered himself into the vacant chair near his father.

"Happy Christmas. How did you spend that lovely day?" Mrs. Cookson chirped.

Trevor raised his eyebrow. "Lovely?"

She patted her damp, snowy curls and nodded. "Yes. Jesus' birthday is such a wonderful day, isn't it? What did you do to celebrate?"

Dad rescued him. "We had a quiet day enjoying each other's company. What did you do besides baking these tasty delicacies for two lonely gents?"

"First, I read the Christmas story in the three of the Gospels where the nativity is described. I find it so exciting to get the different viewpoints. Then I sang." She cackled. "Well, if truth be told, it was more like squawking than singing. My Leonard used to say, 'Helen, it's a good thing the Lord doesn't have a requirement for our joyful noise to be in tune.'" She pointed to the teapot. "Would you like me to pour?"

"I believe it's my turn, Mrs. Cookson, but thank you for the offer." Dad deftly put a dollop of milk into the bottom of each delicate cup, following with the aromatic, amber liquid from the pot. "No sugar today, I'm afraid."

She gave a dismissive wave. "I haven't had sweetener in ages. I won't miss it. Besides, we'll get our sugar from the scones, won't we?"

He distributed the tea and scones, and they partook of the simple fare in companionable silence for several minutes. Dad moaned and put his empty plate on the tray then slumped in his chair. "I do believe you've outdone yourself, Mrs. Cookson. These are quite good."

The old woman beamed. "I may not be able to sing, but I can bake." She dabbed the linen napkin to her lips then turned to Trevor. "I read in this morning's paper about the skeleton found under the house on High Street. You must surely be involved." Her eyes glowed.

Trevor crossed his legs and tugged on his sweater. "You know I can't discuss ongoing cases."

"Is it true he was only wearing his boots?"

His eyebrows came together in a deep frown. "What did I just say?"

She shrugged. "I'm only asking about what's in the paper."

He blew out a deep breath. "The boots were all that were left. Everything else had rotted from being in the damp ground for so long."

"So he's been there a while."

"That's what the MO said."

"How about the picture? Can I see it?"

Trevor sat up straighter. "Mrs. Cookson!"

She looked contrite. "Sorry. My Leonard always said I had a penchant for getting into things I shouldn't."

Trevor patted her arm. He should not have barked at the woman. "You like to be helpful, don't you?"

She brightened. "Exactly. Leonard didn't understand that. You know, I've lived here all my life. I might recognize the men in the photo. The paper said you didn't know who they were."

"What else did the paper say?"

"It was most likely murder since his skull was cracked, and two young ladies found him after the bomb."

Miss Brown's heart-shaped face came to mind, and he waved the thought away. "Anything else?"

She stared off in the distance for a moment. "That's everything. Didn't you read this morning's paper?"

He shot a dark look at his father. "Dad hid it. Said we didn't need death and destruction on Boxing Day."

The old woman chortled. "Good for you, William. Maybe we should wait until tomorrow to look at the picture."

Trevor rose. "Now is a fine time. I'll be back in a moment." He climbed the stairs to his bedroom and opened the gleaming cherry-wood secretary that stood against the far wall. He pulled out one of the narrow drawers and extracted the magnifying glass he used with his stamp collection. Retrieving the photo from his pocket, he held the glass to it, drew it slowly toward himself, and watched the tiny figures expand. Perfect. If Mrs. Cookson identified anyone in the photo, it would spare a tremendous amount of man hours. He would have to caution her to keep the information to herself. Trevor shook his head. That would be like holding back the tide.

He descended the stairs and rejoined the two in the living room, where they were deep in conversation. Correction. Mrs. Cookson chattered like a magpie while his father listened.

Dad leapt to his feet. "Trevor, got that photo?"

"Yes, and a magnifying glass."

Trevor gave the items to Mrs. Cookson, and she leaned forward to hold them under the light of the polished brass candlestick lamp. She peered through the magnifier. Her head reared up, and she yelped. "Goodness me! They jump right off the paper, don't they?"

"Let me show you." He gently guided her hands to hold the glass about a half inch from the yellowed photograph. "Now, slowly move the picture toward the glass until it comes into focus. It won't be as startling."

She nodded and squinted through the glass, head tilted. "Much better."

The rhythmic tick-tock of the mantle clock cut the heavy silence while Trevor waited while the elderly woman studied the faded faces on the paper. Minutes passed. He watched her frown in concentration, her eyes darting back and forth. When he thought he could stand it no longer, she sat back and grinned.

"You recognize them?"

She tapped the photo with an arthritic finger, indicating the two young men in the middle. "Not all of them, but I'd know these two anywhere. Nigel Winchester and Ian Belvedere. I haven't thought of them in years. They were two peas in a pod. See one, you'd see the other. Closer than brothers, they were. It surprised everyone when they chose to attend different colleges, but not me."

"Sounds like you knew them well."

"As well as anyone, I suppose. They liked my cookies. The lads would come around after school. I lost track of them when they left for college. Looks like they enlisted together. Not surprising."

"What were they like?"

Mrs. Cookson took a final glance at the photo then handed it to Trevor with the magnifying glass. "They were good boys. They'd get into mischief from time to time, but it was never serious. Besides, Nigel usually managed to talk their way out of trouble. He was a smooth one."

Her face grew wistful as she picked up her cup and saucer. Her gnarled hands absently rubbed the edge of the plate. "Ian was a dreamer. He loved art, all kinds. He was good at it, too. Nigel was the only one who didn't make fun of Ian about drawing pictures. Ian carried a sketchbook and a pencil everywhere. His father was none too keen on his choice of vocation. Ian finally agreed to get a teaching degree. That's why they didn't go to the same college. Nigel became an engineer."

A stray tear trickled down her wrinkled cheek. "And we're losing our young men again to the ravages of war. Sometimes, I think I've lived too long."

William nodded. "It's a terrible thing, to be sure."

For many moments they sat in silence broken only by the tapping of rain against the glass panes. The solitary lamp did little to mitigate the growing darkness. Trevor rose and circled the room, stopping to draw the blackout curtains at each window. He switched on another lamp before he turned and cleared his throat, looking once again at the photograph. "They appear to be wearing American uniforms. They were British, were they not?"

"Nigel is British, but Ian's mother was an American. Maybe they joined an American unit."

"Possibly." His brow furrowed. Or did they lose their jackets? Or worse, steal the ones they were wearing?" Every answer prompted more questions.

"Is there anything else you can tell me about them, Mrs. Cookson? Where did they live? Did you know their parents?"

She pursed her lips then shook her head. "I'm afraid that's all I know, Trevor. I could try to remember where they lived. It wasn't far from where Leonard and I set up housekeeping, but as far as an exact address…" Her shoulders slumped, and dejection marked her face.

"You've been of great assistance, Mrs. Cookson." Trevor spoke in a gentle voice. "Certainly anything else you can think of would be appreciated, but don't lose sleep over this." He grinned. "That's my job."

A tentative smile creased her face. "You wouldn't be trying to assuage an old lady's feelings, would you?"

Trevor moved to where she sat and took the teacup from her. He set it down with a soft clink and clasped her papery-soft hands in his. He stared into her eyes, rimmed with weariness. "I would not." He lifted his head and cocked an ear. "I believe the rain has finally come to an end. You should go home and rest. You've had a full day."

"I am quite tired. Must be the excitement of sleuthing with you."

Trevor laughed. "No doubt."

Dad stood and offered the octogenarian his arm. "Let me see you home, dear Mrs. Cookson."

"You're most kind." She took the proffered arm and pulled herself up from the sofa then smoothed her skirt before tottering with him to where her slicker clung to the hall tree. Dad lifted the still-damp garment and held it open for her to slip into. She buttoned it to the neck and turned toward Trevor. "I'll give some more thought to the lads." She grimaced slightly. "Unfortunately, my memory is not always what I would like it to be."

Resigned sadness etched lines on her face. Before Trevor could respond, his father patted her shoulder. "Tsk. Never you mind. You've been a big help, for sure. Hasn't she, son?" Trevor turned toward his father, who stared at him with wide eyes, imperceptibly jerking his head toward the old woman.

"Please believe me, Mrs. Cookson. You have truly been of assistance." He rubbed his stomach and smacked his lips. "And thank you for sharing from your larder. Your generosity in these lean times is most appreciated."

Her countenance brightened. "That was a tasty treat, wasn't it?" She patted his arm. "You're a gracious man, Trevor Gelson."

He smiled, and she slipped out in front of his father, who stood near the open door. It closed with a sharp click behind them, and Trevor busied himself with clearing away and washing the dishes. As he dried the last plate, his dad came back into the house with a bang. Trevor hung the soggy towel on the hook by the sink and greeted him with a raised eyebrow. "How is she? I didn't mean to wear her out."

Dad shrugged himself out of his charcoal-colored suit jacket and unfastened his vest. He loosened his tie and massaged the sagging flesh of his neck. "You didn't. She'll be fine after she has a lie-down for a bit."

He sighed, stretched himself onto the couch and squinted at Trevor through cracked eyelids. "I could use some shuteye myself. You're no good for conversation now that she's got your mind going on that photograph."

Trevor snorted. "You were just as bad when you were on the force, Dad."

"That I was. Glad to be done with it on most days. It's a hard job with a family." Grief marked his face.

"You're thinking of Mother."

"Indeed. She was a strong woman, but I could see her straining to be cheerful when I left for work each morning, wondering if I'd come home safe again in the evening."

"She understood. You were a policeman when you married."

"She did, but that didn't make it any easier."

Trevor eyed his father and saw his gaze take on a distant look, a ghost of a smile playing on his lips. His own memories of his mother grew fainter with each passing year. Without the photo of his parents' wedding, he'd have forgotten her face.

Scraps of past events flitted through Trevor's mind, but they were mostly sounds. Mother singing him to sleep. The clatter of pots and pans in the kitchen as she readied the meals. Her face was a blur, and his heart gave a guilty tug at the thought. It almost seemed like it had always been just he and his dad. What he did remember with crystal clarity, as if it were yesterday, was the night the telegram came confirming her death.

His father's face had turned ashen and crumpled when the delivery boy handed him the black-edged message. They'd held out hope for nearly a week after the *Titanic* went down. Listening intently to reports on the wireless and pouring over casualty lists, they waited to receive notification she had somehow survived the disaster until hope turned to trepidation.

Dad was so proud of having saved enough money to send her back to America to visit her family. She had not been home since marrying the up-and-coming sergeant in 1897.

Trevor swallowed the lump in his throat. "Maybe it's a good thing I've never married."

His father pulled a clean white handkerchief from his pocket and wiped his eyes. He shook his head as he folded the linen and tucked it back in place. "No, a man needs a family, especially a wife. Granted, I lost a piece of me when Mary died, but I'm a better man because of having loved her."

He wagged his finger at Trevor. "It wouldn't hurt you to find a good woman. Not all of them are like Charlotte. Turn your pain over to the Lord, son. He can open you up to love again. You know, that American reporter sounds like a pip. Your mum had that kind of fire."

Arms crossed, Trevor scowled. "When did this become about my love life? Besides, I thought you were going to take a nap."

William grinned, and his eyes twinkled. "I'm just saying that the love of a good woman is worth any amount of pain."

Trevor kneaded his knuckles, and a vision of Miss Brown standing in front of his desk, hands on her hips and eyes flashing, swept through his mind. "I appreciate your concern, but I have no time for courtships. Anyway, her friend would be the better choice. She has manners, to say the least."

When his father opened his mouth to protest, Trevor grimly made a chopping motion. "End of discussion. And since you're in such a talkative mood, you can help me gather my thoughts about this case."

Dad rubbed his hands together. "Manners are overrated." Then he made a zipping motion across his lips before he picked up the fountain pen from the table and plucked the top sheet from the stack of notepaper beside it. He unscrewed the lid from the pen and scribbled several words before he looked up at Trevor with expectation.

"Ready!"

Trevor joined him on the couch and smiled at his father's enthusiasm, pleased to see the light in his eyes chase away the shadows of bittersweet memories. Dad often spoke of the contentment in his life despite the loss of his wife, but Trevor marveled at the strength of his father's faith that held the deep grief at bay. He, on the other hand, didn't need the complications of a woman in his life. Charlotte was proof of that. And God had bigger things to do than pick out a wife for a lonely detective inspector. Trevor swallowed the lump in his throat and clapped his father on the shoulder. Together they created a list:

1. Search for the Belvedere and Winchester families.
2. Search the military records on Ian and Nigel.
3. Search the town records for information on the two men and their families.
4. Try to determine the identification of the other two men.
5. Get the MO's report as soon as possible.
6. Track down dental records for Ian and Nigel to determine if one of them is the victim.
7. Interview the American reporter and her friend again.
8. Revisit the crime scene.

William yawned and scratched his head. "'Tis a full list of things to do, son. Where do you plan to start?"

"I'll call Christopher to see if he can begin the autopsy tomorrow— that report is the key. Then I'll try to contact the women. That reporter knows more than she's letting on."

"Is that the only reason you want to see her?"

"Dad."

Hands held up in mock surrender, his father snickered. "Your mother was American. Maybe we Gelson men have a penchant for that."

"Dad!"

Rising from the couch, Dad chuckled and walked to the stairs. "I think it's time for that nap."

Trevor shook his head. A penchant for Americans? Hardly. He lifted the telephone received and spoke into it, "Operator, connect me with Whitehall."

Chapter Five

The next afternoon, Trevor stood in the morgue while Christopher hunched over the skeleton, white lab coat stretched taut across his shoulders. The cool, windowless room, tomblike, was located in the basement of the hospital. Stone walls rose from a floor made of cement. Stainless steel shelves and gurneys gleamed in the bright lights. A glittering array of knives, probes, saws, and other evil-looking instruments were lined up on the wheeled table at the doctor's elbow.

Trevor sniffed the sharp, chemical-scented air and cringed. Its pungent scent permeated his clothes. How Christopher could work here day after day was a mystery Trevor had never solved. As far as he was concerned, clean air and fresh breezes were necessary for survival.

It was the far side of lunchtime, and his stomach growled. Hesitant to distract his friend now that the autopsy had finally commenced, he chewed on the inside of his lip. Christopher had agreed to start the proceedings today only if Trevor would assist. The morning hours had been spent meticulously removing dirt and grime from the bones with brushes and tiny picks. There were worse ways to spend a day, but he couldn't immediately come up with one.

Christopher tossed a long, curved blade of some sort onto the tray with a clatter. "Ready?" His voice rumbled low in his chest.

Trevor gave a curt nod and gripped the pencil as he waited to take the doctor's dictation.

"Skeleton weighs five and one half kilograms and measures one hundred seventy-seven point eight centimeters. Narrow pelvic bones. Large occipital bones and skull shows two slightly open sutures. Kidney-shaped groove in sinus cavity. That should help with identification. No signs of arthritis. Got that?"

"Yes." The pencil scraped over the paper as Trevor's hand flew across the page, desperate to keep up with the staccato recital of facts.

Christopher continued, "Minimal bony ridges on the wrist bones, but his feet have definitely seen some wear."

The doctor selected a small lancet and pointed to the indentation in the skull. "There is a fracture between the left temporal and parietal bones caused by blunt-force trauma. The break is deep enough to have possibly caused a rupture or tearing of the epidural artery."

Trevor leaned toward the remains to get a closer look. "Can you tell what sort of weapon was used?"

Brows drawn together, Christopher shrugged. "I can't be certain, but it wasn't very large. A thin pipe, perhaps."

"A fireplace poker rather than a cricket bat?"

The doctor nodded. "Exactly."

"What else can you tell me?"

Christopher turned back to the skeleton and pushed up his spectacles with the back of a gloved hand. He pried open the victim's mouth and chose a hooked probe from the cart. With gentle care, as if the patient could still feel pain, he examined each tooth.

"His teeth are somewhat worn down, but not overly so. He's missing a few."

Trevor leaned forward. "Is that of interest?"

"Might help us with identification, although if he was poor, he wouldn't have had access to professional dental care."

Trevor gestured with the notebook. "Anything else I need to record?"

The doctor stripped the gloves from his hands and flexed his freed fingers. "Not at the moment. Have you been able to locate a dentist for either of the two men in the photograph?"

Trevor tossed the pad and pencil onto the nearest cart with a thump, shook his head, and frowned. "The holidays have taken care of that. They're all closed until tomorrow—and there are dozens of them. Who would have thought a town this size would have so many dentists? And who knows how many closed up shop to head to war?"

"Too many to count, I suppose."

"The lads will start with offices closest to the house where the victim was discovered. With any luck, we'll find the man sooner rather than later."

Christopher smirked as he shucked his lab coat and hung it on the back of the closet door. "I see that look in your eye. You're irritated today is Boxing Day, and you can't do anything about it."

Trevor scowled. "Death doesn't take a holiday. How can we?"

Christopher laid a towel over the used instruments and tossed his gloves into a nearby rubbish bin. "We didn't, remember? I came in on my day off to start your autopsy." He beckoned to Trevor and strode into the small adjoining office. "I'm parched. Join me for some tea."

"That sounds like an order."

"Don't be petulant."

The doctor washed his hands at the sink then busied himself at a tiny two-burner stove in the corner of the office. He filled the battered, black kettle with water and placed it on the heat with a bang. A pair of equally battered cups sat on the shelf. Christopher reached up and pulled them down with one hand, the porcelain clinking as he set them on the counter. He gestured toward the threadbare, brown sofa across the room. "Have a seat. I'll only be a moment."

Trevor approached the couch with suspicion lumps and sags evident in the cushions. He pressed his hand into the padding, grimacing when it gave way to the springs underneath. One could get injured on a piece of furniture like that. "You actually sleep on this thing?"

Christopher snickered. "When exhaustion overtakes me."

"That's what it would take, I would imagine." Trevor lowered himself and perched on the edge of the sofa, his arms resting on his thighs.

Moments later the pot whistled, and Christopher carried it and the cups to the wooden table next to the sofa. He settled on the end of the couch and ran his hands through his hair, leaving it in spiked disarray.

Trevor dug into his pocket and retrieved his notepad and pencil. He cocked his head at Christopher. "I'd rather not wait for your late, badly typed report. Mind giving it to me over tea?"

Christopher snorted. "I'd be insulted if you weren't spot on about my typing. I'd be happy to give you my take on this poor soul. But first, the tea. It should have steeped enough by now." He poured the aromatic, amber liquid into their cups, the steam wafting lazily toward the ceiling.

Trevor took the proffered drink and sipped it carefully. The hot fluid soothed his dry throat. Christopher would speak when ready, so Trevor masked his impatience with a smile.

"Ha! I know what you're doing, Trevor."

"I beg your pardon?"

"You know pushing me for information doesn't work, so you're trying to appear sociable and patient in the hope that I'll start giving my report. Can't we simply enjoy each other's company and a cup of tea? Life is not all about work."

Trevor shook his head and drank deeply to give himself time to collect his thoughts. The china cup rattled when he returned it to the saucer. "Listen, I'm the middleman." He spoke in measured tones. "Despite the Allied victories at Tobruk and El Alamein, the assistant commissioner is very much aware of the morale of the British people, and he expects quick results. I'm constantly called on to justify my actions and those of my men. Do I not understand how important it is to solve a murder? Would it not be in everyone's best interest to find a murderer sooner rather than later? Indubitably." He pointed to Christopher. "That means you get caught in the cross fire."

"I don't have to like it."

A grim smile formed on Trevor's face. "We're in agreement there."

Christopher shifted and set his beverage on the table with a muted clunk. "It's about priorities. For example, take the holidays. Next to Easter, Christmas is the most important day for us Christians. Yet we find ourselves caught up in shopping and parties and resenting the day off from getting work done. Don't you think God would honor our efforts if we stopped to celebrate His Son's birth?"

"An interesting concept. In your scenario, thieves and murderers would take a respite on Christmas and Easter."

"You misunderstand me. Maybe my theology is off. Or maybe I'm naïve. But I feel that if we're following Him like we should, He will give us the thoughts we need to solve this problem. Not like a magic pill or anything…" He flopped back against the couch and crossed his arms, a defeated look on his face. "I'm not articulating this well at all, Trevor."

"You're doing fine. Jesus spoke about this in Mark when He said, 'Render to Caesar the things that are Caesar's, and to God the things that are God's.' I appreciate your candor. You've given me a lot to think about. Do you want to call it quits for the day?"

"No." He swallowed the last of his tea and rose to set the empty cup on the counter. "Finished?"

"I'm still nursing the dregs."

Christopher rubbed his hands together. "Let's get to it, then, shall we?" He leaned back against the wall and spoke. "As I thought, your victim is most probably a twenty-five to thirty year-old male, and weighed eleven and a half to twelve stone. He spent a lot of time on his feet, but he doesn't seem to have done much manual labor. He could have been a shopkeeper or postal worker. Hard to say. He was killed by a blow to the head as you saw. The broken arm was recent, no doubt as a result of the young woman's fall through the floor. But his right leg shows evidence of having been broken, perhaps a few years prior to his death. Otherwise, there is no other trauma to the head or body."

Trevor brightened. "The information about his leg should help." He tapped the pencil against the pad. "Mrs. Cookson may be able to shed some light on that."

"Who?"

"My neighbor. She knew two of the lads in the photograph."

"Excellent. A thread to pull to see how this unravels." Christopher winked. "Maybe that lovely, young reporter can be of assistance."

"I have a feeling she's going to be a hindrance rather than a help."

"What makes you say that?"

"Have you ever known a reporter to be something other than a nuisance? I certainly haven't. Her beauty won't change that."

Christopher chuckled. "So you agree she's an attractive woman. That's a good sign. I thought you had sworn off the fairer sex."

"I have, but I'm not blind."

Trevor rose and retrieved their coats. He tossed Christopher's to him and slipped into his own. "I appreciate your taking part of your holiday for this, my friend. And your words."

Christopher donned his coat and reached out to shake Trevor's hand. "Off to interview your Mrs. Cookson?"

"That will wait until tomorrow. I believe I'll spend some time with Dad and work on my stamp collection."

Christopher turned off the lights and closed the door as the two left the morgue and made their way out of the building. "Still chasing down and cataloging bits of colored paper, are you?"

"They're more than that. Have you ever examined some of the commemorative stamps? The design, the engraving…they're miniature works of art. Did you know that the American president, Mr. Roosevelt, is a stamp collector? I'm among an elite group." He smiled to take the arrogance out of the pronouncement.

The doctor shook his head. "I'll take your word for it. Enjoy your day. As for me, it's back to the house to give Lois a break from the kids." He clapped Trevor on the shoulder and hurried away.

Trevor walked slowly in the opposite direction, noting the beauty of the bobbing flowers for the first time in weeks. Breathing deeply, he picked up the pace, suddenly eager to see his father to discuss the autopsy results. Maybe Dad could shed some light on how someone twenty-five years ago could hide a decomposing body in their house.

Chapter Six

The day dawned bright and clear, yesterday's downpour a distant memory. A cold breeze nipped at Trevor's face as he tramped across town to the house where the bones had been found. He hunched inside his coat. Despite the chill, it felt good to be outdoors. The youngsters in the neighborhood agreed. The streets and sidewalks were swollen with them, their shouts and laughter bouncing off the buildings' façades.

Women were hard at work, sweeping and clearing away the debris of fallen branches and leaves in front of their homes. Each homemaker seemed to take pride in keeping her environs well ordered, even in the midst of the war's continual assault of dirt and rubble.

Or maybe because of it.

Sunshine warmed his back and glistened on the water droplets that still clung to some of the shrubs lining the walkway behind the iron balustrade. It was one of the few railings in the area not confiscated during the never-ending scrap drives.

Trevor dodged a small boy who raced in front of him in focused pursuit of a runaway ball. He smiled at the little one's determination. Clothed in mismatched trousers and jacket and wearing scuffed, heavy, brown boots, the child tackled the ball with a triumphant cry. Trevor applauded, and the boy rewarded him with a delighted smile.

Several blocks later, Trevor stopped in front of a house three doors down from the bomb site. He rapped on the black, wooden door. Muffled footsteps approached, and the door swung open to reveal a stooped, heavily wrinkled, old man.

Trevor held up his police identity card. "I'm Inspector Trevor Gelson. I'd like to ask you a few questions."

The man gripped the doorknob and blinked owl-like at him from behind thick eyeglasses. "Who?"

"Gelson. Detective Inspector Trevor Gelson."

"Never 'eard of you."

"No, I don't expect you have." Trevor pocketed his card.

"Am I under arrest?" The man looked eager.

Trevor shook his head. "I need to ask you some questions, if you have a moment. Mr...?"

"Harry Porterhouse."

"May I come in, Mr. Porterhouse?"

"Don't see why not. I've got all the time in the world. Don't do much these days."

"How long have you lived here?"

Harry screwed up his face and scratched his head. "Can't rightly say. Maybe ten or twelve years. I used to live in Bath. Edna and I moved here to be closer to our daughter." His face fell. "My wife died shortly after we got 'ere. Pneumonia."

"I'm sorry. That must have been difficult. Does your daughter live with you?"

"Yes. She sold her place, so we could all be together." Harry cocked his head and peered at Trevor. "Is this about the skeleton they found?"

Trevor nodded. "We're looking for residents who lived here between 1917 and 1925. Would you happen to know if any of your neighbors were here at that time?"

Harry stepped to the window and pointed to a small brownstone across the street. "Polly Armstrong. She's over there, but she's away for the 'olidays. Always goes to visit her son in Wales. She won't be back till after Candlemas."

"Anyone else?"

"You could try Dorothy Pearson." He gestured toward to a sagging brick house directly across from where the victim was found. "The Pearson family 'as been here since Queen Victoria was a child."

Trevor smiled. Maybe the day would not be a total loss after all. He handed Harry a card then touched the brim of his hat. "If you think of anything else or Mrs. Armstrong returns, would you be kind enough to ring me up?"

Harry squinted at the card then nodded. "I 'ope you find what you're looking for, young man."

"Thank you." Trevor stepped out of the house and heard the door close with a click as he turned toward Dorothy Pearson's home. He climbed the steps and straightened his clothes before knocking. Moments passed. He knocked again, louder this time. Nothing. He peered through the slight separation between the white lace curtains dangling in the window. The interior was dark. He recorded the address in his notebook and huffed. The holidays interfered again. He wrote a quick note on the back of one of his cards asking Mrs. Pearson to contact him at her earliest convenience and pushed it through the mail slot on the door.

A breeze tickled his face, and Trevor sniffed the air. The tangy aroma of cabbage filled his senses and took him back to his childhood. Somewhere, preparation for the midday meal had begun, and despite the coolness, someone had opened her window. Mother had fixed cabbage every Saturday night. At the time, he hated the sameness of it. Now, he relished the thought of routine and simpler times.

Trevor stowed his notebook and descended the stairs. Nothing would get done mooning over his past. The same couldn't be said of the poor soul lying in Christopher's morgue. History was going to be the key to solving the man's murder, but how far back would he have to search?

<hr>

Later that afternoon, Sergeant Phillips braked the police car, then he and Trevor climbed out. One of the men had managed to track down Ian Belvedere's father who'd informed the officer his son had been missing since shortly after the Great War. With any luck, the lad's father would give them enough information to determine if his son was their victim.

Trevor surveyed the area, noting the tidy yard and worn but well-maintained cottage, its thatched roof thick and full. He stepped toward the building, and the door swung open.

"I'm Edward Belvedere. I've been expecting you." The man's smile was tentative and did not reach his grief-filled eyes. He was tall and lanky with a sparse crown of graying hair. His out-of-date brown tweed suit was of good quality, his shoes buffed to a high shine.

Trevor displayed his identity card. "The name is Gelson. Detective Inspector Trevor Gelson. This is Sergeant Phillips."

"Yes, yes. Won't you come in?" Belvedere stood back and gestured for the men to enter.

"Thank you." Trevor stepped into the house and removed his hat. Phillips was close on his heels as they followed Ian's father into the parlor. The small room was sparsely furnished. A pair of olive-green channel-back chairs flanked an oval drop-leaf table, its surface covered with stacks of newspapers. A large dining table stood against one wall and was crowded with more newspapers, magazines, notepads, and scattered pencils. A glass bowl held a collection of straight pins with colored heads, many of which had been used to cover a world map that nearly filled the far wall.

Edward gestured to the chairs. "Won't you sit down? I could get you some tea."

Phillips shook his head and positioned himself near the door while Trevor seated himself. "That's very kind but unnecessary. We'll try not to take too much of your time."

Edward lowered himself into the other chair. "If it solves my son's disappearance, you can take as much time as you need."

"When was the last time you saw him?"

"Made it through the war without a scratch, he did. Had a couple of close calls, but always managed to dodge the bullet." Edward heaved a sigh. "Christmas of 1919 was the last time I saw him. He and Millicent…that's his wife…seemed to have patched things up. They were going to take a trip to ring in the New Year. He didn't tell me where."

"Did she accompany him on his visit?"

He shook his head. "No, she never came for Christmas after the first year they were married. Said she didn't want to hear all that 'mumbo jumbo.' Our tradition has always been to read the story of Jesus' birth from the book of Luke. She would have none of it."

"Is that why they had to patch things up?"

Edward hesitated for a moment. "During the war, she and my boss took a fancy to each other. At first, it seemed harmless—an occasional lunch or walk about the park. One morning when I came into work, they were getting off the bus together. She was wearing the same dress from the day before. I kept it to myself as long as I could, but then I wrote Ian and told him."

He stood and began to pace in front of Trevor. "I shouldn't have done that. What could Ian do about it while he was fighting the Germans? Stupid of me, really. Ian wrote to Millicent and begged her to stop. She must have told my boss because the next thing I knew, I was being transferred to the company's other location."

"Where was that?"

"Brighton."

"What happened next?"

Edward stopped pacing and shrugged. "Nothing of consequence. The war finally ended, and Ian came home. He knew where to find me. I had written to tell him of the move. Anyway, Millicent claimed the affair was over and asked Ian to take her back, which he did. But I could tell things weren't like that before the war. They bickered constantly, but when Ian showed up that year at Christmas, he was in a jolly-good mood and told me about his upcoming trip with Millicent. Said it would be like a second honeymoon."

"Did he vanish before or after the journey?"

"About two days before they were supposed to leave, Millicent called me in hysterics saying Ian had gone and left her. I told her I'd help her find him, but she put me off. Said I had done enough. I guess I knew what that meant." He collapsed into the empty chair and swiped a hand over his pallid face. "I waited for him to contact me, but he never did."

"Is that unusual?"

"We were very close. He would have sent a note, even if he couldn't risk seeing me."

"Did you contact the authorities?"

"I thought about calling the police, but I didn't have any real reason to suspect foul play. I thought Ian would be in touch eventually. But the days turned into weeks and then months. Then it was too late." Edward leaned forward, his hollow eyes boring into Trevor's. "Tell me the truth, DI Gelson, is that my son you dug out of the ground?"

"That's what I'm trying to determine. Did he suffer a fall before he disappeared or mention getting hurt during the war?"

"No. Why do you ask?"

"At some point, the victim had broken his leg, and it appears the break occurred not very long before his demise."

Edward shook his head. "Ian never broke his leg that I'm aware of. Maybe when he was overseas, but if that's true he never mentioned it to me."

"What can you tell us about his friend Nigel?"

"They were thick as thieves, the two of them." Edward's face took on a faraway look. "Different as day and night, but something connected them. They did everything together. Except college. Nigel went to engineering school."

"I'm aware of that. What else can you tell me?"

"He's done well for himself. He teaches engineering at City University. We exchange Christmas cards. I can dig out an address and send it to you, if you like."

"That would be most helpful." Trevor pulled out the photograph of the four men and passed it to Edward. "Can you identify the other two men?"

Edward looked at the picture for a long moment and then stroked his son's face on the paper before handing it back. "The one on the right is Millicent's younger brother, Hugh. I don't recognize the other fellow."

Trevor tucked the photo back into his pocket and rose. "You're sure about that?"

"Quite sure. He came round to see Millicent on a regular basis. I couldn't tell you where he is now."

"What kind of man was Hugh?"

"A straight sort. He'll inherit his father's title one day. I think manages the estate or some such thing. It seemed to me he was always trying to prove himself."

Trevor handed his business card to the man. "We've taken enough of your time, Mr. Belvedere. You can contact me at that number with the address or any other information you remember that might be helpful. Don't get up. We'll see ourselves out." He turned and gestured to Phillips.

"DI Gelson?" There were tears in Edward's voice.

Trevor turned back. "Yes?"

"Ian was a good boy. He didn't always make wise choices, but he was a believer, and in his heart he knew what was right."

Trevor nodded at Edward and donned his fedora as he walked toward the door that Phillips held open.

No man should have to outlive his son, and Mr. Belvedere deserved to know what happened. Lord, give me a clear mind. Help me see the clues for what they are. Help me solve this terrible crime so that justice is done, and the victim can be laid to rest. Then I can rest, Lord.

Rest in me.

Trevor rubbed his burning eyes. When would he learn to rest? To be content. He sighed. Probably never.

The two men left the house and crawled into the car. Phillips turned to Trevor. "Where to, sir?"

"Town records. Let's see what we can find out about Ian and his wife."

Chapter Seven

Ruth arrived at the crime scene and gazed at the devastation that had been her home. The area was still cordoned off with wooden blockades. Someone had swept the sidewalk, but the exposed furniture and personal items remained coated with gray dust. The familiar scent of burning coal hung in the air.

She stuffed her gloved hands into her pockets to warm them. Christmas was three days past, and she'd spent the morning feverishly working on her article about the deprivations and sacrifices of the British people during the holiday season. She stopped at the newspaper office to transmit her piece before setting out for High Street.

A large magpie swooped back and forth in the overcast sky, harsh chattering breaking the silence. Its glossy, black head and breast glistened with a metallic green-and-violet sheen in stark contrast to its pure white belly and wingtips. She laughed at his antics then turned toward a movement she caught from the corner of her eye. A short, stocky man approached from the south. Enormous, bushy white eyebrows hung over rheumy, blue eyes. Wisps of white hair dotted his freckled scalp. A book was tucked under his left arm.

"Why are you laughing, young lady? Don't you know a magpie's an ill omen?"

Her smile died. "Is that a fact?"

"Ah, an American. Of course, you don't know."

"Why don't you tell me about it?" Her reporter's curiosity prickled.

He nodded solemnly.

> "One for sorrow,
>
> Two for joy,
>
> Three for a girl,
>
> Four for a boy,
>
> Five for silver,
>
> Six for gold,
>
> Seven for a secret never to be told."

His brows drew together as one giant caterpillar above his eyes. "You only saw one, you see. Now, do you understand?"

"The magpies are everywhere. How do you explain that?"

"These are terrible times, are they not? And the birds know it."

"Terrible times, indeed." Her heart squeezed. He reminded her of Ralph, the gruff correspondent who had befriended her when she first arrived in London. She still couldn't believe he was gone, a casualty in North Africa. "Do you live around here?"

The man pulled his bulky overcoat closed and nodded. "I'm Andrew Wingate, and my home is about three blocks over. The weather causes havoc with these old joints, but I get restless this time of year. A man can stay inside only so long." He brightened. "Would you join me for a walk in the park?"

Ruth hesitated then shrugged. He seemed harmless enough. "I would welcome that. My name is Ruth Brown."

"It's a pleasure to meet you, young lady."

They walked away from the house, sauntering past several groups of children who played in the empty street, their progress slowed by Mr. Wingate's limp. Shouts and laughter faded as they reached the end of the block and turned right.

"Have you lived in the neighborhood long, Mr. Wingate?"

"All my life." He stopped and pointed to a white spire that rose behind the rows of houses. "I was the vicar at that church, like my father before me."

Ruth's heart beat faster. Would he know about the poor man who had died in her lodging establishment? "Is it a large congregation?"

"Sometimes. The ebb and flow of members changes with the times. I lost many a parishioner during the Great War, as if they blamed God."

"Don't judge them too harshly. I was guilty of that myself not too long ago."

Mr. Wingate scrutinized her face. "I leave judgment to God. We're all guilty of wrongdoing or sins of omission at one time or another. Fortunately, God is gracious and forgives us our shortcomings, doesn't He?"

"That He does."

They walked in silence for several moments, their footsteps crunching in the grit on the sidewalk. Ruth sighed. The English must feel like their country might never be clean again. She would no longer take the beauty of her native New Hampshire for granted.

"Here we are." Mr. Wingate stopped in front of a small grassy area surrounded by a low stone wall. Garden plots were roped off, and a few women worked among the fledgling plants. "There's a bench under a grove of trees at the other end."

"Perfect."

He beamed, and they strolled along the cobblestone path leading to a slate patio.

They seated themselves, and Mr. Wingate pulled out a slim volume.

Ruth squinted at the worn spine. "What did you bring to read? The book looks quite old."

"I'm a student of the classics. This is *Paradise Lost.*"

"A wonderful poem, but not a light read by any means."

Mr. Wingate nodded. "Perhaps not. My grandfather learned to read later in life and as a result became quite the bibliophile. Family lore has it that he sometimes went without necessities to purchase a book. He passed that love on to his son, my father, who in turn passed it to me." A shadow crossed his face. "Sadly, thanks to the Kaiser, I no longer have a son."

"I'm sorry to hear of your loss."

Mr. Wingate shook his head. "It was a lifetime ago. The current war brings up too many memories for this old man." He motioned to the book. "I've learnt to be content with my lot. Let's celebrate today—that we are both alive and well at this moment. Tell me why a lovely young woman like yourself is in our dilapidated country."

She stared across the park. "There's not much to tell. I'm a writer for my hometown newspaper and had an opportunity to come here to cover the war. I arrived this past June before Eisenhower took over as supreme commander. My job is to put a face on the war for my readers at home. Would you like to be in the paper?"

He sat back and chuckled. "No one wants to read about an old man whiling away the hours in England, do they?"

"It's up to you. You've seen a lot." She tilted her head and studied him. "I'd wager you might have even served during one of the British conflicts. Am I right?"

"The third Burmese War, as a matter of fact." The wind rustled the branches overhead, and Andrew shook his stubby forefinger at Ruth. "But you're a sly one. We're back to talking about me."

Ruth lifted her shoulders. She grinned and dropped her voice. "You can't blame a girl for trying."

"There is something I would like to talk about, if you don't mind."

He gave her a wary look. "Yes?"

"The skeleton that was found in the house where I was standing when you saw me."

His eyes twinkled, and he sat back with a grin. "I heard about that."

"My friend, Varis, and I rented a room there."

"Oh, my. How is your friend?"

Ruth shifted on the bench. "She's fine. But about the skeleton—I'd like to find out who he was. Do you know who would have owned the house around 1920 or a little later?"

Mr. Wingate rubbed his jaw. "I believe the Belvedere family lived there—a big lot, they were. Edward and his wife had five boys. As a matter of fact, his wife was an American. Can't say which state she hailed from."

From her purse on the ground, Ruth snatched her pad and pencil. "What were the boys' names?"

"Hmmm. There was William, Colin, Robert, Ian, and…ah…what was that last youngster's name?"

"Ian?" She could not believe her luck. That was one of the names she managed to decipher on the back of the picture.

"Yes. He was a good lad. An artist and a dreamer. He accompanied his mum to America for a visit with her family. He must have been eight or nine years old at the time. Became quite enamored with the country, he did. Ian spent many happy hours in my home reading as many books as he could by American authors. The other lads made fun of him. I believe he moved there after the war."

Ruth's pencil hovered over the paper. "To America?"

"I think so." Mr. Wingate smiled. "You're taxing this old brain of mine, young lady."

She looked down at her notes.

"I'm teasing. No need to fret. What else can I tell you?"

"You said he was a dreamer. Was he a loner? Did he have any friends?"

"Just one. Nigel something or other. They joined up together." Andrew gazed up at her through thick white eyebrows and whispered conspiratorially, "I think he was a spy."

Chapter Eight

Ruth's eyes widened. "A spy?"

Mr. Wingate crossed his arms, a furtive look on his face. "That one wasn't to be trusted."

"Is that why you think he was a secret agent?"

"It runs in the family; his great-grandfather worked undercover. It's a fact."

Ruth shook her head. "You've lost me, Mr. Wingate. Nigel's great-grandfather was an operative for the British government?"

He gave a sagacious nod.

"And you think Nigel was one, too?"

Another nod.

"How does Ian fit into all this?"

"Ian?"

"Yes, Ian Belvedere. The boy who lived in the house where the skeleton was found."

Mr. Wingate blinked vacantly at her. "There was a skeleton?"

She leaned forward and touched his arm. "Mr. Wingate, are you all right?"

"Yes, why do you ask?"

Ruth sighed. Her grandfather suffered like this. One minute perfectly lucid, the next unsure of where he was. How much of the information he'd shared was credible? She'd begin her search with the names he mentioned and go from there. She rose and reached for her coat. "Would you like me to see you home?"

"No, I'd like to sit a while longer. I've enjoyed our visit. Come back any time."

She donned her jacket and draped the strap of her purse over one shoulder. She glanced at him, taking in the tired look in his eyes. Would he be safe alone and unsure of his surroundings? Maybe she should find a bobby. "Is there anything you need before I go?"

He shook his head and opened his book. "I'll sit and read for a while."

Ruth slapped a hand to her forehead before opening her purse to pull out her card. Now she was forgetting things. She tucked the card between the pages of his book. "You can reach me at this number if you remember anything else about the house on High Street."

"The old Belvedere place?"

She froze. Was he back? "Where the skeleton was found."

"Yes. Edward Belvedere was the man's name."

"Did he have any children?"

"Four or five maybe. I'm sorry. I can't recall exactly."

Her face fell. Another look at his eyes told her he had slipped away again. She would definitely find a police officer to ensure the kind man made it home.

<hr>

Several hours later, Ruth stood at Grosvenor Square admiring the sandstone-colored American embassy. At three stories high and the length of two city blocks, it was a formidable structure. According to Varis, the Duke of Westminster had knocked the old building down in 1936 to construct this one. The Americans moved in two years later.

She glanced across the courtyard. Eisenhower recently established his military headquarters on the other side of the square. Looking back at the embassy, she saw the familiar stars and stripes waving in the slight breeze, and as cliché as it was, she felt her heart swell with pride. Sunlight bounced off the windows, and a pair of stone-faced marines guarded the entrance.

Ruth dug into her bag and found her passport. She drew it out and held it up as she approached the door. The soldier on the right held out his hand, and she gave him the small booklet. He flipped through it and stopped at the page that displayed her photograph. He scrutinized the picture for a long moment then with an impassive look returned the passport. He opened the door, and she murmured her thanks as she stepped across the threshold.

Varis stood in the lobby. Ruth hurried to her, and they moved together to the rear of the cavernous room. Voices and footsteps echoed around them, and somewhere overhead a door slammed. Varis cast a furtive glance at the receptionist and leaned toward Ruth. She spoke in a whisper. "It took some doing, but I was able to obtain service records for Ian and Nigel."

Ruth squealed then clapped a hand over her mouth. Varis held a finger to her lips before saying, "You can look at them, but you must do it at my desk."

Ruth gave a brisk salute. "I understand."

Varis frowned. "This is serious, Ruth. I'm sure we're breaking some rule, if not a law. You can't take notes, so you'll have to use that prodigious memory of yours."

"I only need the next of kin and last known address."

"Follow me and don't ogle, or they'll spot you as an outsider."

They made their way behind the receptionist to a long hallway. Ruth kept her eyes glued to Varis's back, but tried to catch a glimpse of activities with her peripheral vision. Too many doors were closed as far as she was concerned. She grinned to herself. As the British would say, it was all very hush-hush.

Two turns, and they stopped in front of another closed door. Varis tossed a warning look at her before she opened the door to a room that held a sea of desks. Ruth understood Varis's concern. There was no privacy. No one looked up as Varis gestured for Ruth to sit in the wooden chair next to the closest empty desk. Varis sat and slid two folders across the desk then busied herself with a stack of paperwork.

Ruth selected the top file filled with yellowed sheets of paper. She scanned the contents, her eyes racing down the pages. Finding the information she needed, she stared at it for several minutes committing it to memory then exchanged the folder for the second one—nearly identical to Ian's file. She memorized the name and address before returning the dossier to the desk. With an attempt at nonchalance, she smoothed her slacks and stood. "Want to grab some lunch?"

Varis shook her head and beckoned to Ruth. "I'm swamped. I'll need to eat at my desk. Follow me, I need to escort you out."

"Varis."

Varis and Ruth whirled.

A woman glared at them from the desk a few feet away. "Not sure what you gals are up to, but I'd be careful about letting outsiders look at files they shouldn't."

Varis drew herself up, a withering stare on her face. "Thanks for the advice, Pauline, but everything is under control." She pulled on Ruth's arm and led her out the door.

———◆———

Trevor sat at the dining room table bundled against the chill. His mind appreciated the logic of conserving coal, but his body would have liked the ration quota to be a bit more generous. He surveyed his stamp collection spread across the table. He pulled the album toward himself and began to page through it. It wasn't a mint collection; he preferred used stamps, the uniqueness of each cancellation telling its own story. It also wasn't a British collection. With a nod toward his mother's American citizenship, he focused on the United States' commemoratives. Challenging to get during peacetime, the stamps were nearly impossible to find during war.

He turned to the section in the book called National Parks Issue of 1934 and stared at the blank spot for the Grand Canyon stamp encircled by the rest of the set. Issued during National Park Year, each stamp was a miniature work of art—the intricate engraving, the nuances of color, and the majesty of its subject. Trevor almost felt the spray on his face as he looked at the one labeled Old Faithful. A satisfied smile on his face, he picked up the envelope he had tucked between the pages several days earlier. He opened the flap and eased the bright red stamp from inside with a tiny pair of tongs.

The craggy, striated cliffs of the Grand Canyon were nearly centered on the stamps, and the cancellation mark was crisp and clear. He read the date and grimaced—August 2, 1934—the day Hitler became president of Germany. If only the world had known what that event had portended.

A sharp rap at the front door interrupted his thoughts. Trevor laid down the stamp, rose, crossed the room, and opened the door. Sergeant Phillips gave a brisk salute and spoke with excitement. "Sorry to bother you at home, sir, but I thought you'd want to hear the news as soon as possible."

Trevor widened the door, and Phillips marched into the room and removed his hat. Smoothing his hair, he turned. "We've unearthed the identities of the other two lads in the photograph. A Devon Smythe and Hugh Davenport. We don't have much on Smythe, but it turns out that Hugh was Ian's brother-in-law."

Trevor frowned. "I thought Ian was one of five boys."

"He was. However, Ian's wife has a brother. Bit of a bounder from what we can find out thus far. It seems that he's trying to make it on his own, but hasn't had a lot of success. He walks a thin line of legitimacy with his business interests." Phillips pulled a folded slip of paper from his pocket and passed it to Trevor. "He's dabbled in a number of different industries. This includes the company names and dates."

"Well done, Sergeant. Keep at it with Smythe. I'll be in the office first thing in the morning."

"Very good, sir." Phillips moved toward the table where Trevor had been working. "You must be pleased. You've completed the series. Where did you find the last one?"

"A lead from one of the lads in the philatelic club. It's a beauty, isn't it?"

Phillips saluted and clamped his hat back on before opening to door. "If you say so, sir. Enjoy the rest of your day, sir. I'll see you tomorrow."

Trevor returned the salute and closed the door behind Phillips. He walked to the table and studied the Grand Canyon stamp. It jogged a distant memory that he couldn't quite push forward to his consciousness. Shrugging, he sat down and picked up the stamp, attached a hinge, and pasted the stamp into the book. It had taken eight long years to obtain this particular one, but it had been worth the wait. He stretched, and his gaze swept the table. His eyes fell on the photo of Ian Belvedere and his friends. Trevor picked it up. He held it close and studied the blurred, smiling face of the four young men.

In a flash, he was with them. One minute he and his buddies were arguing and playing cards in the woods, the next they were dodging staccato bursts of machine-gun fire. The boom of mortar fire filled the air as it rained down from the sky. Men screamed in agony, others dropped without a sound, their lifeless eyes glassy and staring.

Ian's face came back into focus, and Trevor tapped the photo. Had he ever been that young and carefree? Could he learn to be carefree again, or at least content like Dad? He rubbed his eyes. He'd think about that another day. He had a murder to solve.

He picked up the magnifying glass and studied the photo for the umpteenth time. The men. The jeep. The crates. The statue. The statue!

Trevor clambered to his feet. He slid into his coat and slipped the photo and glass into his pocket. He knew just the fellow to tell him about the sculpture.

Chapter Nine

Two days later, Varis had the day off and joined Ruth in her search for Nigel Winchester. They stood in front of a small cottage outside London where, if the nearly twenty-five-year-old files could be trusted, Nigel resided. If not, the hour-long tube ride to Southgate and subsequent trek had been a waste of time. Thanks to the lack of street signs, they made three wrong turns before finding Church Hill Road. Ruth wondered if the street was named for England's revered prime minister.

Ruth sniffed the air. The acrid smell of burning coal that constantly assailed her in the city was not quite as strong. What she smelled was earthy, more organic. Perhaps it was peat. She scrutinized the building that abutted the sidewalk, its front stoop spilling into the walkway. Vacant, rust-filled holes in the stone indicated where the railings once stood. The windows were dirty and smudged, and the peeling paint on the gray door revealed several prior colors.

The battered façade of the house next door was little better. A withered wreath hung from a ten-penny nail stuck through the front door, and plywood covered the first-floor windows. Like most windows in England, the upstairs windows were coated in grime.

Behind her, a horse-drawn carriage clattered past on the cobblestone street, the vehicle's driver bellowing at the animals. Somewhere in the distance, a dog howled.

Clearing her throat, Ruth turned her attention back to Nigel's house. She gave a sharp rap on the door then recoiled as it swung open at her knock. Varis yelped and jumped off the porch.

Ruth looked at Varis with wide eyes then back at the open door. The lights did not appear to be on inside the house, but Ruth detected the faint sound of music. She knocked again. No response. Her heart pounded. She eased the door wider and stepped into the foyer. Framed photographs lined the walls in the entryway. At the end of the hall, there was an empty nail. On the floor below, a torn picture lay among the splintered frame and shards of glass.

"Mr. Winchester? Hello?" Ruth crept forward, Varis close behind her. "Mr. Winchester?"

Varis touched Ruth's shoulder. "We should have called ahead. I don't have a good feeling about this."

Ruth turned to Varis and frowned. "What would we have said on the telephone? 'We found a skeleton and think you might have something to do with it?' Besides, that's water under the bridge, now."

"How about if I go find the nearest police box?"

Ruth's heart fluttered. "And leave me alone in here?"

"You could come with me."

A low moan sounded from the living room. Wide eyed, they froze for a moment. The moan came again, and Ruth rushed forward with Varis on her heels. "Mr. Winchester?"

At the end of the corridor, they turned into the living room. Ruth stopped short, and Varis plowed into her back. The couch was upside down, its pewter-gray cushions torn apart and tossed aside. The padded seats of the two matching chairs were also sliced open. All three drawers from the bulky, wood desk on the far wall had been removed, their contents dumped on the floor. The gray-and-gold needlepoint rug was shoved into the corner.

The soft groaning came from behind the sofa. Ruth hurried around the furniture. A dark-haired man lay face-down, two well-worn canes beside him. A large gash on the side of his head pumped dark blood. She fumbled in her purse for something to staunch the flow. Nothing. "Varis, see if there are clean towels in the kitchen."

Varis rushed out of the room, and Ruth bent over the man. "Mr. Winchester, what happened?"

A chunky glass ashtray sat nearby, its edge covered in blood. Her hand flew to her throat. Someone had intentionally hurt the man. Ruth looked up as Varis clattered back into the room clutching a fistful of towels. She thrust them at Ruth who dropped all but one next to the victim. Ruth folded the cloth several times then pressed it against the wound. She felt a sticky wetness on her knees, and her gaze fell to the blood seeping into the fabric of her slacks. Her stomach roiled at the sight.

The makeshift bandage was soon soaked through. She swallowed against her nausea and reached for another towel. She put the new dressing on the injured area, and the man cried out, flailing his arms. Then all was silent.

Ruth pressed her fingers to his neck. No pulse. She scrambled to her feet and reached for Varis. "Oh no! He's dead! What are we going to do?"

Bloodied and rumpled, they clung together and stared in horror at the man's contorted face, now frozen in its mask of pain.

"I'm going to be sick!" Varis pushed away from Ruth and rushed out of the room.

Ruth squeezed her eyes shut against the bloody man, but the vision was burned into her memory. Trying not to faint, she opened her eyes and reached for the leg of the upside-down couch to steady herself. Running water sounded from the back of the house. Then it stopped, and Varis, wan and shaky, tottered into the room.

A shout came from the front door, and they turned. Two constables and a man in a suit burst into the room.

"Hands in the air, ladies!" The suited man scowled at Ruth and Varis.

Ruth stepped forward. "But..."

"Do as I say!"

Ruth and Varis raised their hands. The uniformed officers, a diminutive woman with blonde hair and a lanky man with sandy brown hair, approached and frisked them.

"They're unarmed, sir," the blonde said.

"Okay, you can put down your hands," the man in the suit said, "but stay where you are."

He jerked his head toward the corpse, and the two bobbies moved to the body and began to catalog the scene. The man glowered at Ruth and Varis. "Who are you, and why did you kill this man?"

"He—"

"We—"

"One at a time!"

"We didn't kill him!" Ruth said. "We were looking for Nigel Winchester. When we knocked on the door, it opened, so we came inside." Her lips trembled. "He was moaning, and we tried to help him. But he died."

"You expect me to believe that?" Sarcasm dripped from his words.

"Yes, sir. I do."

He reached out. "Your identity cards, please."

They scoured the room for their pocketbooks, and Ruth spied them piled next to one of the chairs. She pointed, and the man nodded. She hastened forward and snatched their purses from the floor. Ruth handed Varis her bag and began to dig into her own. They found their passports and held them out to the man.

Ruth cleared her throat. "Sir?"

Still examining their passports, he grunted, "Yes?"

"Would you be so kind as to give us your name?"

He scrutinized her face for a long moment then returned their identification books. "Detective Sergeant Aikens."

"DS Aikens, we've told you the truth. May we leave now?"

"No. Even if you didn't kill him, I need to ask you some questions. Like why you were here in the first place?"

"It's all very simple. In fact, you could talk to DI Gelson, and he could explain everything." Ruth swallowed. The detective inspector would *not* be happy she had found another corpse.

Aikens raised one eyebrow and crossed his arms. "You ladies know DI Gelson? How did you manage that?"

Ruth gave a self-conscious giggle. "He was the officer in charge when a skeleton was found under our house after it was bombed."

His eyebrow rose even farther, and he glanced at Varis who nodded. He glowered. "This is obviously not as *simple* as you claim. Let's take a trip to the station, and we can chat with DI Gelson. How does that sound?"

"Well..."

He clapped his hands. "Good! Let's go."

Ruth tried again. "Detective..."

Aikens gestured toward the door. "Time's wasting." He called to the officers still collecting evidence. "We're going to the station. You know what to do."

"Yes, sir," the constables replied in unison.

Ruth stamped her foot. "Detective!"

His head swung back toward her. "What?"

"Are we under arrest? Do I need to contact the embassy?"

"Not yet."

"But..."

"Look, Miss Brown, I need to question you about this situation, and you've mentioned knowing DI Gelson. I thought we could kill two birds with one stone by going downtown. I thought it also might be a little nicer for you than staying here with the deceased. Don't you agree?"

Ruth nodded. She slung her purse over her shoulder and followed Varis and the detective out of the house, her eyes darting to and fro as she walked. She paused in the doorway and stared at the wall above the fireplace. It was blank, but something had been there. A small nail hole was visible, and a two-foot-square area on the wall was darker where the paint had not faded from sunlight.

———————◆———————

Thirty minutes later, Detective Aikens led Ruth and Varis into the police station. The uniformed sergeant seated behind the wooden counter jumped to his feet and saluted. He peered at the two women before his eyes slid to Talbot. "You want me to book 'em, Detective Sergeant?"

Aikens speared him with a reproving look. "They're not under arrest, Sergeant. Is DI Gelson here?"

"In his office, sir."

"Would you ask him to join us?"

"Yes, sir."

Aikens opened a door to the left then swept his arm to indicate Ruth and Varis should precede him inside. He grunted as he lifted a chair from the hall and carried it into the windowless room that held a scratched table with a chair on either side. He placed the chair on the far side of the table. "Would you ladies care to take a seat?"

Ruth and Varis looked at each another and sat. Ruth slapped her purse onto the table and crossed her arms. Varis kept a firm grip on her bag while Aikens hunkered in the corner. The silence in the room grew as the trio waited. In the hallway, muffled voices sounded and footsteps echoed.

The walls were painted an indeterminate shade of beige. Water stains on the ceiling resembled a series of Rorschach tests. A large sign proclaimed, Prisoners Must Remain Seated at All Times. The stale smell of fear clung to the room as if it had not been long since the last interrogation. Detective Aikens seemed to remember his manners when he turned to them and mumbled, "Would you like some water?"

"No, thank you," the women spoke in unison.

The door opened, admitting Trevor Gelson, and relief split the air when Aikens straightened and executed a stiff salute.

Ruth gave Trevor a frank appraisal. He was impeccably dressed, his bright white shirt clean and pressed, monogrammed cuff links at his wrists. His herringbone suit was chocolate brown, set off with a pale-green tie. Salt-and-pepper hair, mostly pepper, was cropped close to his head. When she met his intelligent gray eyes, she realized that very little escaped his notice. She wondered at the sudden urge to ensure her hair and makeup were in place.

Trevor tossed a glance at Aikens then looked back at Ruth and Varis. "Good afternoon. Have you ladies been offered anything to drink?"

Varis straightened in the chair. "Yes, Detective Inspector. We've been well taken care of."

Ruth swiveled toward Varis who pointedly ignored her, so she turned back to the inspector and spoke through stiff lips. "Apparently, we're fine."

Trevor leaned on the end of the table and crossed his arms. "Then let's get down to business. Why were you in Nigel Winchester's flat? If I remember correctly, we agreed that you would contact me if you thought of anything."

Ruth pasted a sweet smile on her face. "We didn't want to waste your time in case this was the wrong Nigel Winchester."

Trevor raised an eyebrow. "I'm supposed to accept that as fact?"

"Believe whatever you'd like."

"How did you know to look for him?"

"I met a man on High Street near the house, a Mr. Wingate, who said he knew Ian Belvedere and his family. We chatted a bit, and he told me about Ian's friendship with Nigel."

"Just like that, he told you all about Ian and Nigel."

"First, he invited me to take a walk with him."

"Are American women in the habit of stepping out with strange men, Miss Brown?"

Ruth huffed. "You make it sound inappropriate. He's eighty years old if he's a day, and it was all quite innocent."

"Detective Inspector, we'd be delighted to give you the information you seek." Varis intervened. "However, there is little to tell." She gestured at Ruth. "Ruth was at the house, and an elderly gentleman stopped to speak with her. They discovered a mutual love of books and took a stroll. He said his name was Andrew Wingate. I'm sure your records will confirm this. Anyway, their conversation turned to the bomb site, and Mr. Wingate indicated he had lived in the neighborhood for many years and knew the family. That's when he told her about Ian's friend Nigel. I'm sure he would talk to you."

"Perhaps. What else did he say?"

"Ian is one of five boys, and his mother was an American." Ruth licked her lips. "He thought Nigel was a spy."

"Who did? Ian?"

"No. Mr. Wingate. He said that Nigel's great-grandfather had been an agent and that it ran in the family."

Trevor's eyebrow went up again. "Really?"

"Yes. But he drifted in and out of lucidity, so I'm not sure how useful that tidbit will turn out to be." She hesitated. "Now do you see why we thought we'd visit Nigel before passing the information to you?"

"No, I don't. But I can see how you would. Reporters like to validate the truthfulness of their sources. But they also like to get their scoop, even if it means interfering with a police investigation. I've had occasion to run up against your type in the past."

Ruth swallowed her irritation. "Exactly. I didn't want to give you a faulty lead."

"I'm sure that's what it was." He grimaced. "Tell me about what you found at Nigel's place."

"I already told Detective Aikens."

"I'd like to hear it from you."

Ruth sighed and recited what she and Varis experienced. "We were only there a few minutes when the officers arrived."

"Did you see or hear anyone? Besides the victim, of course."

"No."

Trevor looked stern. "If the killer had still been there, you could have been hurt. Or worse."

From the corner of her eye, Ruth saw Varis shudder. "So you don't think we killed Mr. Winchester?"

"No. But this is the second time you've found a murder victim. I'd rather that didn't happen again. Please promise to leave this investigation to me."

"Yes, sir," Varis piped up.

Trevor smiled at her before turning to study Ruth. "Miss Brown?"

Ruth shook her head. "I'm not investigating. I'm working on a story."

Trevor's face darkened. "I could charge you with interference..."

"You wouldn't!" Ruth's heart leapt into her throat.

"Or murder."

Chapter Ten

With the car barely at a standstill in front of Nigel's house, Trevor opened the door and stepped out. The memory of yesterday's verbal dual with Miss Brown surfaced. He grit his teeth and cinched his trench coat. He walked to the front window and motioned for the driver to roll it down. "Wait here. I won't be long." The officer nodded and turned off the engine.

Trevor settled his hat on his head and glanced at the barricades blocking the victim's home. A worn sign leaned against the wooden barrier, its message clear: WARNING! Looting Is Strictly Prohibited and Is Punishable by Hanging.

He approached the house to the right. Despite the morning's brilliant sunshine, there were no reflections on the dirty second-floor windows. Like many of the buildings along the street, boards were nailed over the first-floor windows—or at least where windows had been at one time. The rubble along the curb confirmed Hitler's flying henchmen had been here.

With any luck, today would be more productive than yesterday's interview with the reporter and her friend. Trevor huffed out a breath. Annoying and attractive. A lethal combination.   He rapped on the door.

Moments passed, and he knocked again. Louder. From inside, he could hear footsteps and a high-pitched voice called out, "I'm coming!"

The door swung open to reveal a plump woman who could be forty-five to sixty-five years of age. Dark circles rimmed golden-brown eyes, and her oval face was splotched and lined. A few silver threads ran through the woman's faded-black hair.

"Yer a policeman, aren't you? I can tell just by looking at you."

Trevor nodded as he produced his identity card. "Yes, ma'am. I am DI Trevor Gelson."

The woman preened. "*Ma'am?* Nobody's called me that in a bit. I'm Mrs. Collingsworth." She stepped back and beckoned him inside. "Won't you come in?"

He removed his hat and stepped over the threshold. His eyes prowled the room as she led him to a pair of upholstered chairs. The furnishings were few, but a multitude of framed photographs cluttered the walls and stood on every horizontal surface. Trevor waited for Mrs. Collingsworth to sit down before lowering himself into the other chair.

She put a work-roughened hand to her throat for a moment. "Dear me, where are my manners? Would you like some tea?"

"No, thank you. I'd like to ask you a few questions, if I may."

She arranged herself on the burgundy floral cushion and crossed her ankles. "This is about the poor boy next door, isn't it? Such a shame. He was a nice young man."

"You knew him?"

"Not well. He kept himself to himself, really. But when he saw me, he would speak. Once or twice he picked up items at the market for me, even though he was, you know, crippled. He was especially kind after Harry joined up."

"Harry?"

She pointed to a picture on the table nearby, and grief passed across her face. A young man in an army uniform laughed at the camera, his hat pushed back on his head. "My son."

Trevor sighed. "Where did you lose him?"

"Dunkirk."

"I'm sorry. You must miss him very much."

Silence blanketed the room then she tapped the photo and smiled. "He was a lovely boy. I'm quite proud of him, you know."

"I'm sure you are."

She folded her hands in her lap. "Enough about that, Detective Inspector. What can I tell you?"

"Did Nigel Winchester have many visitors?"

She shook her head. "No. There was one lad who came every Saturday to play chess. They would set up a table outside on nice days. Boring, if you ask me, but they would remain there for hours."

"Do you know the lad's name?"

"It's in there somewhere." She rubbed her forehead for a moment then shook her head. "I'm sorry. I can't recall."

Trevor crossed his arms and leaned against the chair. "Was there anyone else who visited?"

About a month ago, a man from the army came to see him. I was surprised at that. Did you know Nigel was injured in the last war? He could barely walk. He never talked about it, but I know it bothered him."

"His canes were in the flat."

"Of course." She continued to prattle. "Anyway, the man was an officer, a major. His uniform was starched and pressed, and he had lots of medals and ribbons. I wondered why he'd come to see Nigel. The poor boy certainly couldn't join up. Why do you think he came?"

Trevor shrugged. "Perhaps he was a friend."

"I don't think so. He only stayed for a short time. What kind of friend does that?"

"Indeed. Did you happen to see his name badge?"

She looked crestfallen. "No."

"That's fine. Can you tell me more? How old do you think the major was? Could he have served in the last war?"

"He looked to be about Nigel's age."

"Are you certain about that?"

"Yes. He was definitely in his mid-forties or early fifties. I could tell."

"Let's talk about the night Nigel died. Did you hear anything unusual?"

"I didn't think about it at the time, but Nigel may have been arguing with someone."

"May have been?"

"His voice was raised. I couldn't hear the words. Then nothing. And then he'd start shouting again. I never heard another voice, so maybe he was just mad at himself."

Trevor leaned forward. "Was he in the habit of shouting at himself? Was he bitter or angry because of his legs?"

"No. He was a quiet sort. Seemed resigned to his fate. He had built a life with his job at university and his chess matches." She frowned. "It's always the good ones who die, isn't it, Inspector?"

"Sometimes it feels that way, Mrs. Collingsworth." He reached into his jacket pocket, pulled out a card, and handed it to her. "If you think of anything else that might help, please contact me."

He rose and gestured for her to remain seated. "I can see myself out."

"Have a good day, Inspector. I hope you find who did this. It's bad enough we're at war. Do we have to kill each other?"

"Unfortunately, Mrs. Collingsworth, some people think that we do."

"Hugh!"

Trevor stopped at the door. "Pardon?"

"The young man who plays chess with Nigel. His name is Hugh."

Chapter Eleven

Across town, Ruth shivered on a wooden bench outside the American embassy. A cold wind wrestled with her long, navy-blue wool coat and nipped at her face. She tightened her scarf against her neck then wrapped her arms around herself. Two uniformed marines who guarded the entrance stood at ramrod attention. Despite their taut and impassive expressions, she never doubted they watched her like hawks—ready for action at a moment's notice.

Late last summer, Ruth had seen a mother with her toddler son rushing to the embassy gates. Disheveled and sobbing, they were bruised and dirty. The terrified woman screamed, "I'm an American. Let me in. Please, let me in!" In an instant, the guards came alive. One of them swung open the wrought-iron gate while the other whipped the rifle off his shoulder and cocked it. The woman staggered through and collapsed into the soldier's arms. He gently led her into the building as another marine came out to take his place as sentry. The man who'd been chasing the woman scowled and slunk away.

Ruth waved away the memory. The sidewalks were empty. She stood and paced. Although high in the sky, the sun provided little warmth.

Movement at the embassy caught her eye, and she smiled. Varis descended the stairs and left the embassy grounds to cross the street.

As usual, Varis was the picture of beauty and professionalism. Her brown hair was swept into a smooth victory roll, and wispy bangs covered her forehead above perfectly arched eyebrows. Her black wool coat was buttoned over the burgundy suit Ruth had seen her put on that morning.

Ruth hugged Varis. "How can you look so good after a full morning at the circus?"

Varis giggled and mugged a pinup-girl pose. "Don't I always look this good? Anyway, the ringmaster was out of the office this morning. That reduces the atmosphere from frantic to crazy. It's also why I'm able to eat lunch with you today." She looped her arm through Ruth's. "Let's not waste a minute of it."

They hurried along the sidewalk, weaving their way through the lunchtime crowds. The scent of food tempted them as they passed several small restaurants. The pungent smell of cabbage mixed with the tantalizing aroma of fresh bread. On another street, marinara sauce clashed with fried fish. Above it all clung the bitter odor of coal dust. A car rumbled past and from inside the vehicle snatches of Glenn Miller's "You and I" floated toward them.

Ruth cocked her head. From one of the homes came the rumbling voice of Edward R. Murrow.

"Is it much farther?" Varis said.

"I think the place is on the next block. It's hard to say, for the usual reasons." Ruth nodded at the covered-over street sign.

"The authorities don't want to make it easy on the Germans if they do invade."

"I know, and I agree with the sentiment. But it sure creates a problem when I'm in a new neighborhood."

They continued walking. Restaurants gave way to shops—book shops, dress shops, toy shops. Some had boarded-up windows proclaiming, Open for Business in hand-painted scrawls; others displayed their minimal wares nestled among red, white, and blue bunting.

Varis pointed across the street. "There it is. Vine's Stationery and Paper Goods."

"Excellent." Ruth winked at Varis. "Here goes nothing."

They entered the shop, and the door closed behind them. The store was impeccable, but only slightly less cold than outside. A waist-high counter circled the room, and the walls were lined with shelves stained a dark brown. In the center of the room were three display cases, their glass clean and sparkling. The stock of notebooks, pencils, fountain pens, sheaves of paper, and scissors was sparse but tastefully displayed.

The woman behind the counter wore a gray tweed suit with a pale-pink blouse. Her straight blonde hair fell to just below her chin. Her smile reached her coffee-colored eyes. "Good afternoon, ladies. I'm Miss Packer. How may I be of service?"

Ruth approached. "You have a lovely shop. Are you the owner?"

Miss Packer shook her head. "No. I've only worked here since last summer. One of the girls lost her husband and left London to live with her mother in Marlow."

Varis said, "How sad."

Miss Packer nodded. "They had only been married a year, and she has a little boy. Now he'll grow up never knowing his father."

Ruth and Varis murmured their sympathy. Ruth cleared her throat. "I'm looking for someone, but I noticed you carry typewriter paper. Could I see what you have?"

"Of course. How much do you need?"

Ruth held her thumb and forefinger about a half inch apart. "Is that too much? I don't want to take more than my fair share."

"I can sell you a dozen pieces. Will that be enough?" She pulled a sheet of paper from two different piles. "We offer paper from a couple of suppliers. One is a bit higher quality than the other, but maybe you'd rather save a few pence."

Ruth reached into her purse and drew out some coins. "I'll take the less expensive one. I'm sure you understand."

Miss Packer nodded and counted out the appropriate number of pages. "That will be five shillings. Is there anything else I can help you find?" She wrapped Ruth's purchase into a large envelope. She tied a string around it and laid it on the counter.

Ruth handed her the coins and picked up her stationery. "Not from the shop, but as I mentioned earlier, I'm looking for someone. Does Millicent Belvedere work here?"

"Not since Christmas. She didn't return after the holiday, and no one has been able to contact her. She's a lovely woman. Worked here for years, from what I understand."

"Did you know her well?"

"Not particularly. Mr. Marshall—that's the owner—he expects us to stay busy even when the shop is empty. That doesn't give us much time for chatting."

"What can you tell me about her?"

Licking her lips, Miss Packer leaned toward Ruth and Varis. "The girls say she came from money. When I heard that I wondered why she was working here, but Lucille said Millicent gave up everything to marry beneath her station—that her parents cut her off when she did. But her husband ran off, and she had to find work. Her parents still don't speak to her. Terrible, isn't it?"

"How long ago did he take off?"

Miss Packer tsked and said, "It was ages ago. Sometime after he came home from the Great War. Can you believe it? She waits all that time for him to return, and he makes it through without getting killed. Then he up and leaves her. It's unfortunate, really."

Ruth shifted the package in her arms. "Did she give any indication before the holiday that she wouldn't be back?"

"Not to me. Mr. Marshall might know or Cecile Cook. They seemed to know each other well. Millicent and Cecile often took their lunch together."

Ruth brightened. "Will either of them be in today?"

Miss Packer squinted at the watch dangling from the chain around her neck then nodded. "Cecile should be here momentarily, but we never know when Mr. Marshall will visit the shop. I think he pops in and out to keep us on our toes."

Varis smiled. "Bosses are like that, aren't they?"

"I'm not complaining. He's a good man. Gave me this job when I didn't have any shop experience."

"That was nice of him. What did you do before?"

The woman shuddered. "I worked at one of the munitions factories. Made good money, I did. But it was dangerous work." Her bottom lip trembled. "I lost my best friend in an explosion. That's when I quit. I don't earn as much here, but now I just have to worry about the Jerries. I'll take my chances with them rather than sit on a powder keg every day."

Varis patted Miss Parker's arm. "I'm sorry for your loss. These are terrible times."

Miss Parker dabbed the tears from her eyes with a worn handkerchief and nodded. She sniffed loudly. "I'm sorry for weeping. I don't know what came over me."

"No need to apologize. We've lost loved ones also," Ruth said.

The bell on the door jangled, and a stocky, dark-haired woman entered the shop. She peeled off her brown wool coat to reveal a blue plaid dress that accentuated her roundness. Her feet were shod in heavy-soled brown oxfords. She smiled at the three women and hung her coat on a hook behind the counter.

Miss Packer gestured to Ruth and Varis. "Miss Cook, these young ladies are looking for Millicent Belvedere. I thought you might be able to help them."

A shadow crossed Miss Cook's face. "And you are…?"

Ruth lifted her hand. "My name is Ruth Brown, and this is my friend, Varis Gladstone."

"You're Americans? What are you doing over here?"

"I'm a journalist, and Varis works at the embassy."

Miss Cook narrowed her eyes. "Why do you need to know about Millicent?"

"We're trying to help her. We understand that she thinks her husband left her many years ago, but we think we've found him."

Miss Cook straightened, and her face darkened. "Found Ian? Why would you want to tell her? You need to leave well enough alone. She's done with that part of her life. He was no good. He hurt her bad by leaving."

Ruth cleared her throat. "Actually, Miss Cook, he's dead. And has been for a long time."

"I don't understand."

"I can explain," Varis said. Several nights ago, the building where our flat is located was bombed. Ruth fell through the floor and discovered a skeleton. We believe it is Ian Belvedere."

Miss Packer's eyes widened. Miss Cook sagged against the counter.

Varis looked apologetic. "We're sorry to tell you like this, but now do you see why we need to contact Mrs. Belvedere?"

Miss Cook straightened and smoothed her dress. "Yes. Of course. I don't know what came over me. Mr. Marshall may know how to contact her. He must have sent her wages. We don't know when he'll return, but we could leave a message for him to contact you. Will that be all right?"

Ruth studied the middle-aged clerk, her reporter's senses on alert. The woman refused to meet Ruth's eyes. "That would be fine." Ruth fished her card from the depths of her pocketbook and laid it on the counter. That's my phone number. If you can't reach me there, you can leave a message at *The Times*."

Miss Cook stared at the card for a long moment then picked it up, and without a word, slipped it into the cash register drawer.

Five hours later, the door to the flat opened, and Ruth leapt up from the couch. Varis entered and unbuttoned her coat. Ruth gestured to the dining room table where she had placed two plates of ham sandwiches. A small bowl of roasted carrots stood to one side. "Sit down. I've already made dinner."

Varis hung her coat on the hall tree and turned to Ruth with a raised eyebrow. "Need a favor, do you? Let me wash up, if you don't mind."

Ruth nodded. "I've got another lead on one of the Belvedere's neighbors. She was on her way out when I went by this afternoon, but she said she would see us this evening."

Moments later, Varis dried her hands, and they made their way back to the table. "No wonder you're jumpy. Sit. I'll say grace."

They seated themselves and joined hands. Varis prayed, "Dear Father. Thank You for this food. Thank You for providing ham. What a lovely treat! Keep us safe tonight while we are out, Lord, and again as we sleep. Let us know when it's time to stop pursuing this story. We pray all these things in the name of Your Son, Jesus. Amen."

Varis leaned over her food and inhaled deeply. "This smells heavenly, Ruth. Where did you manage to find ham?"

"The Kaminski's shop. They had a tiny piece. She sliced her sandwich and picked up one half. Now, what did you mean when you prayed to stop pursuing the story? That's my job."

Varis bit into her sandwich and chewed slowly. She seemed to be collecting her thoughts. "Our safety is paramount. Did you forget this is a murder investigation? An unsolved murder, which means the killer may still be out there and, if so, probably doesn't want to be discovered. Have you already forgotten how scared we were when the purse snatcher accosted us this summer? I don't like that feeling."

She put her food on the plate and continued, "I love your excitement for what you do, Ruth. Your tenacity at getting the whole story—not only what happened, but why and how it affects the people involved. However, I'm not willing to put my life on the line for it. Or yours."

Ruth sagged in her chair. "As usual, you're right. I almost got you killed last year during the Coltrain investigation."

Varis grinned. "No, the man driving the car almost killed me. But we probably should have stopped before we annoyed him so badly."

Ruth chuckled. "You're the best, Varis. I promise I'll quit if this story gets too dangerous."

"No, you won't. But I'll try to keep you out of trouble." She pointed at Ruth's food. "Now, eat up! We've got an interview to conduct."

<hr>

Forty-five minutes later, Ruth and Varis walked into Polly Armstrong's parlor. Decorated in shades of blue, a large overstuffed midnight-blue sofa dominated the room. A regal-looking woman with silver-streaked brown hair sat in a chair the color of a robin's egg. The rug was a blend of baby blue, sapphire, and hyacinth.

"Thank you for seeing us, Miss Armstrong. This is my friend, Varis Gladstone."

"Love to meet you, dear." Miss Armstrong gestured to the room. "Sit anywhere you'd like. May I get you some tea?"

Ruth shook her head. "No, thank you. We don't want to take up too much of your time."

Ruth and Varis seated themselves on the couch, and Ruth spied a harp in the far corner of the room. "Is the instrument yours?"

Miss Armstrong gave it a loving glance. "Yes. I used to play with the London Symphony. Those days are long over." She held out her hands, her fingers arthritic and bent.

Varis's clasped her hands together. "The symphony! How exciting. You must have lots of stories to tell about your time with them."

Their host smiled and looked at Ruth. "You wanted to know about Ian and Millicent Belvedere. Is this about the skeleton found in their house the night of the bombing? The neighborhood has been buzzing."

"Yes. We lived in that house."

Miss Armstrong's hand went to her throat. "Oh, you poor dears. You must have been terrified. Have you found a place to stay?"

"Yes. A friend of Varis's has an extra bedroom," Ruth said.

"How fortunate for you."

Ruth leaned forward. "Yes. Did you know the Belvederes very well?"

Miss Armstrong shook her head. "They were quite a bit younger than I was but often went for walks and would stop to chat. That was before the Great War. Then poor Ian went off, and we held our breaths to see if he would return."

"What did Millicent do while he was away?"

"I believe she took a job associated with the war effort. She left the house early in the morning and often did not return until quite late at night. Occasionally, she wouldn't come home for several days in a row. It must have been very important work."

Ruth and Varis exchanged glances, and Ruth said, "No doubt. Did she ever have visitors? Girlfriends who came over?"

"None that I recall." Miss Armstrong sat up straighter and snapped her fingers. "Actually, there was. One time a gentleman friend came home with her. I didn't think anything of it when I saw them. It was common to be walked home that late at night. For safety, you know. But the following morning, Millicent seemed to search me out to assure me there was nothing untoward going on. Which, of course, told me there was." She frowned. "Poor Ian, fighting for his country, his wife gadding about. I didn't think it was a good match from the beginning."

Ruth perked up. "What makes you say that?"

"One sees things. Little things. But they added up. Millicent criticized Ian. Constantly. "Straighten your tie. Comb your hair. Tie your shoes." That sort of thing. You'd think she was speaking to a child." Miss Armstrong pursed her lips. "She didn't seem to respect him."

"But they were in love, weren't they? Why else would they get married?"

"I think he loved her very much. You could see it on his face. Millicent? I think she was in love with the idea of love. I heard she came from money. Maybe she took pleasure in marrying outside her set. Maybe she was bored. Maybe she did love him in her own way. I just know what I saw when he came home. And I'm not surprised he didn't stay home for long after the war."

Ruth raised an eyebrow. "What happened? Do you know?"

The clock tolled eight times, and Miss Armstrong glanced at the brooch watch pinned to her blouse. "Is it eight o'clock already? Goodness, where does the time go? Do you girls have far to go to get home?"

Ruth pressed her lips together. Had they overstayed their welcome? There was still so much she wanted to know.

Varis stood and smoothed her skirt then picked up her purse from the table. "Thank you for your hospitality, Miss Armstrong. You've been most generous." She gave Ruth a pointed look, and Ruth scrambled to her feet. When would she learn to exit gracefully? "Yes, thank you, Miss Armstrong. I wonder, would it be possible to come back for another visit?"

"Perhaps. I'm quite busy. Working with the war orphans, you know."

Ruth reached into her purse and withdrew a card that she handed to Miss Armstrong. "Please call me if you have time to speak with us further.

The woman laid it on the table without a glance then rose and led the girls to the foyer. She opened the door. "I hope you find what you're looking for, Miss Brown. Miss Gladstone."

Varis tugged on Ruth's arm, and they stepped outside with murmured goodbyes. Miss Armstrong closed the door.

"She practically threw us out," Ruth huffed. "Do you think she knows something? What is it with these people? They give us tidbits of information and claim that horrible things happening to their neighbors are none of their business."

Varis beckoned, and they walked toward the bus stop. With any luck it would be running on time tonight. Varis drew her coat closer and said, "It was a different time back then, Ruth. People did mind their business. It wasn't proper to get involved. One looked the other way."

Ruth scowled and repositioned her purse on her shoulder. "Even when a man is being murdered under their very noses?"

"They didn't know that. How could they?"

In a cloud of dust and fumes, the bus chugged toward them. Its slitted headlights were dark, yet the vehicle pulled to a stop directly in front of them. The doors swung open, and the girls stepped on board.

Ruth grimaced. "That's what I aim to find out."

Chapter Twelve

Trevor followed the hulking man to the back of the smoke-filled pub where he knocked then opened the door and gestured for Trevor to follow him. The door closed behind them shutting out chatter, laughter, and music. Their footsteps were muffled on the black-and-tan Persian rug. Paneled in rich mahogany, the room was the antithesis of the cheaply painted bar he had just passed through. This was where the real business was conducted.

A mammoth oak desk dominated the room in front of which two carnelian leather chairs covered in brass rivets, waited. An ornate, crystal chandelier cast shards of light on the man behind the desk. His sandy-brown hair was slicked back accentuating his tall, pale forehead. Small features clustered in the middle of his face. Dressed in a hand-tailored suit, the man sat still as a statue. A diamond stud held his yellow silk tie against his white shirt. In one manicured hand, he gripped a slender cigarette holder, in the other a champagne flute filled with fizzing, straw-colored liquid. The light glinted from his diamond cuff links when he tapped the cigarette into an ashtray. A telephone sat near his elbow.

Trevor removed his hat and strode forward. The brute behind him cleared his throat. Trevor gave him a long hard look. The man broke eye contact and scowled.

The smell from the man's half-eaten meal permeated the room. The remnants of a rare steak lay on one side of the fragile-looking china plate, bloody juices congealing beside a few forkfuls of fluffy mashed potatoes and a pair of green beans. Next to the plate stood a magnum of champagne. What was the man celebrating, or did he drink the stuff every day? Trevor pointed to one of the leather chairs. "Sorry to interrupt your dinner, Young. Mind if I sit down?"

Sidney Young eyeballed the dish then jerked his head toward the door. The guard lumbered forward and cleared the dinnerware before clomping from the room. The door closed with a bang, and they were alone. Young took a deep drag on the cigarette then blew the smoke out through his nostrils. "Champagne, DI Gelson? I could call for another glass."

"No, thank you."

"Of course, you're on duty. Perhaps another time." He narrowed his black eyes, two cold pebbles against his fair skin. "What can I do for you?"

"Nigel Winchester was found dead yesterday. I thought you'd want to know."

Young's hand froze on its way to the champagne glass. "What's that got to do with me?"

"I understand he worked for you sometimes."

Young shrugged. "Sometimes."

"What could you possible need an engineer for in your line of work?"

Young's face darkened for a moment then he leaned back and chuckled. "Good one, Inspector. You had me going there for a minute. Sure Winchester worked for me, but it wasn't anything to frown at. He's a genius, and I've got a couple of development projects in the works. I needed his expertise to check things out."

"Doing your part for the city, are you?"

"Every chance I get. I'm a legitimate businessman. I paid my debt to society, and I want to give back."

Trevor tossed his fedora on the desk. "Sure you do, Young. And you wouldn't even think of using this war as an excuse to make a little extra cash through the misfortune of others."

"No, I wouldn't." Young drained the champagne and set the glass down with a faint clink. "You didn't say how poor Nigel died, Inspector."

"His head was bashed in."

Young winced. "That must have been a mess. I wonder what he did to deserve that."

"You don't know?"

"Why would I? He helped me out a few times reading those fancy engineering drawings, and he teaches at some highbrow school. How can you do that and anger someone enough to want to kill you? Doesn't seem possible."

"He's dead, and it was definitely not through natural causes. Did you make a bad investment because of information he gave you? That would be reason enough."

Young rested the cigarette holder in the ashtray and poured more of the straw-colored champagne into his glass. "Detective Inspector Gelson, I am saddened to hear of Nigel's death. It's a terrible waste. He was a brilliant man. He could be a trifle tedious, if you ask me, but did I kill him? No. You need to look elsewhere for your suspect. Maybe our quiet professor was into something he shouldn't have been. People are not always what they seem, and war doesn't always bring out the best in men. You have firsthand knowledge of that."

Trevor shifted in the chair, and the leather squeaked. He crossed him arms and gave Young a steely-eyed look. "You know I have to ask you. Where were you between one and five o'clock in the afternoon, three days ago?"

Young pulled a small book from his inside breast pocket and flipped through the pages. "Ah, yes. I was here. I had a meeting with my accountant. His name is Lester Berrey, and his place is on Fifty-Ninth Street. You can check with him."

"I will. I know you're well connected. Do you know who any of Nigel's friends or colleagues were?"

"I could ask around, casual-like." Young massaged his fingers.

Trevor swallowed. "Did you and Nigel ever discuss his hobbies or interests?"

Young raised an eyebrow. "Sounds like you already have a possible motive, Gelson."

Trevor gave him an unblinking stare until Young finally shrugged and broke out with a forced laugh. "I like you, Detective Inspector, but I would never play poker with you. All right, in the spirit of cooperation I'll tell you what I know about Nigel Winchester. He had a keen mind in the ways of engineering, but when it came to people he was too trusting, too naïve. He believed in the intrinsic good of people. Can you believe it? After having been to war? Being injured like he was? What a fool! But he could play chess like a master, and he loved to talk about art. Apparently, he had seen many beautiful things while in France: churches, paintings, sculptures. Only the French would leave their valuables lying around during war."

"Are you aware of any art he might have owned?"

"Not, but I don't see how he would have any. His tastes outpaced his wallet."

The phone trilled, and the two men looked at it. It rang again, and Young lifted the receiver. He tucked it under one ear and murmured, "Hold on." He looked at Trevor. "Anything else I can do for you, Inspector?"

Trevor stood and picked up his fedora. "I'll leave you to your business." He stuffed his hat on his head and took his time getting to the door. He turned back to Young, gave a quick salute, and slipped out of the room.

The noise of the bar enveloped him as he passed through it to the street. He squinted into the sunshine and drew his coat closer against the chill. He stepped to the curb where Sergeant Phillips waited in the car perusing *The Times*. Phillips folded the paper and tossed it on the seat next to him then rolled down the window and looked at Trevor. "Sir?"

"I think I'll walk back to the station, Phillips. After that I need some fresh air."

"It's twenty blocks, sir."

"I know. It will give me time to sift through the conversation. My gut tells me he's lying about not knowing that Nigel was dead, or at a minimum there's something he's not telling me. I have to figure out what it is. He did claim he'd check with his cronies to see if they knew anything."

"Only because it's in his best interest. Don't you think, sir?"

Trevor nodded. "Before you go back to the station, swing by the offices of one Lester Berrey. B-E-R-R-E-Y. He's an accountant. Young claims they were together at the time of the murder. I'm sure he's already called Berrey to give him a heads-up, but we have to go through the paces."

"Yes, sir."

"I'll see you shortly." Trevor knocked on the roof and stepped back. He rubbed his arms. He needed a bath after meeting with a guy like Young.

Ideas and theories bounced back and forth in Trevor's mind as he stalked the sidewalks toward the station. He shouldered his way through the crowds, his eyes searching for guilt on each face he passed—a habit he could not break. Maybe Young was telling the truth. As the man said, he'd paid his debt. Trevor snorted, and the man next to him looked over and quickened his stride.

Men like Young did not change. He wanted respect and was willing to buy it, surrounding himself with riches and sycophants. What did the death of one minion mean to the man? Nothing, unless it protected him from something.

What could Young need protection from? Trevor stopped in his tracks, and a stout man bumped into him with a loud complaint. Trevor mumbled an apology and tipped his hat when the man moved past him with a heated glare.

Trevor began to walk again, his pace faster. Money. It had to be a scheme that added to Young's coffers. Black market? Smuggling? How could an engineer be tied to this? War production?

Could Young have something he wanted to sell to the highest bidder, no matter which side of the conflict they were on? Was Young committing treason, and Nigel discovered it? Even if Young's alibi checked out for the day of Nigel's murder, that didn't put him in the clear. He wasn't known for doing his own dirty work.

"Sir!"

Trevor looked toward the voice. Phillips braked the sedan and called to him through the open window. "Sir, there's been an incident."

Removing his hat, Trevor hurried to the car and slid into the back seat. Phillips stomped on the accelerator, and the vehicle shot forward. He met Trevor's eyes in the rearview mirror. "On my way to see Young's accountant, one of the boys flagged me down. He had contacted the station to report in and was told to be on the lookout for a group of five men. They fled the scene of an attack."

Traffic bottlenecked, and Phillips stopped the car. He turned to look at Trevor. "They beat up a conchie, sir. A conscientious objector."

Trevor rubbed a weary hand across his forehead. "Yes, yes. I know what a conchie is. How is he?"

Phillips shrugged. "Billings didn't know. But the victim was taken to hospital. We can visit him there, get his statement." Cars began to move again, and Phillips accelerated. His head swiveled to the left, then right, then left again as he negotiated the sedan through the snarl of vehicles. His face brightened. "Hang on, sir."

Jerking the wheel, he guided the car down an alley. The car bumped and jostled its way down the narrow street. Trevor gripped the door handle to keep from being battered and bruised. "Is this shortcut worth it, Phillips?"

His sergeant grinned. "Absolutely, sir. I use it all the time."

Trevor raised an eyebrow. "Is that why this car needs alignments more than any others in the pool?"

"I wouldn't know, sir."

The alley ended, and Phillips turned right. He gave Trevor a satisfied smile. "See? Wide open."

"Well done, Sergeant."

Fifteen minutes later, Phillips stopped in front of the brick monstrosity that was St. Bartholomew's Hospital. "Would you like me to wait here, sir?"

"Please join me. You can take notes."

"Very good, sir."

They stepped out of the car and climbed the stairs, their feet scraping against the stone. Removing their hats, they entered the building.

Approaching the desk, Trevor smiled. "Good afternoon, Sister. We're police officers, and we're here to see a young man who was brought in a short time ago. He's been beat up."

A frown creased her brow. "Yes, I know who you mean. He's very bad off. Must you speak to him now?"

"I'm afraid so, Sister. We won't take long, but it will help us find the culprits who committed the crime."

She gave them a long, haughty look then stood. "Follow me." Her skirts rustled as she walked, and her shoes chirped on the polished wood floor. She led them down a long hallway. The bare, white walls were broken up by a closed door every few feet. White-coated doctors spoke with nurses in white dresses. A splash of color would go a long way to cheering up the ward.

They stopped at the last door on the left. She turned to them and laid a finger against her lips. "You have ten minutes. Do not agitate him. He needs his rest."

"Yes, ma'am."

She opened the door and gestured for them to enter. "Inspector?"

Trevor looked at the woman.

Her face had softened.

He cocked his head. "Yes?"

"Find the hooligans who did this. No one deserves to be brutalized, no matter what his beliefs." With that she closed the door behind them with a muffled thud.

Propped up in a sitting position, the young man was motionless under the light blue blanket. His left arm was cast from wrist to shoulder, his right lay bruised and lifeless by his side. He studied Trevor and Phillips through one eye, the other blackened and swollen shut. A row of stitches marched across his forehead down to his jaw.

Trevor lowered himself into the wooden chair next to the bed. He cleared his throat. "I'm sorry for your injuries. We will find out who did this, but we need your help. What's your name?"

The man opened his mouth to speak, but he choked and fell into a fit of deep wracking coughs. Phillips snatched the pitcher of water from the cart by the window and filled a glass. He handed it to Trevor who braced the man and held the cup to his lips. The patient sipped for a moment then slumped back against Trevor who eased him against the pillow then set down the cup and returned to the chair.

"Thank you. I'm Colin Bertram." The man spoke in a raspy voice.

"Are you feeling strong enough to tell me what happened?"

Colin nodded. "I was walking home from work, and when I passed one of the alleys, a group of boys came out and began to follow me. At first they just called me names. I didn't want any trouble so I sped up, but that only served to fuel them. They bumped into me a few times. I told him I didn't want any trouble. That's when they started hitting me." He took a shuddering breath. "Two of the boys held my arms behind my back, and the other three took turns punching me. When my legs wouldn't hold me anymore, I fell to the ground, and they kicked me, and kicked me, and kicked me." Colin's voice trailed off, and he spoke in a whisper. "I woke up here."

Trevor frowned. A despicable act by cowards and bullies.

"Can you tell me anything about your attackers? What they looked like? Had you ever seen them before?"

Colin shrugged then winced. "I'm not sure. I thought if I didn't look them in the eye they would leave me alone."

"Take your time. I need to speak with Sergeant Phillips for a moment." Trevor stood and gestured for Phillips to follow him to the door. He whispered, "Call the station and get Sergeant Banks down here. Maybe he can get sketches worked up."

"Yes, sir." Phillips slipped from the room, and Trevor returned to the bed.

"One of my men is going to visit and try to draw what these men looked like. He's quite good at helping victims remember their attackers. You'd be surprised what is buried in your mind."

"Okay. I'll try."

Trevor smiled. "That's all we ask. Now, has your family been notified? Do they know where to find you?"

"I think so. My parents don't have a phone, but there's a shop down the street from where we live that takes messages for us."

"I know you must be getting tired, but I have a few more questions if you're up to it."

Colin nodded. "Sure."

"Do you take the same route home every day?"

"Yes."

Trevor leaned close. "How vocal have you been about your beliefs?"

"Vocal?"

"Do you make it a point to tell people you are a conscientious objector? Attend protest rallies, that sort of thing?"

"No, sir!" Colin broke into another paroxysm of coughing, and Trevor waited until it subsided to pass him the glass of water. Colin drank deeply then cradled the cup in his hand. "I mind my own business and work hard to help support my family. That's all I do."

"Does your family hold with your beliefs?"

Colin's eyes fell, and he rubbed the rim of the cup. "My brother is a pilot with the Fifth Squadron. We haven't spoken since he enlisted in thirty-nine."

Trevor sighed and ran a hand across his face. The war was tearing families apart. When would it end? "What about your parents?"

"They don't understand me either, but they tell me I have a right to my opinion." His face pinked under the bruising. "I think they're ashamed of me."

"What makes you say that?"

Colin did not respond. He closed his eyes and turned his face toward the wall. A single tear trickled down his cheek.

The silence deepened, and weary to the bone, Trevor pulled himself out of the chair. He gazed at Colin. *Lord, heal this young man. Heal his heart, not just his broken body. Heal his family. End this war! I know men have been fighting each other since the beginning of time. It's our own fault—our sinful, prideful selves get in the way of doing right, and we don't deserve Your grace. But send it anyway, Lord. Heal our land.*

Trevor gave Colin's shoulder a light squeeze. "I'll be praying for you, son. And we will find who did this."

The door opened to reveal Phillips. "Banks is on his way, sir. But you've had another call. Dr. Ledger wants to see you. He has additional information about our skeleton."

Chapter Thirteen

The next day, Ruth stood outside the police station. Uniformed officers and civilians brushed past her to enter the facility. Thus far, the structure had escaped unscathed from the bombings. It stood tall and proud next to a two-story office building that had not been so lucky. Bricks were missing, and much of the wooden trim was broken or riddled with holes. Of the eight windows on the front of the building, five were boarded over. The remaining three were crisscrossed with tape to prevent being shattered when the next bombing occurred. *When*, not *if*.

Would she ever be able to enjoy Independence Day fireworks again? Or would she crouch in terror at the colorful explosions in the sky? She shook her head to clear her mind and straightened the collar on her chocolate-brown wool coat. She would not follow that line of thinking. She couldn't.

What she needed was a new story to sink her teeth into. Anything to help keep the morbid thoughts at bay.

A colleague told her that a conscientious objector had been beaten up and "her" detective inspector was on the case. It was a story that needed to be told. Would the good-looking but stubborn man give her the details or stonewall her as usual?

She pulled out her compact and scrutinized her appearance in the tiny mirror. She didn't need to pinch her cheeks for color; the frigid wind had put roses on her face during the walk from the Underground. She straightened her narrow-brimmed, tan fedora on her head and squared her shoulders.

Ruth took a deep breath and ascended the stairs. She pushed opened the door and barreled into a medium-built man in an ill-fitting gray suit. A smattering of freckles danced across his nose, and a tuft of his brown hair stuck up from the crown of his head. He gripped her arms to steady her. "I beg your pardon, miss! Oh, Miss Brown. I didn't recognize you."

"Sergeant Phillips, is it?"

"Yes, miss. Do you need help?"

"I came to see Detective Inspector Gelson."

Phillips's brows came together, and he shook his head. "I'm afraid that's not possible, miss. Could I be of service?"

"I'm here to get details about the attack on the conscientious objector. My readers will want to know about that."

"There's little to tell."

Ruth shook her head. "There's plenty to tell. Are you protecting the inspector, Sergeant Phillips? I will see him."

"No, he's not here. May I leave a message for him?"

Ruth craned her neck around Phillips and searched the faces of the people walking through the lobby. Maybe he was telling her the truth. She looked back at the sergeant and crossed her arms. "What time do you expect him back?"

"I don't know. He doesn't find it necessary to inform me of his plans or schedule."

She pointed to a wooden bench near the intake desk. "May I wait over there?"

Phillips tossed a glance at the bench and shook his head. "This is a police station, not your personal news bureau. I told you I would leave a message for Detective Inspector Gelson. That will have to satisfy you."

Ruth glared at him. He may look like the boy next door, but he was not a pushover. She'd have to try another tactic. One she hated: the simpering female. But it often worked. She hitched her purse over her shoulder, cocked her head, and flashed him a pert smile. "Of course, Sergeant. I apologize for my behavior. Sometimes I get a bit overzealous in my search for a story. You understand, don't you? I'm in a hard place. My editor expects up-to-the-minute news. Perhaps you could help me. That way, I wouldn't have to bother the inspector."

"Well..."

She laid her hand on his arm. "You don't need to divulge any secrets, but if you had any information that would help keep the public safe..."

"Miss Brown?"

Ruth snatched her hand back as if burned and turned. DI Gelson stood in the doorway, a quizzical frown on his face. Sergeant Phillips blushed to the roots of his hair. He snapped a salute and stammered, "Miss Brown was asking about our most recent victim, sir."

"I see. Carry on, Phillips. I can take it from here."

"Yes, sir." Phillips hurried out the door.

Trevor removed his hat and shook his head. "Go easy on Sergeant Phillips, Miss Brown. He's not used to you American women."

"And you are?"

He gave her a level stare. "As a matter of fact, I am."

"Because…?"

Trevor gestured to the bench against the wall. "Don't start investigating me. I will tell you what I can about the poor young man who was assaulted, and then I must ask you to leave. We have business to attend to here."

They walked to the bench and sat down. Ruth dug into her purse to find her notepad and pencil. What was the inspector's story? Who was the American woman in his life? Or was he referring to her? She looked up to find him staring at her. Her face warmed. Now it was her turn to blush. Why did he have to be so attractive? She needed to dislike him. That would make her job so much easier. Instead, she was drawn to his razor-sharp mind, how he was able to cut to the heart of the matter. And those eyes of his. Dark and glittering, they didn't seem to miss a thing. When he spoke, a Clark Gable-like dimple appeared on his left cheek. His hair was creased where his hat had rested, and she stifled the urge to smooth it out.

She gripped her pencil and cleared her throat. "I'm ready, Detective
Inspector."

<hr>

Trevor smiled to himself in spite of his irritation at Miss Brown. If
he were honest, he would admit he was no different from her. Tenacious to
a fault, she didn't back down when it was in the best interest of her readers
to get the information. She was reminiscent of Mrs. Cookson's terrier
when the pup had a bone. But he did not relish the idea of a story like this
in the American newspapers. They did not need to see the seamy
underbelly of England. He would tread with care.

He narrowed his eyes. "I'm not prepared to give you the name of
the victim, Miss Brown. His identity must be protected. I'm sure you
understand the need for that."

She pursed her lips and nodded. He could see she was not happy.
Too bad. She had a job to do, but so did he, and that included protecting
the innocent from probing journalists. "Much like your own country's
checkered past with violent disagreement, a segment of England's
population is not happy with those who label themselves as conscientious
objectors, and they choose to make their opinions known with attacks on
these people. The crime was perpetrated by five young men. Our victim
was on his way home from work, and he was seized and beaten. It
happened at Bedford and Bloomsbury near the museum. Thus far, we have
been unable to find any witnesses other than the poor lad who was
attacked."

Ruth's pencil hovered over her paper. "Will he recover completely? Or could there be lasting results from this terrible incident."

Trevor's fingers tightened on his hat. "I don't know. The doctors say it is still too early to know for sure. He may have internal injuries they haven't found yet. He was well enough to speak to me, but heavily medicated against the pain."

"Was his statement sufficient to lead you to his assailants?"

Trevor shook his head. "I've sent my best sketch artist to work with him, however I don't hold out much hope. Whether through fear or the fact that he truly doesn't remember what they looked like, he was unable to give me any clues."

"Making it impossible to search for them. I could ask one of my colleagues to insert a piece in the London paper asking for witnesses to the event."

"Thank you. We've used the papers in the past seeking the public's help." He blew out a breath. "We are looking for five young men, ages fifteen to twenty-five, maybe thirty. All are of medium build. None exceptionally tall or heavy. Their clothes were in good condition. The incident occurred around six o'clock last night. Anyone who saw something or heard talk about it, should contact Sergeant Phillips here at the station."

Ruth's pencil flew across her steno pad as she recorded the information. A stray golden-brown curl dangled over her cheek as she focused on her work. Her lips were compressed, and her brows were drawn together in concentration.

What would it feel like to tuck the shining lock of hair behind her ear? To run his hands through the tangle of silky strands?

Trevor blinked. She was staring at him. Had she said something? He gave himself a mental shake. He was acting like a schoolboy, and that would never do. He cleared his throat. "Got all that?"

She nodded, so he continued, "Are you familiar with conscientious objectors, Miss Brown?"

"Yes, and I know how the U.S. deals with them. Over here there is some sort of tribunal, yes?"

"Yes, and it is handled much differently than in the last war. The chairman is usually a lawyer or county court judge, and a trade union member must be included. If the CO is a woman, there must be a woman on the tribunal."

"What about the military? Are they involved?"

"No."

"How does the tribunal work?"

Trevor settled back against the bench and crossed his arms. "The applicant is interviewed by the panel, and the decision is made immediately. They have the power to allow a full, unconditional exemption from military service, or they can make the exemption conditional by doing alternative civilian work such as forestry, hospital work, or social service. Some are required to join the military, but they can be exempt from combat duties."

"Making them join the army doesn't seem fair."

"How so?"

"It is a slap in the face. They object to killing as an answer to the situation, and yet they are made to work side by side with those who do the killing. It is also setting them up for ridicule and possibly even assault. Most of the soldiers must hate them."

"I wouldn't know about that, but you see what happens with civilians."

"Any truth to the rumor that the government watches these objectors?"

Trevor shrugged. "I wouldn't know about that either, but I admit it is a possibility. We are at war, Miss Brown. We must know who our enemies are."

Her eyes widened, and her voice hardened. "Are you calling the objectors the enemy? How dare you! These people have a right to their opinion. They have a right to stand up for their moral beliefs."

He held up his hands in surrender. "You misunderstand me. I respect these people; however, I firmly believe there are those who would escape service by claiming a belief they do not honestly hold."

Ruth straightened. "Don't the British people believe someone is innocent until proven guilty?"

Trevor shook his head. "That's not the situation here. We're not talking about a crime; we're talking about a belief system. A person's life should reflect that, and many of the people who raise their hand as a CO have not lived according to that belief, which leads me to think they are seeking a way out."

"I thought the police were to simply follow the clues and look at the facts."

"What's that supposed to mean? I do look at the facts, and the fact is that many people claim CO status because they are afraid to fight. It can be a way to do their part without getting shot at, unless they have the misfortune to be selected for the military as a medic."

He watched emotions flicker across her face: Anger, disappointment, disgust. What did she know? Another typical journalist waging war against something which she knows nothing about. He rubbed his jaw, feeling the stubble against his hand. "If everyone believed as they do, no one would be left to go up against Hitler's evil forces. What about the greater good—the need to defeat the Nazis?"

Her face darkened, and she jumped up from the bench sputtering, "So you think a person's ideals should be put on the shelf when they don't agree with their country's policies? If that's the case, then the British government is no better than Russia...or...or Nazi Germany!" She bent and snatched her purse from the floor where it had fallen.

Trevor stood and laid a hand on her arm. She recoiled and sneered at him. "If you approach all your cases with flawed assumptions, it's a wonder you solve any of them. It's a good thing Varis and I visited Millicent Belvedere's former employer."

"What?"

"I said—"

"I know what you said. And I said that you and Miss Gladstone were to leave the investigation of this case to me and my men. You agreed to that. Do you want to be arrested for obstruction of justice?"

She stamped her foot like Sergeant Phillips's four-year-old son when he didn't get his way, and he stifled a grin. "I can do that, you know."

Ruth stuffed her purse under her arm and flounced to the door, wrenching it open with a quick tug. "Try it, Detective Inspector. See how far that gets you."

Chapter Fourteen

Three days later, Trevor stood in front of a small cottage on the outskirts of the city. The midday December sun struggled to push its rays through angry gray clouds. He eyed the sky one more time and shivered in the damp air. Would the sleet hold off until he returned to the station? He pulled the dark green muffler tighter around his neck and knocked at the door.

A woman bustled past him without a glance. Bundled in an oversized navy-blue wool coat, she clutched a brown paper package against her chest with red-mitten-clad hands. A few steel-colored wisps of hair straggled out from under a blue knit cap. Her worn black brogans had seen many seasons of use. Trevor watched her disappear around the corner then turned toward the door as it swung open.

He held up his identity card and smiled. "Mr. Martin Sampson? Good afternoon. My name is Trevor Gelson. I'm a policeman. May I come in?"

The balding man stared at him for a moment before stepping aside. Trevor entered the house and removed his hat. Sampson hitched up his pants and crossed his arms. "What can I do for you?"

"I have a few questions. Do you mind if we sit down?"

"I'm kind of busy right now."

"I'm sure you are. I won't take much of your time."

A belligerent look marked the man's face. "Then why do you need to sit down?"

Trevor raised an eyebrow and looked past the man. "Is there a particular reason you'd rather I didn't come into your home?"

"Suit yourself." The man stomped down the hall, his left foot dragging.

Once they were inside Sampson's flat, Trevor's eyes scoured the tiny living room. Haphazard piles of newspapers cluttered the floor. A battered square table and four wooden folding chairs took up a third of the room. An incomplete jigsaw puzzle of an idyllic lake scene covered the table. The remaining space held two aged, upholstered chairs and a worn rocker clustered around a low drop-leaf table. Frost lined the windows in the chilly room. Could the man not afford coal?

Sampson lowered himself into the rocker and gestured toward the cushioned chairs. He kneaded his hands and gave Trevor an unblinking stare.

"Thank you for seeing me, Mr. Sampson. Thank you for your service in the last war. I have a few questions about your unit."

Sampson cocked his head. "That was a long time ago. Were you there?"

"I was in the Essex Regiment."

The man's belligerence softened to a look of wary mistrust. "What can I tell you?"

"Records show that Ian Belvedere and Nigel Winchester were part of your platoon. Did you know either of them?"

Sampson scratched his chin. "Why? Are they in trouble?"

"Actually, they're dead."

"What? How?"

"I can't give you the particulars other than to indicate foul play was involved."

"It must be bad if they have a detective inspector looking after them." He rubbed his forehead. "I'll see what I can remember."

Trevor pulled the dog-eared photo from his shirt pocket. "Maybe this will help. Can you identify the two men on either side of Ian and Nigel?"

Sampson held the picture close to his face for a long moment then handed it back to Trevor. The one on the right is Hugh Davenport. The other guy is Devon Smythe. They were quite the foursome."

"Meaning...?"

"They were a bad lot. Sometimes they would disappear for hours at a time then show up just in time for roll call. Later, we'd hear about some illegal incident involving servicemen, but no one could prove who had been there. Most of us figured it was them."

Trevor slipped the photo back into his pocket. "There were hundreds of soldiers. Anyone could have been responsible."

"True enough. I'm just telling you about our unit. When those boys were together, it meant trouble."

"Can you be more specific? What kinds of incidents?"

Sampson crossed his legs and ran a thumb along the crease in his pants. "I hate to speak ill of the dead, Detective Inspector, especially my brothers-in-arms."

"I understand, but it could help us find their killers."

"At first, it seemed to be innocent pranks—tying empty ration containers onto a tank or taking the tires off a jeep. That sort of thing. Went on for months that way. Then the villagers started to complain about items gone missing. Some people might say it was small stuff, but these people had so little. A shirt hanging from a clothesline being replaced by a pair of military skivvies, a loaf of bread cooling on a windowsill taken, apples from the trees."

"I see what you mean. When did it change for the worse?"

Sampson's eyes took on a distant gaze as he stared across the room at the shadow boxes full of medals. "It was toward the end of the war. We had all been there too long. We couldn't believe we were still alive. Anyway, more stuff started disappearing. Chickens, tools—like that. Then a priest showed up and talked to the commander. He was hot. Some of the church's valuables had been taken." He looked at Trevor, his forehead wrinkled. "That's just not right. It's bad enough to steal from people, but to steal from a church, from God? That's worse, if you ask me."

"What sorts of items were stolen?"

Sampson shook his head. "I'm not of the Catholic faith, so I don't rightly know what they are called. But there were a few bowls and a pair of candle stands. There was a statue too, but it was found down the road from the church. I think some pictures were taken, too."

"Where was this?"

"Outside of Somme."

"Were the items ever recovered?"

"I don't know. We moved out not too long after that. Ended up in some tiny French village. The stealing started there, too, once we'd settled in. That's why I think it was those boys. They always seemed to have more cash than the rest of us. How else would they get it, unless they were selling stolen goods?"

"Many a young man has made extra money through gambling."

"True. I hadn't thought of that, but I don't recall any of them playing cards. Like I said, we didn't see much of them except during the fighting. Next thing we knew, the Krauts had surrendered, and we were all going home."

"Do you keep in touch with any of your mates?"

"Not now. For three years after the war we would meet on Armistice Day, but it brought back too many bad memories for most of us. Memories best forgotten." His gaze bore into Trevor's face. "You should know that."

The front door banged open, and a buxom woman carrying a canvas sack clattered into the room. "Martin! Oh...I didn't know we had company. I beg your pardon."

Trevor rose and bowed to her. "I'm Detective Inspector Trevor Gelson."

The woman shifted the bag in her arms and nodded. "Nice to meetcha. I'm the wife. Trudy Sampson."

"How do you do, Mrs. Sampson."

"Is Sampson in trouble?"

"Trudy!"

"What? I'm just asking."

"He wants to know about when I was in the war. Two of the boys from my unit were murdered."

"You don't say." Trudy's eyes widened as she shifted her gaze to Gelson. "And you think my Martin can help you?"

"Possibly."

She looked eager. "Is there a reward?"

Trevor shook his head. "I'm afraid not, Mrs. Sampson. But the department is deeply grateful for your husband's assistance."

"Lotta good that'll do us." She lifted the bag. "If you'll excuse me, I got work to do." She huffed and stomped into the kitchen.

Sampson stared at her retreating back for a moment then turned back to Trevor. "Don't mind her, Detective Inspector. Life's been hard for us." He shrugged. "But who can't say that? Anyway, what else can I tell you?"

"Did Ian or the others ever come to the reunions?"

Sampson nodded. "As a matter of fact, they did. All four of them came the first year, but they missed the next two."

"How did they seem?"

"Same as they were during the war. Kind of standoffish, laughing among themselves. Like they were looking down their noses at the rest of us. Like they knew something, or had something we didn't. Once dinner was over, they skedaddled, and that was okay with us."

"Did any of them bring a wife or girlfriend?"

"Gals weren't invited. It was just for the members of the unit." He snapped his fingers. "Come to think of it, Ian's wife showed up once. Dressed to kill, she was. He was none too happy to see her. He hustled her out of there right quick. Can't remember her name...it was kind of hoity-toity–Marguerite or Meredith. Something like that."

"Millicent."

Sampson smiled. "Yep, that was it. Have you seen her? She's quite a looker, or at least she was then."

"No, I've not had the pleasure. What do you know about her?"

"Nothing. I only know it was her, because we all could hear the argument. Him yelling at her for coming. Said she'd ruined everything."

"Did you hear her response?"

"Everyone heard it. She slapped him and ran out the door. You could've heard a pin drop after it happened. He got real red in the face and followed her. That's the last time I saw him."

———————◆———————

Back at the station, Trevor hunched over his desk and rubbed his throbbing forehead. His skin felt as if it were on too tight. He stared at the diagram he had drawn onto the paper. He had solved more than one case by creating these primitive drawings. They cut through the clutter and brought clarity to the situation. Relationships were the key. He couldn't quote the statistics, but a large percentage of murders were committed by people who were acquainted with their victims.

Ian and Nigel had been killed by someone they knew. Of that he was certain. It had to be the same person. The discovery of Ian's skeleton had somehow started a chain of events. What was that chain?

A knock sounded at the door, and he looked up to see Phillips waiting with hat in hand. "Is everything all right, sir?"

Trevor gestured for him to enter the room. He tapped the page on his desk. "My usual artist's rendering of the participants in this little drama. Still looking for the common thread. We're missing an important piece to the puzzle, Phillips."

"Another headache?"

Trevor nodded. "What can I do for you?"

"I wondered if you needed me any longer this evening."

Trevor glanced at his watch and grimaced. "Seven forty-five. Where does the time go? Valerie will have my head for keeping you so long."

Phillips smiled. "She's very understanding, sir. Truth be told, she misses the excitement."

"I miss her. Her women's intuition clinched more than one case, didn't it? I should be angry at you for marrying one of my best officers. Then to go and have a baby, so she's too busy to work for me..."

"Maybe Miss Brown can help. She's quite keen."

Trevor pretended to throw his pencil at Phillips. "I could have you dismissed for that suggestion. Miss Brown has *helped* more than we need."

Phillips shrugged. "If I remember correctly, that's what you said about Valerie in the beginning."

Trevor waved Phillips away. "Go home, Sergeant. Enjoy your family."

The sergeant smirked and gave a brisk salute before spinning on his heel. His footsteps faded as Trevor's eyes fell back to the page. Help from Miss Brown? If anything, he needed help to ensure she stayed out of police business. Yes, until the war's end he'd have to make do with his understaffed team.

Ruth's face came to mind. Her sparkling blue eyes that seemed to change color with her mood. He smiled to himself. The last time he saw her they were nearly black with anger. She did get her dander up, but Phillips was right. She was an intelligent woman.

He pushed the thoughts of the tall, curly-headed brunette out of his head and looked back at the diagram. His eyes strayed to one name in particular, and he bolted upright.

Chapter Fifteen

Ruth took a bite of her limp sandwich and laid it on the brown paper, chewing slowly. Varis poured over the newspaper ads for housing. Rick and Louise had informed them that morning they would need to find somewhere else to stay.

They had been overly apologetic, but the embassy had ordered them to house a refugee family. They would be arriving by the end of next week. That didn't give Varis and her much time to find new housing.

She shivered and pulled her sweater closer. Would she ever get used to the dampness in England? New Hampshire might be cold, but it was not a seep-into-your-bones chill. Her eyes strayed from Varis to the others in the embassy cafeteria. Where did they live? Had any of them been bombed out? Of course they had. What was she thinking?

With a red pencil, Varis circled three of the listings. Rooms were often filled before the ink dried on the newspaper. *Lord, forgive me for my doubt. You know we need somewhere to stay. Please provide the right place. Thanks for taking care of us.* Her heart lifted as it always did when she remembered to turn her troubles over to God.

Ruth sighed. If only she would remember more often. God understood she was new at trusting Him, but even with His infinite patience, God must shake his head at her. Her stomach growled. She picked up the sandwich and peeked between the bread slices. Spam again. It was more than many had, so she ate with gratitude.

Varis pushed the paper toward her. "I found some that sound promising. What do you think of these?"

Ruth skimmed the words Varis had circled. Except for their location, they read almost the same. "Room for Rent. Female. Non-smoker." She shrugged and slid the paper back. "Okay by me. I'll call this afternoon to set up appointments. Will you be able to go tomorrow?"

"I don't know. You may have to handle this without me."

"What if you don't like the place I pick?"

Stuffing her food wrapper into the bag, Varis smiled. "I trust you. Besides, we don't have the luxury of deciding whether we like a place or not. We need a roof over our heads we can afford and is close enough to my work that I don't spend hours getting here and back."

"Let's stop by the board in the lobby. Maybe there are ads posted."

"Good idea." Varis stood and brushed crumbs from her navy blue, pleated skirt, an item from before the war when fabric was not in short supply. Ruth looked down at her own clothes. Still serviceable but woefully out of date. Fortunately, fashion wasn't something she worried about.

They tossed their trash in a bin by the door then walked down the long hallway toward the reception area. Varis squeezed Ruth in a quick one-armed hug. "Thanks for taking care of our housing situation. I've got my fingers crossed."

"Sure." Ruth shifted her purse on her shoulder and wandered to the board that hung on the wall. With a critical eye, she contemplated the scraps of paper pinned to the cork. *Male Wanted...Married Couple Wanted...Male Wanted...Male Wanted.* With the number of men who worked in the embassy she wasn't surprised that most of the notices were aimed at them, but that didn't lessen her disappointment.

Females Wanted: Elderly woman with extra bedroom looking for one or two girls to share house. Short walk to the tube. Meals included. Enquire in person.

Perfect. Ruth fumbled in her purse for her notepad and pencil. She opened the pad and scribbled the address on the first blank page. Her eyes scanned the rest of the ads. Two more listed a room for one woman, but she jotted down the information anyway. Maybe they would know of other availabilities.

She stuffed her writing gear back into her bag. This search for a home was becoming a full-time job.

Ruth hung up the phone and crossed out the last listing. She ran a hand through her hair then massaged the stiffness from her shoulders. Every listing Varis selected was already rented. She glanced at her watch. If she hurried, she could go by the housing commission before they closed. Maybe she'd actually get some writing done after that.

The phone trilled, and Ruth lifted the receiver. "Hello?"

"Ruth? I'm glad you're there. One of the secretaries here told me about a couple of rooming places. Got a pencil?"

"That's great, because I struck out with the ones from *The Times*."

"Both of them are only a few blocks from our last place." Varis's voice squeaked in excitement. "Here are the addresses." She rattled off the information then said a breathless goodbye and disconnected. Ruth stared at the phone. Things were obviously hopping at the embassy, which meant Varis would probably be home late again.

Ruth stood and grabbed her coat and purse before letting herself out of the house. Thirty minutes later, she loitered outside a three-story stone-face building.

"Here goes nothing!" She adjusted her hat and ran a hand over her coat to smooth it down. She rapped on the door then tried not to fidget. The door opened to reveal a teenage girl in a plaid skirt and blue blazer. Her white blouse was open at the neck. "Yes?"

"I'm here about a room you might have available. My friend works at the American embassy, and she said you might have something."

A voice thundered from deep inside the house. "Teresa! Who is it?"

The girl shouted over her shoulder. "A lady about the room."

Heavy footsteps sounded, and a large woman with dull brown hair appeared. She wiped a hand across her upper lip. "You're too late. Room's already rented. About an hour ago."

Ruth cringed. "Would you be aware of anything else?"

"Try the housing commission." The woman closed the door in Ruth's face.

"Well! I think I'm glad she didn't have a room." She pulled the crumpled paper from her purse and checked the second address. Only three blocks away. Ruth squared her shoulders and plunged off the stoop.

The wind nipped at her face as she hunched into her coat and rushed down the sidewalk. Within a few moments she stood in front of another three-story stone-faced house. *Lord, is this the place?*

She knocked then studied the building while she waited. The railings were missing, of course. Another victim of some long ago scrap drive. The windows were crisscrossed with tape. Yellow floral curtains were pulled closed on the inside. Ruth pounded on the door again. Silence.

Was that good news or bad? If the owner wasn't home, maybe the room hadn't been rented yet. She tore a sheet of paper from her notepad and scribbled a brief message on it. *Am interested your room for rent. Ruth Brown, Journalist, Associated Press.* She looked at the note then added her telephone number and pushed the paper through the mail slot.

Now what? She stood for a moment on the porch and tapped her front teeth with one finger. Should she put this aside for now and try to get a story done?

A smile flashed on her face. "That's it! I can write a story on the housing shortage. That's sure to resonate with my readers. I wonder if any of the press boys know of any rooms. At this hour, the office is sure to be packed with correspondents phoning in their dispatches.

A cacophony of deep rumbling voices, the shrill ring of telephones, and the clatter of typewriter keys greeted Ruth as she stepped off the elevator onto the third floor of the Broadcast House. Most would find the noise abrasive, but to her it was a symphony. She smiled and bustled toward the sound, her heels percussive against the tile floor.

The hazy room was filled with correspondents, cigarettes clenched between their lips. A line formed near the phones, and nearly all the typewriters were occupied. Someone had opened a window in a fruitless attempt to let in fresh air. She coughed and waved a hand in front of her face. Oh, to be able to take a clean breath in an open field without the pervasive smell of tobacco or coal dust.

A desk opened up near the window, and she hurried to claim it. The man at the next station glanced over and gave her a brief nod before looking back at his work. Pale with dark smudges under his eyes, he squinted at the paper curled around the roller. Sweat darkened his tan shirt against his back and made circles under his arms. His Brylcreemed hair was plastered to his scalp.

She dug into her purse for her notepad and opened it to a clean page. Her pencil raced across the paper as she jotted down the outline for her housing story.

"Hey, Brown. You gonna use that machine or just take up space?"

Ruth looked up to find the burly reporter from the *Chicago Tribune* scowling at her. She grabbed her purse and stood. "Yeah, I'm going to use it but not right away. Be my guest."

He bent in a mock bow then dropped into the chair. "Thank you very much."

One of the more seasoned reporters, the man had a no-nonsense attitude and confidence that bordered on superciliousness. She couldn't believe he actually remembered her name. She decided to risk censure. "Hey, Vince, my roommate and I lost our billet. Our leads have all been a bust. Know of anything?"

Vince continued to hunt and peck at the keyboard. She held her breath hoping he'd come through when he was ready.

He continued to type as he said, "I'm assuming a smart girl like you already checked with the housing commission."

"Yes, and the postings at the embassy where my roommate works."

"The embassy, eh? Friends with Ambassador Kennedy, are you? Maybe he can put you up."

Ruth pressed her lips together to stem the retort that leapt to her mind. No need to antagonize the man, no matter how insulting he was. She needed a place to live.

"Not going to rise to the bait? Good girl. You'll go far." He stared at her over round, gold-rimmed glasses. "There's a place I heard about on Park Street. Let me finish my piece, and I'll get you the information."

A crooked smile hovered on her lips. She had passed the test.

One of the telephones across the room pealed, and the reporter seated at the desk picked it up. He listened for a moment then hung up and turned to Ruth. "Hey, Brown. That was your roommate. She says to get back to the embassy right away."

Chapter Sixteen

Telephone to his ear, Trevor drummed his fingers on the desk while he waited for someone to pick up the phone. He had been holding for Army Information for nearly ten minutes. How long did it take to look up a couple of files?

A fly bumped and buzzed against the windowpane, dancing up and down the glass in a fruitless attempt to find its way outside. Trevor cocked his head. Where had the poor creature come from in the middle of winter? "I know how you feel, little one."

From the receiver, a tinny voice said, "Sir? Are you still there?"

He spoke through clenched teeth. "Yes, I'm here."

"Thank you for your patience. Someone will be with you shortly."

"I don't—"

Dead air changed into the buzz of a dial tone. He resisted the urge to throw the equipment out the window. Incompetent fool! Now he'd have to call back and start the wait all over again.

Footsteps echoed in the hall, and Phillips appeared in the doorway. "Sir, do you have a minute?"

"Thanks to the idiot at AI, I have plenty of time."

The sergeant's brow furrowed. "Sir?"

Trevor heaved a sigh and waved Phillips into one of the chairs across the desk. "Forgive me, I shouldn't take my foul mood out on you. I was trying to get information about our four lads from AI, and I waited for what felt like forever. When the man came back on the line, he managed to disconnect us. How do those folks get anything done?"

Phillips grinned. "It's called Army Information, sir, not Army Intelligence."

A guffaw sprang from Trevor, and he shook his head. "You're a good man, Phillips."

The man looked pleased with himself. "Thank you, sir."

Pencil stub in hand, Trevor began to doodle on the pad in front of him. "What can I do for you?"

"I have news about our lads. I found another of their platoon mates, and he shared quite a story."

Trevor dropped the pencil and sat upright. "That's excellent news. How did you find the man?"

Phillips opened the folder in his hand. With a stubby finger, he pointed to a list of names on a dog-eared typewritten sheet. "I had Brookes cross-reference the men in Belvedere's unit with the telephone book. With names like Taylor, Williams, Evans, and Davies, it took a while, but we found a couple of the soldiers still living in the London area."

"Well-done, Sergeant. Tedious work, to be sure, but well worth it. Does Brookes understand that?"

"Yes, sir. He'd like to make detective one day, so he's willing to do just about anything. He seemed to find great satisfaction in ferreting out these men."

Trevor nodded. "We should find other opportunities for him. Wouldn't you agree?"

"Definitely."

A door banged, and the clamor of voices sounded from the foyer. A shout rang out, and Trevor raised an eyebrow at Phillips, who cracked a smile. "An unhappy customer, sir. They were booking him when I walked through. Protesting his innocence even though he was caught red handed. Apparently, our criminal isn't very good at his trade. His victim felt the pull and was able to grab the man's hand as it connected with his wallet. Perhaps if he had been more light-fingered, he wouldn't have been caught, although the poor sod we arrested claims it's all a misunderstanding.

"Isn't it always?" Trevor chuckled. "Why don't you shut the door to cut out the noise, and tell me what you discovered?"

Phillips leaned back and pushed the door closed. The cacophony died to a dull murmur. He tossed the folder onto the desk and rubbed his hands together. "It seems our foursome went absent without leave one too many times. They often disappeared but usually managed to show up for roll call or just before the fighting started. Since they did their bit during combat, no one complained about their absences. Most men were too busy keeping themselves alive to worry about these blokes."

Anger and revulsion welled up in Trevor. Who were these men? Did they think war was a game? An inconvenience to be fought in between jaunts? Is that what got them killed? Was someone as disgusted as he was at their cavalier attitude about serving their country? Some days it was difficult to remain neutral during an investigation. Today might prove to be one of them.

"Just before the armistice, these men were seen going into a village east of Reims. Combat had been severe. One account notes that the fighting was as if the Germans wanted to inflict as much damage as they could before the war was over."

"It was like that where I was."

Phillips chewed on his lower lip for a moment then said, "I wish I didn't have to bring up disturbing memories for you, sir."

"It's not your fault. Besides, they are never far below the surface. Who saw the men?"

"The gentleman I met with and a friend of his. They were on guard duty. According to this man, the foursome seemed furtive, like they were up to something, so he watched for them to return. They were nearly two hours late from leave which meant they were AWOL. When they finally got back into camp, their backpacks seemed heavily loaded. Sure enough, they were caught with items of value, some from one of the churches. The other items were personal in nature: jewelry, paintings, that sort of thing."

"Were they charged?"

Disgust covered Phillips's face. "They spent a couple of days in the brig, but their commanding officer released them with a reprimand. He required them to return the items with an apology.

"Have you tried to find the commander?"

"He was killed a week later in a jeep accident."

The picture from the crime scene lay on the desk. Trevor drew it close and pointed to the crate with the statue on top. "These men have a taste for thievery. They must have been feeling invincible to have their picture taken in front of all these goods. That's a big risk, don't you think?"

Phillips picked up the photo and peered at it before placing it back down. "That it is. Maybe that's the motive we've been seeking. No honor among thieves—that sort of thing. Did one of them get greedy?"

"It's a thought. Or maybe there was an argument. Did Ian get a guilty conscience? Or did he want to do something different with the goods?"

"There's one more thing, sir. The commander's son was fingered as the fence for the items, but it was never proven. The man I spoke with was of the opinion that the boys accused him in an effort to deflect their own guilt. Most in the unit agreed with him."

The chair creaked as Trevor leaned forward and reached for the file. "Interesting. Did the man have anything else to say about the commander's son?"

"The lad was well liked among the troops. Very brave. Probably trying to prove his worth, rather than cash in on his father's position."

"Might be worth pursuing. See what else you can uncover about him."

The telephone jangled. Phillips retrieved his folder and stood. "I'll leave you to it, sir."

Trevor tucked the photo into his breast pocket and lifted the receiver. "Detective Gelson speaking."

"Gelson? Assistant Commissioner Forester here." The nasal tones of the AC's voice warbled in his ear.

A sigh broke out from Trevor. Now what?

"Gelson, what in the name of all that's good were you thinking when you called Army Information? I just got off the phone with their commander. I'm still stinging from the tongue-lashing. He very nearly handed me my head."

"Sir, I—"

"I'm not finished."

"Sorry, sir." Trevor made an effort to sound contrite.

"AI has better things to do than answer your petty questions about a man who died twenty-five years ago. There's a war on, you know. What have you got to say for yourself?"

"I'm well aware of the war, sir. However, that doesn't make this man's murder any less important. If we allow the killer to go unpunished, we're not doing the job we're paid to do."

"I'm not suggesting you let this go." The AC's voice rose to an imperious squeak. "I'm simply asking you to do it without interfering in the war."

Trevor could picture AC Forester's lanky frame reclining in his mammoth burgundy leather chair, polished shoes crossed and propped on top of the mahogany desk. As was his habit, the man's manicured hands probably stroked his small push-broom mustache. His dark, thinning hair would be combed and plastered over his scalp. Forester had the unfortunate tic of wiggling his long pointed nose when agitated, which gave him the air of a nervous mouse.

However, there was nothing nervous about his boss. He had climbed through the police ranks with savvy aplomb, taking credit where none was due in order to rack up a high case-closure rate. Political to his core, Forester managed to compliment his superiors without simpering. Disliked by the rank and file, he was revered by the administration that never missed an opportunity to tout him as one of the youngest to achieve assistant commissioner in the history of the London police.

"Am I clear?"

"Crystal clear, sir."

"Surely you're clever enough to solve this case without the help of the military. We don't want them meddling in our affairs; we should give them the same courtesy."

"It's about the records, sir. I have a lead that the victim and his friends may have been involved in stealing and selling artifacts during the last war. I believe it is an integral piece of the puzzle. I simply need to know if they were ever charged or disciplined for that. As you said, we don't want to interfere with the war, so I don't need to speak with anyone. I thought a low-level clerk could retrieve the file for me without undue hardship to AI. I apologize for any inconvenience."

Forester's voice continued to squeak. "An integral piece for the case, you say?"

"Yes, sir. Quite important."

Silence filled the line for a long moment then the AC said, "Let me see what I can do for you, Gelson. I have a few friends over there. You know, if you had come to me in the first place, this wouldn't have happened. I'm a resource for you fellows in the ranks. You should take advantage of that."

"I don't know why I didn't think of that, sir. I appreciate anything you can do for me."

"We're a team, Gelson. Don't forget that." Forester hung up without another word.

Trevor glared at the receiver then slapped it into the cradle. "A team. Right." With any luck, Forester would figure out a way to get him the file while making himself look like a hero. Then they'd both get what they wanted. Meanwhile, he had another card he could play.

Chapter Seventeen

The following day, sunshine warmed Ruth's back from a cloudless robin's-egg-blue sky as she and Varis wheeled their bicycles to a stop in front of a large stone manor house in the outskirts of the city. Varis had been awarded some unexpected time off. No one was talking, but the rumor mill indicated that several high-level officials had scheduled a conference, and Ambassador Kennedy did not want to take chances that information from the meeting would leak. Nonessential personnel had been granted leave.

Willow baskets hung from the handlebars of the old and slightly dented bikes they had borrowed from the embassy's collection. Patches of rust marred the dark blue paint, but the seats were new. They had left the ever-present smell of coal dust and rubble behind, and Ruth took a deep breath to fill her lungs with the fresh, brisk air reminiscent of New Hampshire. She relished the opportunity to stretch her legs and get some exercise after being cooped up in the office.

Varis shielded her eyes from the bright rays as her gaze rose higher and higher to take in the imposing home that had somehow survived Germany's bombs unscathed. She pointed to the six chimneys that dotted the ochre-colored tiled roof. "I wonder if she has the wood to fill those fireplaces."

"It must cost a small fortune to heat a place this immense. But it looks to be in one piece—one of the benefits of being this far out of the city, I would imagine."

"And peaceful, too. Perhaps worth the time it took to get here."

Ruth took another deep breath and rolled her bike toward the entrance. Varis followed her. They propped their vehicles against the thick hedge of yews that snuggled around the entire structure, reached into their baskets to retrieve their gas masks, and ascended the twenty-foot-wide steps that led to the columned porch spanning the front of the house. A holly wreath festooned with a green plaid bow hung on the glossy red door. Like windows all over England, the panes were crisscrossed with tape.

She lifted the brass knocker and rapped on the door. A moment later, a maid, dressed in a dark blue dress covered with a matching apron, opened the door.

The woman's smile did not reach her green eyes that were sunk deep in her wan face. Her gaze raked them, registering disapproval with their appearance. "Here about the room, are you?" A light brogue peppered her words.

"Yes, ma'am, if it's still available. May we see it?" Varis said.

The woman sniffed. "That's not up to me. It's the missus who will decide that. Follow me." She turned and trudged toward the recesses of the house.

Ruth and Varis looked at each other then entered the foyer. Varis closed the door, and the women hastened toward the disappearing maid. They passed closed door after closed door, their steps muffled on the aged carpet. The eyes of unsmiling men in gilt framed oil paintings followed their progress.

After making several turns, the trio arrived at a large parlor. The maid minced forward and curtsied to a gaunt woman with snowy white hair seated on a burgundy floral sofa. "Mrs. Caulfield, these ladies are here about the room to let."

Mrs. Caulfield sent her away with a dismissive wave and stared at Ruth and Varis through narrowed eyes. "Come closer, girls." Her voice was low and querulous as she spoke through thin lips. "My vision isn't what it used to be."

They hesitated as they watched the servant leave the room. The woman clapped her hands. "Step lively, I haven't got all day."

Ruth and Varis started and moved toward Mrs. Caulfield. She crossed her arms and looked down her nose at them "Who are you, and why should I rent you one of my rooms?"

Varis answered, "My name is Varis Gladstone, and this is my friend Ruth Brown. We have been bombed out of our house. We're quiet and respectful and are fully employed. We need somewhere to live. We have been staying with a friend of ours, but she can no longer keep us. You have a lovely home, and we hope you can help us."

A look of disdain flitted across Mrs. Caulfield's face. "You're Americans?"

"Yes, ma'am. I work at the American embassy, and Ruth is with the wire service."

"A reporter?" The woman's countenance morphed from disdain to disgust, and Ruth jammed her hands into her pockets so their hostess could not see them clenched into fists.

With a soothing tone, Varis continued, "Is the room still available, ma'am? If not, we'll be on our way."

Mrs. Caulfield stroked the pearl necklace at the base of her neck and studied them. "You Americans were late to the last war and late to this one."

"Yes, ma'am."

Ruth stifled a sigh and let Varis continue to negotiate. The woman was a positive dragon, but the home was beautiful. With fresh air and woods in which to roam, perhaps it would be worth putting up with the owner's crotchety nature.

Movement past the window behind Mrs. Caulfield caught Ruth's attention. She strained to catch a glimpse of who or what hovered outside. Then she saw him. A stooped, hoary man wearing a uniform was creeping past the shrubs. He carried a sword in one hand and a pistol in the other. Should she be amused or alarmed?

"Pardon me, Mrs. Caulfield, but there's a soldier in your garden. He's armed."

Varis's head whipped around. The man had disappeared. "Are you sure?"

Mrs. Caulfield blanched, and her lips thinned. Without a word, she rang the small silver bell on the table at her elbow. Moments later, the maid who had answered their knock hurried into the room. With a brief curtsy, she said, "Yes, ma'am?"

"Mr. Fairborn is in the garden. Edna, see to him."

"Right away, ma'am." The maid sprinted from the room. An awkward silence descended before their hostess cleared her throat. "Now, where were we?"

Edna and a strapping lad of perhaps twenty years old dashed past the window. A moment later they reappeared leading the elderly warrior by the arm. The pistol had been holstered, and the young man held the sword. The soldier's face was serene.

Ruth tore her gaze away and gestured toward the door. "Perhaps you'd like us to come back later."

The woman's haughtiness drained. "There's no need. The situation is under control. Are you ladies still interested in the room? She named a price. Rent is payable on the first. Breakfast and dinner are included."

Varis and Ruth exchanged a glance, and Varis's head moved in an imperceptible nod.

Ruth spoke for them. "Yes, ma'am. You have an exquisite home, and we would be honored to share it with you. We can move in immediately."

Lord, there I go judging again. I thought Mrs. Caulfield was a pompous, difficult woman, yet it is obvious she is hurting. Forgive me, Father, and help us serve her.

Mrs. Caulfield rang the bell again, and a different maid entered the room. Dressed in burgundy with white collar and cuffs, this one was middle aged with graying-blonde braids wrapped around her head. "Yes, Mrs. Caulfield?"

"Ah, Mrs. Swenson. These young women will be joining us in the most recently vacated room. Would you kindly show them upstairs?"

"Yes, ma'am."

Ruth and Varis murmured their thanks and followed Mrs. Swenson out of the parlor. She turned and glanced at them. "No, luggage?"

Varis shook her head. "We didn't want to presume. The rooms we've attempted to see have already been rented by our arrival."

"Aye. There's not much to be had in these parts. Our rooms don't remain empty for long."

"Where did your last tenant go?" Ruth said.

Mrs. Swenson pressed her lips together and shook her head. "The poor dear. Her husband was killed at El Alamein. She went home to live with her parents in Chatham."

Murmuring sounds of sympathy, Ruth thought about the nameless woman whose life had been devastated by the war. One person's tragedy became another person's good fortune. Trevor's face sprang to her mind, and she tried to bat the vision away to no avail. She and Varis had lost their house and most of their personal effects, yet that had led her to her meeting the detective inspector. Was he a boon? More like an annoyance, albeit a handsome one.

At the top of the stairs, the landing split to the right and left. They turned to the right, which led to the back of the house and past six closed doors on each side of the hall. Behind them, Ruth could hear muffled female voices.

"Mrs. Swenson, I have a question."

She stopped and turned to Ruth. "Yes?"

"Are there only young ladies staying in the house?"

The woman's brows came together. "Absolutely. And when menfolk come to visit, they must be met in one of the two parlors. There is to be no entertaining in the rooms. And all guests must leave by ten o'clock. No exceptions."

"That won't be a problem, ma'am."

Near the end of the hall, they stopped in front of an open door. Mrs. Swenson gestured for Ruth and Varis to enter. Both gave a sharp intake of breath.

Two pencil-post twin beds covered in white spreads stood against the far wall with a nightstand in between them. At the end of each bed stood an armless bench topped in saffron-colored cushions. A pair of gleaming cherry-wood bureaus lined the wall to the right, and to the left two wing-backed chairs the hue of whipped buttercream, nestled around a floor lamp. A row of hooks stretched behind the door. The single window shone like a diamond in the sun.

Varis clapped her hands. "How lovely! Wouldn't you agree, Ruth?"

"Absolutely."

"The bathroom is two doors down on this side of the hall," Mrs. Swenson said. "You share it with those in the room next door, but you probably won't see your neighbors. They work the night shift at one of the factories. If there's nothing else, I'll leave you to it."

The girls shook their heads, and she left quietly, closing the door behind her.

With outstretched arms, Varis twirled in the center of the room then flopped on one of the beds. Her hair splayed out around her face, which brightened with excitement and joy. "Didn't I tell you God would provide a place for us, Ruth? And He went overboard."

"That He did."

Varis sat up and patted the mattress beside her. "Let's thank Him, right now."

Ruth sat on the bed, and they clasped hands. The clock tick-tocked while Varis prayed. "Father God, thank You so much for Your blessings and provisions. Thank You for Your generosity. You not only met our need—a roof over our heads—but You met our wants: an exquisite, homey place to live. Praise You, Lord. Bless Mrs. Caulfield, and show us how to serve her. In the name of Your Son, Jesus, amen."

"Amen."

They grinned at each other

"Let's go get our stuff," Ruth said.

When they entered the empty parlor where they met Mrs. Caulfield, Ruth beckoned Varis inside. "Check out this painting, Varis. It looks very old."

"Ruth! We can't start skulking around the house before we've even moved in."

"But we can afterward? Besides, we're not skulking around. This is one of the parlors where we'll visit with our 'gentlemen callers.' I just want to take a look at the painting. There's something about it that intrigues me."

Varis stood with hands on her hips. "Make it snappy. I'd like to get back in time for dinner."

Ruth walked to the pastoral scene and peered at the signature. Difficult to read. She studied the landscape and wondered why it was so familiar to her. Furious waves crashed around a man who stood on a pile of rocks with his back to the painter. The black-coated figure leaned casually on his walking stick.

"Since when are you interested in art, Ruth?"

"Normally I'm not, but this is stirring a memory for me I can't retrieve. Have you seen this before?"

Varis shrugged. "No, but I slept through most of our art appreciation class."

Snapping her fingers, Ruth exclaimed, "That's where I've seen it. In our textbook." Her eyes widened. "I think it was one that went missing sometime during the late eighteen hundreds. What's it doing in London?"

"You girls! Get away from there!"

Ruth and Varis turned and froze. Mrs. Caulfield's brother filled the doorway, his sword gripped in one hand. His face was drawn into a black scowl, and his eyes shot daggers at them. He lunged toward them. "I said, step away."

Chapter Eighteen

Ruth and Varis dropped to the floor behind the sofa. Varis gripped Ruth's arm and spoke through clenched teeth. "Perhaps taking a room here isn't the best idea we've ever had."

"Maybe that's the real reason our room is vacant."

Concern and fear were etched on Varis's face. "What are we going to do?"

Footsteps thundered down the hall and into the parlor. "Mr. Fairborn, what are you doing in here? Don't you know? It's time for your snack."

The girls peeked over the back of the couch. The young man they spied earlier gently led Mr. Fairborn from the room. They exhaled loudly. Varis tittered. "That was a close one!"

"Do you think he's harmless?"

Varis shrugged. "I guess time will tell. But for the moment we have a place to stay, so let's be grateful, if not cautious."

"What do you mean 'he's dead'?" The next day, Ruth stood in the administrative offices at a woolen factory deep in the heart of London.

The rest of yesterday passed uneventfully while Rick helped them move their meager belongings to their new room.

Once unpacked, she looked at the painting in the parlor again but hadn't managed to find any answers to her questions. A visit to the art section of the nearest library was next on her agenda.

Meanwhile, she was at an impasse with the beady-eyed, self-important manager who glowered at her from behind the desk. "Just what I said, lady. Smythe is dead. There was an accident here yesterday. It was his own fault, and that's all I'm going to say." The man crossed his arms and clamped his mouth shut, his face set in mulish lines.

Ruth's reporter senses went on alert. There was a story here. Maybe connected with her investigation, maybe not. But the man was hiding something. She just needed to find it, and being antagonistic wasn't going to help.

Dropping into the chair in front of her, she slumped over her purse and looked at him from under lowered lashes. "I apologize for my behavior, Mr. Gantry. I'm surprised. That's all. I'm not here because of the incident in your warehouse. I've been trying to find the colleague of a man who died under my house, and I thought I was so close, and now you're telling me he's dead. Needless to say, I'm disappointed."

Gantry lowered himself into his chair. "Your house fell on someone?"

"No, but I did. You see, our house was nearly obliterated by a bomb a few weeks ago. I fell through the floor and landed on a skeleton."

She shuddered. "The poor thing had been there for years. I'm trying to get his story. It deserves to be told."

The skepticism on Gantry's face faded as he seemed to search her face. "You didn't know anything about yesterday before you got here today?"

Ruth drew the yellowed photograph from her purse and passed it to him. She really should return the picture to DI Gelson, but she always seemed to need it. "That was found with the body, and I'm trying to identify the four men. I received a lead that one of them was a Devon Smythe." She cocked her head. "I guess I should have realized there would be many Devon Smythes in the London directory."

The last of the anger drained from his face, and he returned the picture to her. "You must understand my caution, Miss Brown. We're a government contractor. I can't have the press crawling about, especially after the accident. An investigation is being conducted to find out exactly what happened, and until we determine that I can't have you here."

"I understand the need for discretion, but not secrecy, Mr. Gantry. However, if you'll help me with information about Devon Smythe, I'll leave you to your inquiry."

"What sort of information?"

"His next of kin, home address, that sort of thing."

In a flash, Gantry wheeled his chair to a cabinet in the corner and yanked out the bottom drawer. He fingered the tabs on the folders inside and pulled one marked with Smythe's name then rolled back to the desk and opened the file. "He's not married, so it's his parents you'll be after. Devon Smythe Sr. and Harriet Smythe. They all lived together." He slid the folder toward her and pointed to the address.

Devon Smith Sr.? Ruth scribbled as he talked. If the victim was young enough to be living at home, he was obviously not the man she was looking for, but maybe his father was. One step closer.

———————————

Humming Bing Crosby's "White Christmas," Ruth walked with a light step as she left the factory and made her way toward the bus stop. A uniformed bobby touched the brim of his helmet in silent greeting as he walked his beat. A policeman. She should contact DI Gelson with the information about Smythe, or he'd threaten to lock her up again. He might actually follow through one of these times.

A stiff wind tugged at her coat, and she drew it closer against the chill. The crowd pressed against her and provided warmth the murky sunlight could not. A glance at her watch told her she had ten minutes to wait for the bus, so she huddled deeper into her scarf and stomped her feet to keep the circulation moving.

"Excuse me, miss, but aren't you that reporter who was asking about Devon Smythe?"

Ruth turned. A short, wiry man, bundled in a black pea coat and a wool cap pulled low over his brow, stood beside her. His pinched lips were tinged blue.

Her heart sped up. "Perhaps I am. Who might you be?"

"My name's not important, but what I have to say is." He tossed a look over his shoulder and lowered his raspy voice. "I'm sure the powers that be told you it was an accident. I'm here to say, it wasn't."

"Wasn't—"

"Shhh!" The man made a chopping motion with his hand to cut off her words. "Just listen. Follow the money, and you'll find the answers you're looking for. They didn't like what Devon had to say about them, so they shut him up. Accident? Bah!"

"I promised I'd let Mr. Gantry conduct his investigation."

Although shorter than Ruth, the man gave her the distinct impression of looking down his nose at her. They glared at each other for a moment then Ruth said, "Who do you suggest I speak with first?"

"You're a smart lass; you'll figure it out." With a smirk, he slipped through the crowd and trotted down the street.

Ruth searched the throng of people and tried to determine which of them might work at Gantry's company. Earlier than anticipated, the bus rolled to a stop at the curb. The door opened with a squeak, and the group jostled and pushed to get on board. When the last person had climbed the stairs, Ruth moved forward then hesitated.

The bus driver scowled. "You getting on or not? I'm on a schedule, you know."

She felt her face flush then stepped back and waved him away. The door closed with a bang, and the vehicle chugged forward with an oily cough.

Now what? Uncertainty gripped her. She couldn't go back to the factory after her promise to the general manager. Perhaps she could loiter at the bus stop to await the next wave of employees. Another glance at her watch told her she'd have hours until the next shift change. No good.

Should she report to Trevor then visit the Smythes? The opportunity to see the handsome detective was tempting, but there might be workers to interview. What could the man have meant about following the money? The company already had the contract. Was there a possibility of better terms? And what about Devon Smythe? Why did he need to be "shut up" as the man said?

Ruth sank into a nearby bench and finger combed her hair to massage the tightness of her scalp. *I need some help here, Lord. I can't go back on my promise, but if there's injustice here, it should be uncovered. I can't be like other journalists who go back on their word for the sake of a story.*

"I can't have you here." That's what he said, but that doesn't mean I can't search elsewhere. Tension became excitement as she devised her plan of attack. A trip to the police station to see Trevor first then to the Smythes. Her face split into a smile. Maybe they could visit the family together. Drat. He'd never allow that, and she certainly didn't need the handsome detective getting in the way of her story.

⸺◆⸺

Trevor resisted the urge to drum his fingers on his thigh as he sat in the foyer at Army Information. The receptionist's clicking of the typewriter keys echoed off the marble walls. A look at the clock told him a long three minutes had passed since the last time he checked. Stifling a sigh, he inspected his shoes. Polished to a high shine, they reflected the overhead lights.

The telephone shrilled. The stern-faced woman at the desk lifted the receiver and whispered into it. She hung up with a click then turned toward Trevor. "He will see you now."

Trevor rose and walked toward the opaque glass door. It opened to reveal a freshly shorn young sergeant who clicked his heels. "Please follow me, sir."

The hallway was dim, tomblike. The empty light sockets confirmed that even the military was rationing supplies. At the end of the hall, the pair stopped in front of another closed door. The soldier knocked once then opened the door and stepped aside, signaling for Trevor to enter.

"Ah, Detective Inspector Gelson. Good to see you again."

The door closed behind Trevor with a muted thud.

With a crisp salute, Trevor greeted the balding man seated behind a mammoth desk littered with maps, files, empty coffee cups, and pencils. "Thank you for agreeing to meet, Colonel Hood."

The man gave a dismissive wave. "We're alone. You can drop the formality, Trevor. We've known each other far too long for that. How've you been?"

Trevor shrugged and lowered himself into the only uncluttered chair in the room. "Still wishing I could do something for the war effort,

Owen. I love the challenge of solving crimes, but occasionally I feel like I'm treading water."

"The problem is you're too good at your job. You're needed where you are. However, I'll keep my ear to the ground."

"I'd appreciate that."

Owen shuffled through the riot of papers in front of him. "Blasted paperwork. I've got the information you're looking for somewhere in this mess. If I could actually find it." He continued to sift through the piles while Trevor surveyed the room.

Overflowing built-in cabinets lined the walls. He couldn't read the spines but assumed the books were filled with regulations, laws, and procedures. The military lived and died by their procedures. A twelve-foot table took up one end of the immense room and was just as cluttered as Owen's desk. It was a wonder he could find anything. Teetering stacks of paper and files threatened to topple at any moment.

Four Queen Anne chairs huddled around a small oval table near the single window. Trevor peered out the window at another building, a twin to the AI facility. Bare ivy branches straggled up the stone edifice. Curtains or shades were drawn in almost every window.

"Ah, here it is." Owen held up a folder in triumph. "Maybe if I let my secretary in here on occasion I would be more organized." He swept papers to the side and laid the folder on the cleared spot. Running his finger down the page, his lips moved silently as he perused the record.

Trevor fidgeted while he waited. Finally, Owen stabbed at the paper. "I remember now. There were several reports about this particular unit. Seems that artwork and other items of value went missing wherever this bunch was stationed. However, no one was ever charged."

"Why ever not?"

"According to the platoon officer, the MP in charge mishandled the investigation."

"How so?"

Owen frowned and slid the folder toward Trevor. "He interviewed most of the men together, so they were able to corroborate each other's stories. And to make matters worse, he didn't speak with all the witnesses. Unfortunately, none of the missing items were ever found either."

"I'm surprised there's a report at all. One of his platoon mates told me the men were caught just before the cease-fire, and the commander chose not to file a report."

Owen shook his head. "Tsk. It pains me to hear such things."

"Does the report include the name of the MP?"

"A Lieutenant Whiston, but before you get too excited, I checked, and he was killed in action not too long after the incident."

Trevor's eyebrow shot up. "Do you think that's a coincidence?"

"We were at war, Trevor. Men got killed."

"I know, but I would still like to review the report involving his death."

Owen nodded and pointed to the folder. "I thought you might, so I had my secretary include it."

"You know me too well."

A knock sounded at the door, and the men turned as it opened to reveal General Markham. A bulldog of a man, he filled the doorway with his girth. His hat was tucked under one arm, and his face was set in a deep frown.

Before Owen and Trevor could scramble to their feet, he barked, "As you were."

The floor shook as he strode into the room to stand by the window. He leaned on the ledge and sighed heavily. "What are you men doing with sealed files?"

Trevor shifted under the general's dark stare but would not blink. "Investigating a murder, sir. A skeleton was uncovered after a home was bombed. The MO has indicated the man probably died of blunt-force trauma to the head around 1920, and the victim was found with a photograph from the war—he and three of his mates. I'm trying to determine if something happened during the war that precipitated the crime."

For a long moment, Markham's gaze shifted back and forth between Trevor and Owen. Then he tossed his hat on the desk and crossed his arms. When he spoke, his low voice held an edge of cold steel. "I won't ask how you managed to secure the file, Colonel Hood. That way you won't have to implicate anyone. But to show it to a civilian? You're way out of line. I could have you court-martialed."

"Yes, sir."

"And you." Hood's deep-set eyes bore holes in Trevor's face. "I've heard about you. Not one to go by the book, are you? Rather unconventional ways of doing your job. But your case-closure rate is among the highest in the entire force. That's the main reason I won't have you sent to Wandsworth Prison for twenty years of hard labor. Find out who killed this poor man and do it quickly. But keep me apprised. Understood?"

Trevor unclenched his hands. "Understood."

"Excellent. Then I will leave you to it." The general snatched his hat from the desk and stomped out of the room.

Wordless, Owen and Trevor stared at one another, then Owen slumped back in his chair and blew out a loud breath. "I thought we were going to be strung up for sure."

"I don't know about you, but I'm too old for hard labor." Trevor pulled out a handkerchief and mopped his forehead before tucking the cloth back into his pocket. "How well do you know the general?"

"Not at all. I'm not exactly in his circle of associates, even if he is only a one-star. Why do you ask?"

"Why wouldn't he court-martial you and arrest me? We broke military law. Seems like a career man wouldn't let that slide so easily."

Owen sighed again. "Stop looking for conspiracies. Maybe Markham wants to see justice done and has decided the greater good means not punishing the two of us. Take the miracle and be grateful for it."

"Maybe, but I think he may have another motive." Trevor pushed the file across the desk. "Look at the name of the platoon leader—Lt. Horatio Markham."

Chapter Nineteen

Ruth studied the wax figure of King Louis XIV then turned and smiled at Varis. "You certainly picked somewhere unusual to commemorate your birthday."

"Madame Tussauds is one of my favorite places to visit. You know that."

"And to think it survived the Blitz with only the loss of the cinema and some molds."

"Too bad the same can't be said for St. Paul's Cathedral. Praise the Lord, they were able to diffuse the bomb that hit it in September 1940, or the church would have been obliterated."

Leaning over, Ruth hugged Varis and said, "Enough sadness. It's your special day. We need to celebrate. Which exhibit would you like to see next?"

"Hmmm. Let's go visit Mrs. Tussaud herself."

They linked arms and sauntered from the room. Their footsteps were muted by the carpet as they threaded their way through the lunchtime crowd. While they stood in front of the figure of the museum's founder, Trevor walked around the corner.

Holding his fedora in one hand, he bowed slightly. "Miss Brown. Miss Gladstone. Your landlady told me I might find you here." He smiled at Varis. "Happy Birthday."

Varis pinked and returned the smile. "Thank you."

"I apologize for interrupting the festivities, but I wanted to find out what else you've discovered." He winked. "Since I know you're still digging around despite our conversation."

She opened her mouth to protest, and he held up his hand. "I also wanted to update you on the case, as I promised." He gestured to a bench a short distance away.

Ruth lost herself in his modulated Ronald Colman voice, and her face heated.

Worry marked Trevor's face. "Are you feeling all right, Miss Brown? You're flushed. We could do this another time."

Using the museum's brochure, she fanned herself. "Yes, I'm fine, just a bit warm with all these people around." She had to stop getting distracted by the inspector's good looks. It was difficult enough to be taken seriously in the ranks of the seasoned war correspondents on her own merit. She'd be skewered by her colleagues if they thought she was in a relationship with a detective inspector to get a scoop on the police blotter.

The lines of concern disappeared from Trevor's face. "Very well, then. We've discovered the four men in the photo had a penchant for stealing items of value during the war. Unfortunately, they got off light for their last escapade. The statue and numerous crates in the photo lends credence to the theory that they may have been involved more deeply than anyone surmised. So, until a different motive surfaces, we're going to assume relationships between at least two of the parties soured enough to prompt murder." He looked at the women with a satisfied smile.

Attraction and irritation fought for supremacy in Ruth. "How long have you known about the men's war activities? That's a key piece of information."

"What?"

"You heard me. When did you find out about the art thefts?" Her eyes narrowed. "Are you feeding me bits about the case to keep me happy, so I won't interfere? I already promised you I wouldn't."

Varis laid her arm on Ruth who shook it off and continued to glare at Trevor. "It's a legitimate question, Varis. Care to answer, *Detective Inspector*?"

"I don't owe you any explanation at all, Miss Brown. If you'll recall, I'm doing this as a courtesy." Trevor scowled and spun away. He barreled into a tall, willowy woman with raven-black hair. Gripping her arms to keep them both upright, he said, "I beg your pardon, miss." He flushed and dropped his hands. "Uh, Charlotte?"

The woman's angular features hardened, and she stepped back. "Trevor, what in the world are you doing at Madame Tussauds? You never took time off for touring museums when we were walking out together." Her gaze fell on Ruth and Varis who had risen from the bench. "Are you with them?" A sneer colored her words.

"No! Well, that is, I came here to...wait. You gave up the right to question me when you walked away from our engagement."

Charlotte sniffed and looked down her nose before wrapping her cloak closer around herself as if to avoid contamination. She slung the end of her jade-colored silk scarf over her shoulder and brushed past Trevor without a backward glance.

Ruth stared at Charlotte's retreating figure. "That was your fiancée? What a princess. Is she always that rude?"

Poking her with a well-placed elbow, Varis frowned at Ruth and shook her head. She hissed between thin lips, "Speaking of rude..."

With a tired sigh, Trevor shrugged. "Let's just say she has a well-developed sense of who she is."

"And who would that be?"

"The daughter of a wealthy baron."

"And that means she can treat others with disrespect? You should consider yourself lucky not to be saddled with her."

An awkward silence grew until Varis cleared her throat. "I'm sure the inspector would like to get back to the matter at hand instead of discussing his personal life. Did you have more information for us, DI Gelson?"

"Yes."

"As I was saying, we believe the victim and his friends were involved in some sort of art theft ring. We don't yet know how big it was.

We're interviewing as many of their unit members as we can locate. The men were never charged due to sloppy investigative procedures."

Ruth rolled her eyes. Probably a cardinal sin in his book. He was brilliant at what he did, no doubt solving every case that came his way. When would she stop letting her temper get the best of her? It was a wonder he didn't arrest her for obstruction or some other charge.

Forcing a smile, Ruth nodded as Trevor continued, "And there's something else. We may have found one of the other men in the photo."

Ruth bolted upright. "Really?"

"Possibly. We're still in the early stages of following this lead. You know about the accident at the wool factory that involved a young man named Devon Smythe. We have reason to believe that his father, Devon Smythe, Sr., is one of the four men."

"Have you seen him?"

"No. Devon was still living with his parents, and we went to the house, but his father hasn't been home since the day after Christmas. His wife claims she doesn't know where he is, but her behavior suggests otherwise."

"How can you tell?"

"I'm a police officer, Miss Brown. People lie to me on a regular basis. I've learned to recognize the signs."

"What are you going to do?"

"We'll pay Mrs. Smythe another visit, but we must give her some time to grieve the loss of her son. With any luck, Devon's death will bring his father home. At the very least, Mr. Smythe may be in contact with his wife."

"Will you be looking into the accident that killed Devon?"

"Not at this time. The company is conducting their own investigation. They'll keep us apprised."

Ruth stood and tucked her pocketbook under one arm. "Do you really think they'll admit to any wrongdoing?"

"Such as?"

"What if Devon's death wasn't an accident?"

Trevor's brows came together. "Why would you think that?"

"First the skeleton came to light, then Nigel turned up dead. Now Devon Smythe's son, whose name is the same as another of the men in the photograph, is dead, too. Is that a coincidence?" She shook her head. "I don't think so."

Chapter Twenty

The following day, Trevor stepped out of the car in front of the grandiose home of Millicent Belvedere's family. His feet crunched on the circular gravel driveway as he walked toward the arched entryway. Sunlight glinted off the windowpanes, and although dormant for the winter, the surrounding gardens were mulched and clean, without a stray leaf in sight. Two large yews pruned into precise squares stood guard on either side of the walkway.

Millicent's parents had finally seen fit to schedule a meeting to discuss their daughter. What sort of people weren't concerned about a missing child, even one who was an adult?

Phillips had been disappointed not to be allowed to tag along, but Trevor knew better than to clutter the room with police officers. These were the sort of folks who expected tradesmen and constables to use the back entrance.

Sighing, Trevor approached the door and gripped the large brass knocker. He banged three times with it and let his hand drop. After a long moment, the oak door swung open to reveal a young servant with hair the color of cinnamon. She wore a navy dress with a crisp white apron overtop of it. A small white cap sat on her head.

"May I help you, sir?"

"I am Detective Inspector Gelson. I have an appointment with Lord Davenport."

The woman's eyes widened, and she stepped back. "Won't you come in, sir?"

Trevor removed his hat and stepped across the threshold. His feet sank into thick brown carpet that contrasted with the creamy walls covered in expensive-looking artwork. As he followed the maid, he peeked into the rooms they passed and caught sight of Louis XIV furniture and framed oil paintings. The war did not seem to have affected the lives of these people.

The servant girl led him into what appeared to be a man's office. The walls were lined with bookshelves, and a large mahogany desk took up a third of the room. Behind the desk a black leather chair waited for its master. A dark green love seat and two matching chairs were clustered in front of the fireplace. The maid moved forward and pulled a box of matches from the mantle. She struck one and touched it to the newspapers wadded up beneath the logs. Flames gobbled up the paper and soon engulfed the wood.

"Lord Davenport will be with you in a moment. May I take your coat and hat, sir?"

"No, thank you. I won't be here long enough to make it worth the effort."

"Very good, sir." She left the room on soundless feet and closed the door.

The fire snapped and popped, and the earthy smell of burning wood drifted into the room. Trevor approached one of the shelves and studied the books' spines. An entire section was made up of ledgers and journals dating back fifty years. What he wouldn't give to peruse those. The other shelves were devoted to a wide range of subjects from political science and philosophy to Shakespeare.

A clock on the mantle struck eleven. Would his host play the busyman game and keep him waiting, or would he be the affable host and show up on time?

The heavy oak door opened, and Baron Davenport entered the room, his arm outstretched and a wide smile on his face. "Detective Inspector Gelson, sorry to keep you waiting."

The two men shook hands, and Trevor said, "You're right on time, sir. Thank you for seeing me."

Lord Davenport led Trevor to the chairs at the fireplace, and the men lowered themselves into the seats. His face sobered. "You have news about my daughter?"

"I'm afraid not, sir. I was hoping you could answer some questions that would assist us in locating her."

Settling back into the padded Queen Anne chair, Lord Davenport tugged at his jacket sleeves and crossed his legs. "I haven't seen her in years. What could I possibly know that would help you?"

Trevor leaned forward, his hat dangling between his knees from loose fingers. "Maybe nothing, but we have to explore all avenues. When was the last time you saw Millicent?"

"It must have been 1915 when she ran off and married that Belvedere boy. That was before the Great War."

"You didn't approve?"

Lord Davenport's face darkened, and he smacked his thigh with a fist. "We had already planned an advantageous match with Baron Chittendon's son. It was an embarrassment, really. Fortunately, the announcement of their engagement hadn't been made public when she eloped, but the incident changed our relationship with the baron and his family. It's never recovered. We were quite put out."

Swallowing his distaste for the man's elitist attitude, Trevor said, "Were you aware she was seeing Ian Belvedere?"

"Her mother and I didn't have the faintest idea. Although we're not surprised the marriage didn't last. His father was some sort of clerk, and we don't know anything about his mother. The boy had no education to speak of—what sort of life could he offer her? Millicent liked fine things, beautiful things. In fact, she had begun to show an interest in art collecting. We attended an art show together shortly before she left. With advice from me, she purchased a small piece by Rindisbacher. If she still has it, it would be worth a goodly sum. Anyway, after we discovered Belvedere had left, we wrote and told Millicent she would be welcomed home—that we'd overlook her mistake—but she never responded."

"He didn't leave her, Lord Davenport. He was murdered, and his body was recently unearthed after a bombing raid."

Lord Davenport blanched. "Murdered? When? How?"

Trevor studied his host's face. "As far as we can determine, he was killed two or three years after returning from the war."

"And he came to light after a raid? I don't understand."

"He had been buried in the basement of the house Millicent and Ian lived in. The bomb tore up the ground and uncovered the body."

Lord Davenport passed a trembling hand over his face then removed a handkerchief from his pocket and dabbed at his forehead. "I'm sorry to ask so many questions. This is all quite sudden, you know." Looking at Trevor, Lord Davenport asked, "Do you have any information at all about my daughter?"

"We believe she's alive. Or was at Christmastime. According to her employer, she hasn't returned since the holiday. But I'd like to go back to when Millicent eloped. Were you and your daughter close? Did her behavior change in any way prior to her leaving?"

His host's jaw tightened, and he sighed heavily. "Do you have any children, Detective Inspector?"

"No, I've not had that privilege."

"Millicent was different from us. We tried to understand her, but it was difficult. She was volatile, given to arguing every decision we made on her behalf, even as a small child. We only wanted the best for her, but she would have none of it. Frankly, we were not surprised when she left. Disappointed? Hurt? Yes. Surprised? Definitely not."

"She had a temper, then?"

Chagrin marked her father's face. "That is one way she and I are very much alike, I'm afraid."

"You have other children, yes?"

Lord Davenport brightened. "Two. A son and a daughter. Both a real joy. My daughter lives with us. She was widowed several years ago."

"Did your children get along with Millicent?"

"Yes, but..."

A sharp rap on the door sounded. It opened, and a tall, fair-haired woman of perhaps forty swept into the room. Her blue eyes were wide set in a pale face. She wore a gray wool skirt and white linen blouse. "Daddy? Mother says there is a man here about Millicent. Have you found her? Is she all right?"

Trevor stood and gave a small bow. "Detective Inspector Trevor Gelson, ma'am. I take it you don't know where she is either?"

A frown darkened her face. "Not since she left when I was a child. What are you implying, Detective Inspector?"

"Sometimes sisters have a special bond. They might keep in touch even if their parents had severed ties with one of them."

Her eyes held a hint of fear for a single moment, then it was gone. He'd struck a nerve. Now, perhaps, he would get the information he needed. Turning back to Millicent's father, he gestured to the oil painting hanging over the fireplace. "I'm not familiar with this piece. Can you tell me about it?"

Lord Davenport stood and approached the artwork. "This was done by Ludwig Geyer. It is very valuable. Or was. He was a German artist. Nothing of German heritage is worth much these days. A shame."

"Do you have others by him?"

"Yes, I like his work."

"You collect German paintings?"

His host nodded. "Would you like to see them?"

Trevor donned his hat. "I believe I've taken enough of your time. I will keep you apprised, sir."

"I'll show the inspector out, Daddy."

"Thank you, Victoria. I do have some business to attend to. ."

With a bow, Trevor said, "Good afternoon, Lord Davenport."

The man mumbled a response, and Trevor followed Miss Davenport to the front entrance. When they reached the door, she whispered through thin lips. "How did you know I've been in contact with Millicent?"

"I didn't. I took a chance that you might be."

Her shoulders slumped. "You don't know where she is?"

"I'm afraid not. Anything you can tell me might be helpful in locating her. Do you have a current address?"

"You won't tell my father?"

"Not at the moment."

Miss Davenport's eyes bored into his, her face questioning. She reached out and gripped his arm. "You must find her."

Without a word, Trevor slipped his notepad from his pocket and handed it and a pencil to Victoria. She flipped to a clean sheet and scrawled on the page. "This is the last address I had, but she hasn't answered any of my letters. Nor has she returned my calls. Find her," she repeated and pressed the pad and pencil back into Trevor's hands before opening the door. He stepped over the threshold, and she put a finger to her lips before closing the door.

Trevor trotted down the stairs to his car. Deep in thought, he glanced back at the house, and movement in a top-floor window caught his attention. A younger version of Baron Davenport stood at the glass. Millicent's brother, Hugh. It had to be.

Chapter Twenty-One

The wind gusted, and dust swirled at her feet as Ruth approached the construction site behind the woolen factory where Devon Smythe had fallen to his death. The company was obviously doing well, since they were building an addition onto the plant. The sweet smell of sawdust hovered in the air. A dozen men swarmed over the three-story frame, shirts clinging to their backs with sweat. Hammers banged in a symphony of staccato drumbeats.

A burly man on the ground shouted at the crew on the scaffolding, and they scrambled to the ground where they retrieved their lunch pails before breaking into pairs and threesomes for their lunch break. Ruth tightened her grip on her pocketbook, took a deep breath, and walked to the nearest group.

"Good afternoon, gentlemen. I wondered if you might have a moment to speak with me."

A wiry man with red hair and several missing teeth squinted up at her. "And who might you be?"

"My name is Ruth Brown. I'm a journalist with the Associated Press, but that's not why I'm here."

A second man dressed in dark gray work pants and a torn black shirt spoke through the bulge of food in his cheek. "Then why are you here?" He wiped his mouth with the back of his hand and took a deep swallow from a dented canteen.

"I'm following up on the accident that killed Devon Smythe."

Black Shirt shook his head and studied his sandwich. His partner busied himself in his lunch pail.

Ruth's eyebrow went up, and she leaned toward the men. "Can you at least tell me if you know where he lived? I'm trying to get in touch with his next of kin."

"Marcus could tell you that, isn't that right, Bruce? He's the foreman."

"I understand it was an accident. Can any of you tell me what happened?"

Bruce shrugged. "We're being paid to put up this here building, not to put our noses where they don't belong."

Fumbling in her purse, Ruth drew out a card with her name on it. She scribbled Mrs. Caulfield's telephone number on the back and held it out to Black Shirt. "Will you call me if you think of anything that might shed light on what really happened to Devon?"

He took the card with dirt-encrusted fingers and stuffed it into his pants pocket. "You'll most likely find the foreman in the little shack behind those trucks. He doesn't like to spend a lot of time supervising the job." The man rolled his three middle fingers to his palm, his thumb and pinky outstretched and held his hand to his lips then tipped it as if pouring something into his mouth.

Her eyes widened, and she whipped her head around to look at Bruce who gave an imperceptible nod. Ruth leaned over and pitched her voice to a whisper. "Are you telling me the man has a drinking problem?"

The men swallowed the last of their meal and stuffed their napkins into the bottom of their pails before standing and brushing crumbs from their pants. Black Shirt jerked his head toward the vehicles. "We're not telling you anything. We have families to support, and we've spent too much time with you already. Go talk to Marcus. Maybe he'll tell you something." Without another word, they turned and walked toward a trio of workers seated under a nearby tree.

Ruth chewed on her lower lip. Her gaze raked the groups scattered over the job site. Would all the men be as reticent to speak as these two? Probably. She slung the strap of her pocketbook over one shoulder and picked her way across the uneven ground toward the collection of battered drays and panel trucks.

Rounding the vehicles, she spied a shack that looked unable to withstand a stiff wind. The door was a piece of plywood with a window just large enough to see through. She was surprised to hear voices from within because the structure didn't look big enough to hold more than one person.

Torn between guilt for eavesdropping and curiosity, she stood rooted in place. She didn't have long to wait. The door burst open, and the burly man who had called the crew to lunch rushed outside, a deep scowl on his face. He stopped short when he saw her, and his eyes narrowed. "Who are you, and what are you doing on a construction site? Visitors are not allowed, especially women."

Ruth drew herself up to her full height. "I'm here to see your foreman: Marcus, is it?"

The man jerked his head toward the building and stalked off without a backward glance. Ruth walked to the door and rapped sharply on the frame. A voice rubbed in sandpaper barked from within. "What?"

She opened the door and peeked inside. A hulking man with dark hair plastered to his head glared at her from behind his desk, if that's what it could be called. Two wooden frames held a warped board on which blueprints were strewn. Dozens of pencils were stuffed in a chipped mug that stood next to a metal flask. The man snatched the bottle and slipped it into his front pants pocket. The pungent smell of his unwashed body filled the room.

"Who are you?"

Ruth held out her hand. "My name is Ruth Brown. I wondered if you could help me."

The man ignored her hand, and Ruth dropped it to her side. He tipped his chair and crossed his arms, his gaze never leaving her face. "You do realize this is a construction site, don't you, lady? If you're looking for directions, why don't you use one of the police call boxes? We've got work to do. We're already behind."

"I'm not lost, but I am looking for some people. Two of your men suggested you might know how to find them."

He narrowed his eyes. "And who might you be looking for?"

Ruth licked her dry lips.

Before she could speak, Marcus brought his chair to the floor with a loud thud and leapt to his feet. "Who are you really? Are you from the insurance company? We already told you people what happened. Are you trying to shut us down?"

Ruth recoiled. Spittle formed at corners of the man's mouth, and his face reddened. He continued to rail at her. "I'm not authorized to give you that information. You'll need to speak with the owner."

"I'm not with any insurance companies, but I can wait to talk to the owner. When do you expect him? Or can you tell me where I would find him?"

The man swung his glance to the time clock mounted on the wall. Relief washed over his face. "He should be here any moment."

"Then I'll wait, if you don't mind."

"Suit yourself. Just stay out of the way." The man dropped back into the chair and began to study the drawing on top of the stack.

Ruth crossed her arms and leaned against the wall. With any luck the owner wouldn't be long. She cast her gaze around the tiny room, but the walls were bare except for the building permit nailed in place. Scooting closer to the desk, she tried to make sense of the blueprint. At her movement, Marcus glanced at her and frowned then dropped his eyes back to the drawing.

The door opened with a bang, and a thin man with receding blond hair stepped into the room. Round wire-rimmed glasses balanced on his long, pointed nose, and he wore a dark suit and red bow tie. He pointed a manicured finger at her. "Who are you, and what are you doing on my job site?"

Marcus scrambled to his feet. "She's here about Devon Smythe, Mr. Harrington. I haven't told her anything."

Ruth straightened and met Harrington's glare. "My name is Ruth Brown. I'm trying to get some information about Devon."

Harrington looked down his nose. "We don't hand out personal information to every Tom, Dick or...Ruth who asks. Who are you with? Are you from the insurance company?"

She shook her head, intrigued with the men's concern about the insurance company. They were obviously worried about something. "I'm not with any company. A skeleton was unearthed when my house was bombed. I think whoever it was knew Devon's family."

"So why are you mixed up in it?" He crossed his arms and narrowed his eyes. "Find yourself a new house, and mind your business. Let the authorities deal with your skeleton."

"I can't do that."

Harrington looked mulish. "And why not? If you're here, you must know Devon is dead, and yet you haven't given me a valid reason as to why I should release any information about him."

Ruth chewed the inside of her lip then blurted, "All right. Yes, I know he's dead. That's why I'm here. The skeleton under my house showed evidence of foul play. Until I knew he was dead, I was hoping Devon could help me figure out what happened. Now I'm wondering if his death has something to do with the discovery of the skeleton."

Harrington paled, but his face remained impassive. "Let me advise you to leave this to the police, Miss Brown. You don't need to get involved with the likes of Devon Smythe and his family. I bid you good day."

"You're hiding something. I can tell. I think my readers would want to know about this."

"What! You're a reporter? Get out this instant."

Ruth drew herself up. "Afraid I'll find out what really happened here, Mr. Harrington? I've done it before. I can do it again."

He exploded, and spittle formed around the corners of his mouth as he shouted at her. "You're that Ruth Brown? With the AP? The one who wrote the article about Coltrain Enterprises?" He shoved the door open, and she jumped as it banged against the side of the shack. "Get out. Get out, right now, or I'll have you forcibly removed. And I don't want to see you on this property again. Do you understand me?"

Ruth clenched her hands to keep them from trembling. "What I understand is there is a story here. I may not find it today, and I may not find it tomorrow. But I will find it."

Chapter Twenty-Two

Trevor stopped pacing and stared at the drawing on his desk. Chaos reigned on the paper. Phrases and stray words intersected with lines and arrows. The process was always like this. He would find the connection; he usually did, but before that happened, the clues and information resembled a plate of spaghetti. He resumed his march around the room then paused at the window when movement outside caught his attention.

A statuesque woman wearing a red beret hurried across the car park toward a dark coupe. Miss Brown? His pulse quickened. What was she doing at the station? The driver's door opened, and a handsome man who looked to be in his thirties stepped out. He circled the vehicle and embraced the woman before giving her a gentle kiss on her forehead. He opened the passenger door and bowed with a flourish.

Clenching his teeth, Trevor tried to wrench his gaze from the scene. No success. He inspected the man, looking for flaws. Who was he? Miss Brown had not mentioned she was seeing anyone. But of course, they'd never discussed their personal lives.

The man's suit was well cut and in excellent condition. Who in England had clothes like that in these difficult times? Maybe he was mistaken; maybe the woman wasn't Miss Brown.

He shook his head. If was definitely the attractive reporter. He'd recognize her anywhere. Even from the back.

She got into the car, and the man shut the door and trotted to the driver's side. He slid into the car and hugged the woman again, knocking the beret from her head. She laughed and tossed the hat into the back seat. The engine roared to life, and the woman's face turned toward the building.

It *was* Miss Brown.

Her face glowed with joy. She was obviously very much in love with the man. Here only six months, and she had found herself a beau. A jolly good-looking one at that. Trevor should be happy for her, but disappointment settled in his stomach.

He turned from the window. Her personal life had nothing to do with him. She was simply cooperating with him in trying to discover how and why Ian Belvedere died. The sooner he could find the killer, the sooner she would be out of his life. Why didn't he relish the thought?

Musing about her wouldn't get the job done. He swept his case notes into a folder and sighed then strode through the hall to the front desk.

"Sergeant, a word, please."

Sergeant Deardon snapped to attention. "Yes, sir. What can I do for you?"

Trevor bit back a smile as the overly anxious first-year officer nearly knocked himself out with his salute. The man's uniform was so starched, it had to be difficult to walk. His buttons and insignia gleamed despite the low lighting. His shoes were hidden behind the counter, but Trevor could guarantee a mirror-like shine on them.

"At ease, Sergeant."

Deardon blanched, and perspiration beaded on his forehead. "Yes, sir."

Trevor reached for the log book. "Was Miss Brown in here?"

Confusion marked Deardon's face. "Miss Brown, sir?"

"Yes. The reporter from America. Her house was bombed, and the skeleton was unearthed."

"No, sir. Not since I came on duty." He glanced at the wall clock. "And I've been here a couple of hours, now. Why do you ask?"

"Are you quite sure? Were you away from the desk at any point during your shift?"

"No, sir. I've been here the whole time."

"Did anyone else come in who might have distracted you?"

The sergeant opened the log and rotated it for Trevor to read. "We haven't had any visitors at all since I arrived. It's been a quiet day thus far."

Trevor slid the book back to the man then drummed his fingers on the countertop. "Hmmm. What was she doing in the police car park?"

"I beg your pardon, sir?"

"Nothing, Sergeant. That is..."

The door opened with a bang, and a brawny man with a deeply tanned face burst in to the foyer. Scowling, he lumbered to the desk. He ignored Trevor and barked at the sergeant, his words loud and slurred. "Who's in charge 'ere? I want to know what's bein' done to charge the culprits what killed my son."

Deardon glanced at Trevor, and the man shouted, "Don't look at him. Answer my question!"

Trevor moved close to the man. "I'm in charge, sir. I am Detective Inspector Gelson, and I'd be happy to help you. Please lower your voice, and show some respect to my sergeant."

The man sneered as his eyes raked Trevor's body. "They must be paying detective inspectors pretty good these days to afford a suit like that. Good at your job, are you?"

"Quite good, as a matter of fact." Trevor refused to rise to the bait and gestured toward his office. "Please step into my office, Mr...?"

"Smythe. Devon Smythe Sr."

"Mr. Smythe. Was it your son who fell and died at the woolen factory?"

Smythe crossed his arms, his head swinging back and forth like a bull raging at the red flag. "He didn't fall. He was pushed."

Trevor looked at Deardon and said, "Sergeant, please bring Mr. Smythe some tea, and ask Sergeant Phillips to join us. We'll be in my office."

Smythe and Trevor entered his office, and Smythe dropped into one of the wooden chairs in front of Trevor's desk. A moment later, Phillips appeared in the doorway. "You sent for me, sir?"

"Yes. This is Mr. Devon Smythe Sr.; Mr. Smythe, Detective Sergeant Phillips."

Phillips gaped at Trevor, then he turned to Smythe. "How do you do, sir?" Phillips seated himself in the vacant chair. Trevor closed the door and perched on the corner of his desk. A knock sounded, and the door opened. Deardon walked in and set a steaming cup of tea in front of Smythe before backing out of the room. The door closed behind him with a thud.

With an inward sigh, Trevor resettled himself on the desk. "Would you please tell us about your son, Mr. Smythe."

Smythe stared at the rising steam, weary resolve etched on his face. "Devon was my only child." He spoke in a low monotone. "His mother and I married late—after I got back from the war—and we were a long time having him. I hoped he could be everything I'm not, but he couldn't keep a job. At the factory, he finally found something he enjoyed. He fixed the machines. He could coax anything mechanical back to life, no matter how badly is was broken." He lifted pain-filled eyes to Trevor. "And now he's gone."

"If he was a machinist, what was he doing at the construction site? On the upper floor?"

His brow furrowed; Smythe shook his head. "That's my point. He shouldn't have been there. Someone must have led him there on a ruse. Or maybe he was coerced. Either way, it wasn't an accident."

"Have you spoken to the company manager? What does he have to say about the situation?"

"That's just it. He won't see me or take my calls. He's got to be hiding something."

"I can understand your concern. I'll send Phillips over to see what we can find out. Would that make you feel better?"

"Yes, thank you. They have to talk to you, don't they?" He turned to look at Sergeant Phillips, who nodded in assent.

Trevor said, "Meanwhile, I'd like your help in another situation."

"My help?"

"Yes. I understand you knew a man named Ian Belvedere."

A shadow crossed Smythe's face, and he set his jaw. "Yes, we were platoon mates back in the war."

"Have you seen him since then?"

"Not recently. Our unit used to hold reunions of a sort, but he didn't come after the first few. I can't remember exactly how many. That wife of his probably stopped him from coming. She wore the pants in that family."

"What can you tell me about her?"

Smythe reached for the teacup and took a sip. He cradled the cup in his palm. "She was a real looker, and she knew it. That kind of took the shine off her for me, if you know what I mean. I think she came from money, or maybe she just wished she had it. Ian was always trying to find ways to earn more so he could buy her nice things. He didn't say much about it, but I think she complained about not having enough."

Phillips looked at Trevor then at Smythe. "Some women are like that, aren't they, Mr. Smythe?"

"That they are. Looking out for themselves, not supporting the man who's supporting *them*."

Phillips leaned forward, his arms resting on his thighs. "Not like your wife. Right? You knew we paid her a visit, didn't you? And that she told us she didn't know where you were. That you had been gone since right after Christmas. But in reality she knew exactly where you were. She was protecting you, wasn't she, Smythe? What were you doing? Why would your wife think she needed to cover for you?"

Smythe sighed heavily. He put the teacup back in the saucer then passed a hand over his eyes. His booted feet clunked against the wooden floor as he shifted in the chair. "Yes. You're right. My Evie is nothing like Millicent Belvedere, and she did know where I was. We had an argument. I was doing a favor for a friend, an old friend from my unit. I wasn't doing anything illegal, but she wouldn't believe me." He wiped his palms on his pants. "He had done time back in thirty-two. But he's clean now. Legitimate. One of his lorry drivers couldn't make a run for some reason, and he asked me to do it."

Trevor said, "Does your friend have a name?"

"Foote. Luther Foote. He works out of Brighton."

"You know we're going to check him out."

Smythe sat up and met Trevor's eyes. "I'm telling you the truth. You'll see."

A knock sounded at the door. Trevor called out, "Enter!"

Sergeant Deardon stood in the doorway. "There's been an incident, sir."

Chapter Twenty-Three

The smell of rotting food assailed Ruth as she stood in front of the pile of rubble that had been her home before the bomb turned her life upside down. The landlord had not begun cleanup efforts, and the bricks, plaster, and thatch still lay in a tangled mess. A fine layer of dust shrouded everything, and she coughed when the wind picked up particles and tossed them into the air.

Down the street, two women swept the sidewalk in front of their houses. An older man bundled in a wool pea coat and dark trousers balanced on a ladder. His green-and-white-striped muffler flapped in the breeze while he covered one of his windows with a board, the nails ringing with every strike of his hammer. Near the end of the block, a group of children tossed a ball back and forth, their faint voices periodically broken by shrieks of laughter.

Ruth looked down at her outfit that was too nice to be rummaging in a bombed-out site and pressed her lips together. Clearly, the wrong clothing selection. But she couldn't traipse around London looking like a chimney sweep. The clothes would have to do. Her gaze cast about for somewhere she could safely leave her pocketbook. Seeing none, she draped the strap over her head so it lay crossways on her body.

She plunged forward, and her ankle twisted when her foot lodged between two bricks. She cried out then clamped a hand over her mouth. Pausing, she waited for the pain to recede. When the pang had subsided to a dull throb, she picked her way with care toward the cordoned-off hole, the uneven ground pulling at her injury.

Barricades blocked the gaping cavity, probably to prevent some poor soul from falling in during the blackout, although most people with any sense weren't creeping through neighborhoods late at night. Ruth drew a pair of leather gloves from her purse and put them on to prevent splinters or cuts from the jagged wood and glass. She squatted in front of the snarl of clothing and broken beams and shoved the wood aside, sneezing as she scattered dust. One by one, she pulled out garments and inspected them to determine what she could salvage. Many were undamaged and with a good laundering could be made useable again—or nearly so. She held up a blouse that had been pierced through the front with a six-inch-glass shard and shuddered.

Breathing a prayer of thanksgiving that neither Varis nor she had been injured, Ruth wrapped the glass in the shirt and set it aside. An hour later, she had finished with the clothes. Her knees burned from the constant pressure of the grit, and her back ached. She stood, favoring her ankle and massaging the stiffness from her shoulders. Looking around, her gaze flitted over the debris.

Bits of charred furniture mingled with shattered pictures that glinted in the sun. She stumbled toward one that she recognized as Varis's reproduction print of Monet's Water Lilies. It was her friend's favorite; with any luck the damage might not be irreparable. Just before she reached the print, her foot caught the edge of a beam, and she pitched forward and landed facedown with a grunt. She tasted blood where she had bit the inside of her cheek, and her knees stung from the impact.

Gingerly lifting herself, she took inventory of her discomfort. Nothing seemed to be broken, but she had wrenched the muscles in her back. Grateful for the leather gloves, she inspected their palms and found them scraped but otherwise unharmed. She couldn't say the same about her trousers. Her knees poked through identical rips in the fabric. She was going to have a lot of explaining to do to Varis, and she might end up looking like a chimney sweep after all.

Her glance riveted on the path in front of her, she inched her way toward the picture. She extricated it from the shattered frame, shook the broken glass from the print, and wiped dirt from its surface. Puckered on one end with a small tear near the top, the rest of the print was in good shape. "I can have it reframed. A late Christmas present."

Ruth's stomach rumbled, and she glanced at her watch. Well past lunchtime. She surveyed the area and frowned. At this rate it would take her weeks to sort through what was left of the house. And that was if she didn't do any investigation or writing. That wasn't going to happen.

Priorities. Now that she had their hanging garments, she should try to find their bureaus to see if she could recover socks, lingerie, and other personal effects. She had her typewriter, so besides clothing, what else did she need?

Her stomach complained again, and she sat back on her heels. It was time to call it a day. Tonight, she'd asked Varis for a list of items she hoped to be retrieved from here. As she climbed to her feet, something glittered in the afternoon sun. Mindful of her earlier fall, she crept across the ruins. She stooped and poked a gloved finger at the small metal disc and discovered several more underneath it. Rubbing one of the discs clean, she gasped.

Coins! They didn't belong to Varis or her. Where had they come from? Her breath came in quick gasps as she dug through the detritus. Hundreds of coins. If she wasn't mistaken, they were *German*. Reminiscent of the coins her father inherited from his grandfather. She popped open her pocketbook and began to stuff them inside.

Trevor's face flashed into her mind, and her heart sped up. She needed to share her discovery with him. Why hadn't his men found the money? Surely, he would not be happy she had unearthed them before he did. Shrugging, she continued to fill her purse. She would deliver them right after she stopped at the library to check out a book about numismatics. Would an English library have a book that included information about German coins?

She reached the bottom of her treasure trove. Pushing aside the rubble, she hunted through the dirt to ensure she hadn't missed anything. Seeing nothing else of value, she stood and tried to lift her purse. Her purse seemed to weigh as much as a bowling ball. She crouched down and pulled the pocketbook into her arms, cradling the heavy bag against her chest. Struggling to her feet, she wormed her way back to the sidewalk.

A bobby approached, and she stiffened trying to appear nonchalant. The man touched the brim of his hat. "Everything all right, miss?"

"Yes, Officer. This was my home. I've been searching for items to salvage, and...uh...realized I should have brought a vehicle. I have a number of things that can be saved."

"Very good, miss. Be careful."

She nodded and clutched her pocketbook tighter. He continued on his way, and she stopped to rest against a nearby letter box. Guilt washed over her. Should she have notified the policeman of her discovery? No. Trevor should be the one she should talk to. A smile split her face at the thought.

<hr>

Across town, Trevor hesitated outside the butcher shop. His gaze took in the queue that snaked from the door into the car park. Women of all shapes and sizes, some in simple floral dresses, others in work attire, clutched baskets or canvas bags as they waited, anxiety etched on their faces, eyes riveted on the building. No one spoke.

The window, crisscrossed with tape, held two signs—Leon's Meats and the warning about the consequences of buying from the black market. He huffed. That's why he was here. An anonymous caller had reported that

Leon was selling meat under the table. The man would deny it, but more often than not these reports proved to be true in the end.

It would be a shame to arrest the man and close the shop. The women would have to go farther to get their meat rations, and a trip could be for naught if the new location didn't have enough. No wonder they all looked worn out. These days, it was an effort just to provide meals for their families.

A few of the women gave him sidelong glances as he approached the door. Anxiety turned to anger. He knew they thought he was cutting in line.

Trevor excused himself and stepped through the doorway. He made his way to the counter, under which an immaculate but empty glass case sparkled. Holding up his identity card, he said, "Are you in charge here, sir?"

The man peered at Trevor's card and scowled. Tall and lanky, his wavy, blond hair straggled over a pink, shining scalp. A graying apron stained with rusty-orange smears hung limply on his frame. "Yes, sir. I'm Leon. I own the place. What can I do for you?"

"We have a report that you're engaged in the trafficking of meat. What do you have to say about that?"

Leon's face darkened, and he shook his head, but he did not meet Trevor's eyes. "I'm an honest man. Aren't I, ladies? I follow the rules, don't I?"

The crowd murmured and jostled forward, seemingly agitated at the turn of events. A dark-haired woman dressed in a worn but well-cut skirt and blouse spoke up, "We don't need your help here. Leon sells his meat fair and square. Sometimes he runs out, and we don't have to like it, but it's the way it is until this terrible war is over. Why do you have to come and make trouble?"

Trevor held up his hands. "I'm not here to make trouble. I know how difficult it is to feed your family with not enough food to go around. But we received a tip about Leon, and it's my job to check it out. If he's on the up and up, he has nothing to worry about, and neither do you. However"—Trevor glanced at the man for a long moment"—if he is selling on the black market or playing favorites, he'll have to answer for his crime. And he could be hanged."

Leon blanched but set his jaw. The woman shifted her basket from one arm to the other and glowered at Trevor. "There's no need to be mean. We're all just trying to get by."

Trevor shrugged. "This is not about being mean. It's about obeying the law. A law that ensures we'll all 'get by' as you say." He touched the brim of his hat. "I bid you good day, ma'am." He strode from the shop without a backward glance, well aware of the black looks shot at his back from the crowd.

Walking to the vehicle, Trevor pulled out his notebook from the inside pocket of his jacket and made some notes about the visit. The man was guilty. His gut told him that. However, he'd need more than intuition to press charges.

He took off his fedora, yanked open the car door, and ducked inside. He turned the key, and the engine roared to life. With a last look at the knot of women outside of the shop, he drove out of the lot. About fifty yards away, a young woman on a bicycle flagged him down.

Her brown wool coat had seen better days, worn at the cuffs and collar. A single button fastened it together in the middle. A pale-blue dress peeked out from underneath, and her sturdy brown shoes had broken shoelaces. Work-roughened hands gripped a square basket that had more than a few broken splints.

The car rolled to a stop next to the woman, and Trevor cranked down the window. Face averted, she scurried toward the car, her hands worrying the handle on her basket.

"I'm the one that called about Leon…uh…Mr. Peters." When she spoke, her voice was barely above a whisper. "He's been selling meat and other items under the table. To anyone who will buy them. And he's giving some of the women special privileges. It's not fair."

"How do you know this? Have you seen it? Or is it hearsay?"

Her face flushed, and she mumbled, "I bought some me self. Only once. My boy, he was sick, weak, and the doctor said he needed meat. Leon helped me out, but I realized it was wrong, so I didn't do it again." She looked at Trevor through lowered lashes. "Will I go to prison? It's only my boy and me. His father is gone."

Trevor searched her face. "Will you testify to Leon's actions in court? If you help me, I can help you."

The woman reared back. "Court? I can't go to court and speak against my friends. They would hate me, turn their back on me. Life is hard enough without that. You'll have to catch him without me." She looked over her shoulder at the shop. "I've said too much already. I have to go." With that, she turned and wheeled down a small lane, her shoulders hunched as she rode away.

He put the car in gear and slowly accelerated as he moved down the road. His mind picked at the situation. How could he catch this man? Could he come back and convince this woman to testify? He'd have to do a house-by-house search to find her. And bothering her would do more harm than good with her life being the way it was.

A battered, black police box caught his attention. He parked the car beside it while he argued with himself. If his plan didn't work or she got hurt, there'd be the devil to pay. The assistant commissioner would probably subject him to another tongue-lashing for going outside protocol. It couldn't be helped. These times called for *creative* police work.

He climbed out of the car and walked to the box. Opening it, he lifted the receiver and spoke into it. Distant ringing sounded, then he heard Phillips's voice. Trevor spoke in a rush before he changed his mind. "Phillips, what are you doing on the desk? Never mind. Didn't you tell me your wife missed the excitement?"

Chapter Twenty-Four

Standing in front of Nigel Winchester's house, Ruth looked up at the night sky. Not a single star could be seen in the inky darkness. Late in the afternoon, a heavy mantle of clouds had rolled in, black and swollen. A vehicle rumbled toward her, and she ducked behind the letter box, holding her breath. The sedan passed. She waited a moment and listened for pedestrians.

The night was silent, so she rose and crept toward the front door. She frowned when she saw an "X" of brown tape sealing the entrance. Drat! Now what? She moved to the window. I couldn't possibly be lucky enough to find it open, could I? Her gloved fingers gripped the top of the window and pushed. It slid up with a screech, and she breathed a prayer of thanks.

Shame washed over her. She was thanking God for helping her break in. Ruth pushed aside her guilt and hoisted herself through the window on her stomach, the rough wood tugging at her sweater. Her hands reached forward searching for the floor. She inched her body across the sill, and her fingers made contact with the cold wood planks. By shifting her hips back and forth she propelled herself forward and tumbled into the room.

The curtains rustled in the breeze, and she reached up to yank the casement closed, another screech filling the air. Rolling her eyes, she breathed out a quiet sigh. So much for stealth. She pulled the blackout material closed and inspected the panels. Satisfied no light would seep between them, she switched on her flashlight.

Glancing at her watch, she smiled. Plenty of time before she had to meet Varis, who would throttle her if she knew what she was doing, but Ruth didn't plan to tell her. Plausible deniability. That way, if Trevor asked Varis about it, she could honestly say she didn't know anything.

Trevor's face filled Ruth's mind, and she shook her head to clear the image and the guilt over his disappointment if he knew what she was doing. After his lackadaisical response to the coins, there was no need to get him involved tonight. Varis. Trevor. The room was getting crowded. She swept the beam around what appeared to be a parlor.

A pair of burgundy chairs sat in the corner, a small round table between them. One wall held a simple wooden table with a glass lamp on one end and a stack of books and papers on the other. A Windsor chair stood nearby as if the occupant had recently vacated it. The far wall was lined with bookshelves. She grimaced. Should she search them all? That could take hours she didn't have.

Better to check the entire house to determine where to start. With her light probing the darkness in front of her, she prowled through the house. She passed through the door into the living room where Nigel had been killed, the furniture still in an upheaval. Her gaze rested on the blank spot above the fireplace. Had he been killed for a valuable painting? Was this simply a burglary gone bad? It couldn't be. Otherwise his death was a coincidence, and experience said coincidences were few and far between.

The dining area was to her right, a six-foot table with claw feet surrounded by four chairs. A swinging door led into the immaculate kitchen. She opened the few cabinets and spied nothing out of the ordinary among the cookery items and canned food. The stairwell stood to her left. She grasped the railing and marched upstairs, her feet scraping against the wood.

There were two bedrooms of identical size with a bathroom in between. Each room held a single bed covered with a patchwork quilt and a nightstand by its side, a horizontal oak dresser and an armoire. The first room held very little–a couple of sweaters in the bureau and a navy-blue suit in the closet. The quilt hung to the floor, so she bent and lifted it to check under the bed. Other than a handful of dust balls, there was nothing to be found. The second room, apparently Nigel's bedroom, looked lived in. Crippled, yet he chose to climb the stairs every night for bed. Who was this man, and what had he done to get himself killed?

A search revealed nothing except his clothing and personal effects. The nightstand held a framed photograph of a family. Ruth shone her light on it and peered closely at the somber faces staring at her. The group stood in front of a small, nondescript house. The man and woman were positioned behind three children, perhaps eight to fourteen years old. The eldest, a boy, was Nigel, his angular jaw the same as in the photo of the four doughboys.

Ruth crept down the stairs and made her way back to the sitting room. She would start with the desk. The police had certainly searched the place, but perhaps they had overlooked a seemingly insignificant clue.

She dropped into the Windsor chair and pulled the files and papers toward herself. Flipping through them one by one, she perused each sheet. Formulas and drawings were scrawled across most of them. Lecture notes filled the notebook underneath. Setting them aside, she turned to the textbooks. Picking up the top one, she held it by the spine and fanned the pages. Nothing. She repeated the action with the remaining books. Nothing.

She tipped it back in frustration, and the chair creaked in protest. Her gaze returned to the bookcase, and she rose. Beginning from the top shelf on the left, she pulled each book out and fanned the pages. After thirty minutes, her back ached and her eyes burned. She had only managed to make it to the bottom of the first case. Ruth wiped her eyes with the edge of her sleeve and moved to the next case.

A scrape sounded at the window. She froze, book in hand, and heart pounding in her chest. Holding her breath, she waited. The window screeched, and the curtains fluttered. She snapped off the flashlight and fled on silent feet into the living room. Her gaze darted back and forth searching for a hiding place. There was none. A soft clunk told her the intruder was now in the house. He muttered to himself.

Racing into the kitchen and up the stairs as fast as she could without making a sound, she held her breath. She turned into the guest room and flung herself under the bed. Would whoever it was think to check under the bed? Her heart quaked at the thought. She tucked the book under herself and clasped her hands in front of her.

Her ears strained to hear what was happening downstairs. An occasional thump told her he was searching for something. Was it the killer returning to the scene of the crime? Sweat broke out on her forehead and under her arms. If that were the case, he wouldn't hesitate to kill again. She strained to look at her watch in the darkness, but it was impenetrable. How long before he ventured upstairs?

Time crawled. He was certainly not in a hurry. A cramp seized her right calf, and she gritted her teeth. Pointing her toes, she rotated her ankle to try to relax her leg. Pain gripped her, and she reached back to massage the clenched muscle.

Footsteps sounded on the stairs, and she stilled. Biting her lip to keep from crying out, Ruth held her breath. Booted feet clomped into the room. A flashlight beam danced on the floor guiding the intruder. He opened the armoire then closed it with a bang, and she flinched. The drawers of the nightstand slid open and closed, then he moved to the dresser, his heavy breathing filling the air.

Her calf seized up again, and tears rushed to her eyes. She squeezed them shut and tried not to whimper. She sent a silent plea to heaven for safety.

The man hesitated at the doorway, the ray of his flashlight stabbing the darkness. His booted feet trod toward her as he approached the bed then dropped onto the sagging mattress with a grunt. Stifling a gasp, she froze when he yanked on the drawer in the nightstand so hard that it dropped onto the floor in front of her. Her eyes widened when he bent to lift the drawer. Would he see her? Surely, he could hear her heart beating frantically in her chest.

Calloused, nicotine-stained hands gripped the drawer, and it disappeared from sight. He muttered an oath as he wrestled the piece into place before standing. Apparently satisfied there was nothing to be found, he stomped from the room. Ruth's breath expelled in a muted sigh, and she rubbed her leg. The intruder bumped about in Nigel's bedroom. Minutes later, he lumbered down the stairs.

Muted thuds filtered up the stairs then the window below squealed, and she knew she was alone. She slumped on the floor, the wood cool against her flushed face. Her heart slowed to its regular steady beat, and tension and fear drained from her body. With careful movements, she slid out from under the bed. Climbing to her feet, she brushed dust off her clothes then bent to retrieve the book.

With the slim volume tucked under her arm, she clutched her flashlight in one hand, gripped the railing with the other, and inched down the stairs. At the bottom, she hesitated for a brief moment before making her way back to the study. She shoved the book back in its place and stared at the case.

Should she continue her search? The man hadn't found anything. Would she? She aimed the beam on her watch face and shook her head. It was nearing ten o'clock. Varis would be worried. Best to leave and come back another day, perhaps when there was less chance of running into someone else in the house.

She looked at the window and chewed her inside lip. Did she want to risk opening it again? The noise it made could wake the dead. Would a fourth time bring the Home Guard? Turning, she walked to the kitchen. There was a small window over the sink. Could she fit through it? She had to try.

Switching off her flashlight, she slid it into her pocket, and hoisted herself onto the counter. The hard surface ground into her knees. She swept the curtains to the side, gripped the edge of the window, and pushed. It rose with a whisper. Yes! Now to cram herself through. She peeked over the sill and sighed. Would nothing be easy? A bare-branched quince bush filled the space below. Better to go feet first.

She pulled her head back inside and rotated her body, her long legs bumping into the spigot, wall, and canisters. With hands gripping the edge of the counter, she looked over her shoulder and aimed her feet out the window. She scooted over the ledge bit by bit. Her flashlight caught on the window frame and stayed her progress. She flapped her legs like a swimmer, and the light released.

Perspiring freely despite the chill of the night, Ruth edged her way outside. Her feet tangled in the bush, and she fell in a heap, the branches pulling at her hair and clothes. The brambles snapped and broke as she disentangled herself, and her face stung where she had been scratched.

Movement to her left caused her to turn. A hulking shadow came at her, and she threw up her hands and ducked. A glancing blow hit her head. Pain, then nothing.

Chapter Twenty-Five

The wan early morning sunlight struggled to dry the dew on the grass as Trevor backed his vehicle to an abrupt stop in front of the hospital. He snatched his gray fedora from the seat beside him and vaulted from the car, not bothering to don the hat before he took the steps two at a time and burst through the front door. The sound of his heels punctured the air as he strode across the lobby to the receptionist.

A gray-haired woman seated behind the desk stared at a worn copy of *Life* magazine through thick glasses, the masked man on the cover lending the periodical an air of danger and intrigue. She tucked a slip of paper between the pages and blinked at Trevor several times as if to bring herself back to the present. He held up his identity card, and her gaze slid from his face to the card. "How may I help you, sir?"

"A patient was brought in last night. A young woman named Ruth Brown."

"One moment, please." With precise movements, the woman pulled a clipboard from a small nail on the wall to her right and checked the list, her fingers walking down the sheet while her lips silently read each name. Trevor pocketed his identity card then clenched his hat in both hands while he waited, his eyes riveted on the old woman.

"Ah, here we are. Yes. Miss Brown is with us." She gave him a satisfied smile and hung the clipboard back in place.

"I'd like to see her."

Her face fell. "I'm afraid that's not possible."

Trevor fought his growing frustration. The woman did not appear to be stonewalling him on purpose, but she was certainly successful nevertheless. "Why is that?"

"Her doctor is not in at the moment, and it's up to him to approve any visitors."

"There must be someone else in charge who can grant my request."

She pulled another clipboard from the wall, and again ran her finger down the page as she read to herself. Shaking her head, she looked apologetic as she said, "No. Dr. Losey isn't due in for another hour, and Dr. McMann is in surgery."

Trevor raised an eyebrow. "You only have one doctor on duty?"

"No, but Dr. McMann is the only one with the authority you require."

"This is a matter of police business," Trevor said, his voice cold. "I don't have time to wait. I insist you allow me to see Miss Brown."

The woman rose and set her jaw. Her demeanor hardened, and she pointed to the line of chairs along the wall. She looked at Trevor over her glasses. "Young man, I'm sure whatever you need is of grave importance. However, Miss Brown's recovery takes precedence over anything you are doing at the moment. Now, you will sit over there and await the doctor's arrival, or leave and return later. Have I made myself clear?"

Feeling like a twelve-year-old in the headmaster's office, Trevor chafed under her glare. "Yes, ma'am."

"Good. And if you are a praying man, I suggest you do so. Miss Brown was seriously injured."

He cast a longing glance down the hallway, and she said, "Don't even think about pushing your way past me, young man."

Nodding, Trevor pivoted and dropped into the closest chair. From the corner of his eye, he saw the woman's face soften as she sat down and picked up her magazine. He sighed. She was only doing her job, but did she have to be so good at it? He tossed his hat into the next chair and massaged his neck with cold fingers before lacing them in his lap. Had the nurse scared off Miss Brown's friend he'd seen from the station?

Slumped against the chair, he closed his eyes and heeded the woman's suggestion, lips moving in silent prayer. *Dear Father, here I am again, bumping up against my will, not Yours. Once more, I've tried to control everything. You are in charge; You are in control. I know I should have learned that lesson by now. Forgive me, Father. Please, heal Miss Brown...Ruth. Only You can work the miracle.*

Ruth's face came to mind, eyes flashing, and hair tumbled about her shoulders. Trevor's fingers tightened. "Please, heal her."

Footsteps stopped in front of him, and he opened his eyes to find a harried-looking middle-aged man wearing a rumpled white coat over brown trousers and a white shirt. A stethoscope was draped around his neck, and his face was gray with exhaustion. Trevor jumped to his feet. "Doctor!"

"I'm Dr. McMann. You are here to question Miss Brown, yes?"

"Yes. No."

The man's eyes narrowed. "Which is it? You are a police officer, are you not?"

Trevor nodded. "Yes, and I'm concerned that Miss Brown was injured as part of a case I'm working on, but that's not why I'm here. Well, not totally. I wanted to see how she's faring." He clamped his lips together. He was babbling like a fool. The doctor would never let him see her.

"You have a *personal* interest in the situation, do you?"

Trevor's face heated. "You could say that."

A smile creased the man's face, and he beckoned for Trevor to follow him. "Then let's get on with it, shall we?"

The tightness in Trevor's chest eased. He retrieved his hat and trotted down the hall behind McMann whose lab coat flapped behind him like oversized wings. A nurse passed, her rubber-soled shoes soundless against the gleaming wooden floor. She dipped her head in greeting.

McMann stopped in front of an open door and put a finger to his lips. "I can give you ten minutes with her. No more."

Trevor's gaze bore into Ruth's face as McMann led him to her bed in the dormitory-style room. The doctor gestured to a wooden chair beside

the cot and with a nod walked toward the nurses' station at the far end of
the room.

White was everywhere, lending an air of clinical sterility. A pair of
white-clad nurses moved the row of beds along each wall, filled with
sighing, moaning, sleeping patients, dispensing care and medications.
Small white tables stood beside each cot and held white pitchers, white
basins, and white towels. The wooden-planked floors were scuffed and
worn but spotless.

Ruth's right hand rested on top of the coarse white blanket. Trevor
sank into the chair and tentatively reached forward to touch her fingers, to
feel the warmth of her skin, to ensure himself she was alive. She stirred,
her eyelids fluttering, and he pulled back his hand as if electrocuted. A tiny
moan escaped her pale lips, but her eyes remained closed.

His breath caught. He let anger build and swirl within him then
tamped it down. The emotion would spur him on, but it must be held at
bay to ensure he did not make mistakes.

With hands dangling loosely between his knees, he continued to
stare at her, drinking in the sight of her face—the dusting of freckles
across her nose darker than usual against her wan complexion. Her mouth
was turned down slightly, and a furrow wrinkled her forehead.

Unbidden, a lump formed in his throat, and he swallowed past it.
Squeezing his eyes closed, he bowed his head. "Lord, what is happening
here? Feelings I thought I would never have again have surfaced. I can't
understand why. She's infuriating. She's pushy, and she never listens to

reason. She doesn't do what she's told. She's stubborn. I can't care for her. It appears she already has a special someone in her life, and I don't know if she believes in You. Help me solve this case and get out of her life."

As soon as he fell silent, Trevor became aware of someone standing nearby. He opened his eyes and flushed. Varis was at the foot of Ruth's bed, worry marking her face. How much had she heard? He'd find out soon enough.

She spoke as he rose to his feet. "Good morning, Detective Inspector. Thank you for coming. I'm sure Ruth would appreciate it if she knew."

He gave her a crooked smile and shook his head. "I doubt that very much; however, it was nice of you to say." Gesturing toward the door, he said, "I'm sure you want to sit with her for a bit, but could you spare a few moments for me. I'd like to know what happened."

Varis nodded, and with a last glance at Ruth, followed him out of the room. They made their way back to the lobby, selecting two chairs in the corner away from the entrance and the prying ears of the receptionist. Varis smoothed her skirt and crossed her ankles. She hugged her arms to herself.

Trevor sagged against the wall, arms crossed, his fedora held loosely in one hand. "I should have kept a better eye on her." He pitched his voice low as he spoke. "I knew she'd keep digging. Phillips said she was found outside Nigel Winchester's house."

Varis's lips trembled, and she rocked slightly in her chair. She met Trevor's eyes with red-rimmed, tear-filled eyes. "After all this time of knowing Ruth, you'd think I would be used to her getting into trouble, getting hurt. She's fearless, and that trait has landed her in harm's way often enough that I should know to watch out for her.

A heavy sigh escaped her lips. "I don't suppose she's told you about her sister's murder. She was shot at and almost killed in an explosion while investigating Jane's death. And there's probably more I don't know about. I didn't even try to dissuade her from going to Nigel's house. I knew it was useless, but I should have gone with her. Maybe if I had, she wouldn't be lying on the bed back there."

"You can't blame yourself for her actions." He squeezed Varis's arm. "If you had gone, the two of you might be back there, or worse. No. You need to leave the sleuthing and protecting to me." He cleared his throat. "Why was she there?"

Varis flushed. "She thought she could find a clue that you and your men might have missed. Something you might not be looking for."

Trevor raised an eyebrow. "Such as...?"

She shrugged. "I'm not sure she knew, but Ruth is bright, and she has an amazing ability to ferret out information. She is able to connect the dots, if you will, that others may not be able to see. She looks at things differently than most people."

Varis snapped her fingers. "She did mention that she thought a painting or picture was missing from above the fireplace. There was an empty nail hole and a rectangle where something had been hanging. She might have been looking for whatever that was."

A tear rolled down her cheek, and she sniffled. Trevor offered his handkerchief to Varis who took it with an apologetic smile. She wiped the wetness from her face. "I'm not usually such a crybaby, Detective Inspector."

"You two are very close. Have you known each other a long time?"

"All our lives. We're from a small village in New Hampshire. There were four of us friends in the same grade." She gave him a watery smile. "We were the four musketeers. Still are. The other two are Grace and Lillian. We'd do anything for each other. You won't be surprised to hear that Ruth is the ringleader."

Trevor chuckled. "No, I'm not surprised." He grew somber. "Is there anything else you can tell me? Something that might help me find these culprits?"

"I'm afraid not." She hesitated then spoke firmly. "I heard your prayer, Detective Inspector. I do not make a habit of eavesdropping; nonetheless, I did hear you. I meant what I said—we'll do anything for each other." Her gaze pierced his face. "Ruth is my priority, not this poor man who was killed and stuffed into our basement. I'm not sure what you think you know about someone special in her life. There isn't anyone, but I can't let you hurt her while you figure out what you feel for her."

"I understand."

"Do you? Because I'm not sure you do."

A nurse approached. Trevor waited for her to pass while he collected his thoughts. Ruth's diminutive friend was more determined than she appeared. He had confused her quiet and gracious personality with timidity. How wrong he was.

"We come from two different worlds, Miss Gladstone, and I don't just mean America and England, although that is a large part of it. I'm a police officer. It's a dangerous profession, even without our being at war. It's not fair to subject a family to that. And I'm not sure how old Miss Brown is, but I can guess, and I'm significantly older. Most importantly, I'm a believer. I follow Jesus Christ."

Varis's face glowed. "Ruth and I are also Christians."

Trevor's eyes widened. "You are? Well, isn't that...something."

"You seem startled. I'm sorry if our lives don't seem to attest to that."

"It's not that. In fact, now that I think of it, your comportment has been above reproach. In my line of work I see very few believers, so I don't tend to look for them."

"I hadn't thought of that aspect of your work. But as to your comments about your age, Detective Inspector, my father is eighteen years older than my mother. It has not been a detriment in their marriage."

The floor matron hurried toward them, her skirts swirling about her legs. She reached their side and spoke in an excited whisper. "Miss Brown has awakened."

Chapter Twenty-Six

A beefy orderly wheeled Ruth outside the hospital, and murky sunlight warmed her face. The antiseptic air from inside was replaced by the coal-scented breeze. She pushed herself from the chair and turned to shake his hand. "Thanks, Warren. And congratulations on your engagement. I told you Lucy would say yes."

The man smiled at her through thick glasses and blushed. "Yes, you did, Miss Brown. I'm beholden to you."

Ruth nudged his shoulder then closed her eyes against the momentary dizziness. "Nonsense, but I do expect an invitation to the wedding."

"Of course." He gestured toward the line of cars at the curb. "Is anyone coming for you?"

"No, I've called a cab. It should be here shortly."

His brow furrowed. "You should have had someone meet you here. What about that nice Miss Gladstone?"

"It's midweek, Warren. She had to work. Besides, I'll be fine. The doctors wouldn't have released me if I wasn't."

He looked doubtful, and she gave him what she hoped was a reassuring smile. A few hours at home on the couch was all she needed.

Then she could get back to the investigation. She was obviously onto something. Why else would someone knock her over the head?

Trying not to wince when she probed the bump on her head with a tentative finger, she said, "I'll be fine. Go take care of the people who really need you."

"If you're sure—"

"Ruth!"

Varis rushed toward them, her normally composed visage held a look of anxiety. Several wisps of hair has escaped her chignon. "I'm sorry I'm late. I had a last-minute report to type."

Ruth's heart lifted as she hugged her friend. "You didn't have to do come get me, but I'm so glad you did." She scanned the vehicles for a taxi. "Where's the cab?"

Varis linked arms with Ruth and guided her toward the parking lot. "I didn't use one. Detective Inspector Gelson sent one of his cars for you. He wanted to ensure your safety."

Ruth stopped short and narrowed her eyes. "And you let him?"

"Yes I did. I certainly couldn't put you on the front of my bicycle, and I thought the bus would be too tiring. The price of a taxi is rather dear these days."

"You're right, of course. I'm sorry to be ungrateful."

Varis squeezed her arm. "I know you don't want to owe the detective inspector any favors. Consider that he might just be doing his job. Now let's not squabble. Perhaps we can take advantage of the situation and ask the officer to stop at the market. Then we won't have to carry our groceries home.”

With a grin, Ruth resumed walking. “That's brilliant. You talked me into it.”

The uniformed bobby waited by the car. As the women approached, he opened the back door and dipped his head. “Miss Brown, I hope you are feeling better. Detective Inspector Gelson sends his regrets for not retrieving you himself, but he had a matter of great urgency. I'm Sergeant Bengsten, and I'm to take you anywhere you wish to go.”

The women slid into the car, and Ruth leaned back against the cool leather. She unwrapped her red knitted scarf, letting it hang loose around her neck. The officer closed the door with a quiet click and climbed into the driver's seat. He met her eyes in the rearview mirror. “All set, ladies?”

Varis nodded. “Yes, thank you. We'd like to stop at Kaminski's market. Do you know where that is?”

“Yes, ma'am…er…miss. Mrs. K makes the best sausages in London.”

The engine roared to life then settled to a deep rumble as Bengsten guided the car into traffic. Ruth watched the vignettes of people as the vehicle passed them—a couple locked in a passionate embrace on a bench, a young woman with a squalling infant on her shoulder grasping a tow-headed toddler in the other hand as she hurried down the sidewalk, four freshly pressed and shorn navy cadets laughing and slapping one another on the back, an elderly man with a thatch of snow-white hair who leaned heavily on a black cane as he inched his way along, a canvas sack with a loaf of bread peeking out the top, slung over his arm.

Varis stroked her shoulder. "Ruth, you look exhausted. Maybe we should go straight home. Then you can rest, and I can do the shopping."

"I am more tired than I realized, but I've been lying down long enough. I need to get back at it. We should take advantage of the car, as you said." She squeezed Varis's fingers. "I'll be okay."

A short time later, the squad car stopped in front of the market. Officer Bengsten climbed out of the car, walked to the curb, and opened the back door. Varis stepped out and reached for Ruth's hand. Ruth slid from the car, aware that every move jarred her bruised head. She tried not to wince as the throbbing increased, and a wave of dizziness washed over her. She waved away Bengsten's offer to help and squared her shoulders.

Varis said, "Why don't you wait with the car, Officer. We'll only be a few minutes."

"Are you certain?"

Ruth nodded, and they made their way into the market. The first rush of morning shopping had passed, so only one other patron perused the goods. Varis grabbed a small basket and led Ruth to the vegetable crates. Several bins were empty, but one held two small bunches of carrots and another a few bedraggled potatoes. Ruth selected the larger bundle of carrots while Varis prodded the potatoes. She tucked four of the least bruised into the basket.

They moved to the shelves lined with canned goods. Ruth's hand hesitated above the display. "Do you have any preference?"

"No, one canned meal is as good, or bad, as another. I know I don't have to remind you, but I miss the fresh produce from home. We didn't realize how good we had it, did we?"

"I, for one, will never take food for granted as long as I live." She fingered the cans then chose several that she handed to Varis who laid them in the basket. "Do you want to see if he has any milk left?"

"That would be a nice treat." They wandered to the back of the store where a small ice box crouched in the corner. Varis opened the door and grinned. A lone bottle of milk stood in the middle of the bottom shelf. "This is too good to be true." She pulled it from inside and placed the bottle with the rest of their purchases as if it were gold.

They stopped at the bread display and put the single loaf into their basket. Varis patted it gently. "I'd say we did well considering the lateness of the hour."

"I agree."

Varis gestured toward the front of the shop. "It's time we left. You look tuckered out."

"I hate to admit it, but you're right." Ruth forced a smile. "I'm ready to be off my feet."

They paid for their purchases and left the store. Bengsten came to attention when they appeared. He took the canvas sack from Varis and put it in the front seat before opening the back door so they could slide inside.

Ruth leaned her head against the seat, her body sagging against the leather cushion. One minute the handsome detective was reprimanding her, and the next he was providing a chauffeured ride home. The man was an enigma, to be sure.

• ◆ •

Reclining on the couch, Ruth snuggled under a blanket and listened to the cabinet doors in the kitchen bang as Varis put away their purchases. The tea kettle whistled then went silent. The clink of china and clank of utensils floated into the living room. Varis entered the room carrying a tray that held the makings of a tea party. She set it on the coffee table and seated herself in the wingback chair.

The warm aroma of tea wafted toward Ruth, and she inhaled deeply. "The Brits may be right. There's nothing a good cup of tea can't cure. I feel better already."

With a giggle, Varis poured a generous serving of milk into the bottom of each cup then lifted the teapot. Before she could add the tea, there was a sharp knock on the door. "Perhaps it's Detective Inspector Gelson checking to see that his charges made it home safely."

Ruth shot a glare at her friend. "I'm sure he has more important things to do. Such as solve this case."

The knock sounded again. Varis set down the pot and stood. "I'm coming." She crossed the room and opened the door. Their landlady stood in the hallway, a deep frown on her face. Her graying hair was pulled back in its usual severe bun. A white apron covered her blue-and-white-checked dress. Her arms were crossed against her chest. "Where have you girls been gallivanting around to? You know I have a curfew, and I expect to be notified if you are not going to be home. I don't house that kind of girl. What do you have to say for yourselves?

Ruth frowned and pushed herself into a sitting position.

Varis stood with her hand on the knob. "We're sorry we didn't contact you, Mrs. Caulfield. We've been at the hospital. Ruth was injured. They kept her for observation because she has a concussion."

The woman deflated, and her arms fell to her sides. Worry flitted across her face then the steel mask dropped back into place. "Is that really what happened? I won't be lied to."

"Yes, ma'am. We have the discharge papers if you'd like to see them."

"That won't be necessary." Mrs. Caulfield spoke through thin lips. "I hope this will not impact your ability to pay your rent."

Ruth raised an eyebrow.

"Thank you for your concern. We'll pay our rent on time." Varis tossed a glance at Ruth then turned back to Mrs. Caulfield. "Would you like to join us? We were just about to have some tea."

"Me?"

"Yes. You work so hard; you must be parched."

The woman eyed the tea tray with uncertainty. Ruth swallowed her irritation and spoke up from the couch. "There's plenty to go around."

"If you insist, but I cannot remain for long."

Varis stepped back and opened the door wider. Mrs. Caulfield marched into the room. Ruth's head still throbbed, but she dredged up a wan smile for their landlady who lowered herself into the wingback chair on the far side of the coffee table. Varis closed the door then went to the kitchen to fetch a cup and saucer for their guest before returning to sit on the end of the sofa at Ruth's feet.

An awkward silence grew while Varis finished preparing their tea. She passed a cup to their landlady and said, "I'm afraid we have no sugar, Mrs. Thigpen."

"That's quite all right, Miss Gladstone, none of us do."

Varis took a quiet sip then set her cup and saucer on her knees. "We're glad you could take time from your busy day to spend a few minutes with us. You're welcome to join us any time you desire some company."

The older woman narrowed her eyes at them, her mouth turned down on the corners. She rubbed a work-worn finger along the edge of the saucer. "Why would young ladies like yourself want to spend time with me?"

"I may be overstepping my bounds, but everyone gets lonely now and again, and we thought…well, you seem like you could use a friend or two."

Their landlady studied her hands and barely spoke above a whisper. "I didn't have any choice about leasing rooms. I could have let the staff go, but they've been with me for years. It wouldn't have been right, by my finances have dwindled, so housing boarders seemed to be a good solution."

"Yes, ma'am. And now we're all together and should make the best of it."

Ruth's heart swelled as Varis quietly broke through the woman's anger and disappointment. She saw Mrs. Caulfield with Varis's eyes, as a woman bereft of any family, forced to share her house in order to save it. Compassion swept over her, and she said, "We're far from our loved ones. It would help us all feel less bereft."

Mrs. Caulfield took a sip of her tea and searched the girls' faces. "

"Let's get to know one another." Varis spoke with gentle tones. "You first, Mrs. Caulfield. You have a beautiful home; the architecture is quite different from where we come from. Have you always lived here?"

"No, I was raised in Brighton. My parents ran a small inn. That was how I met my husband. We moved to London after we were married. His medical practice was here." A shadow passed over her face.

"I didn't mean to make you sad."

"It's all right. He's been gone many years. Even after all this time, the pain is sharp. I couldn't give him any children, but he loved me anyway. Said it didn't matter."

"Sounds like he was a special man."

"That he was. He died of tuberculosis during the last war." Mrs. Caulfield shuddered. "He enlisted, and six months later he was gone. He was too old to go, but he insisted. There's never been anyone else. This is his family's home. His parents and only sister were killed in the Blitz, so it passed to me. Funny what happens. Our house was hit too, but I wasn't home, so I survived. I don't understand."

"It's hard to know why things happen the way they do. Only God knows."

"I used to believe in Him. Then He took Stanley too soon and left me to take care of my brother who was never the same after the war. A childish response, but I struggled to reconcile a loving God with one who would take my husband from me."

Ruth heaved a deep sigh and rubbed a weary hand over her face. "I know how you feel. My sister Jane was killed last year. I was angry at God for a long time about that. I still don't understand, but He has given me a peace I can't explain. There's a bigger picture I can't see. I may not ever know why she was allowed to die, but I know I will see her again in heaven. That gives me hope. Frankly, that's what keeps me from losing my mind in grief."

Mrs. Caulfield blinked rapidly, and a single tear rolled down her cheek. "My heart aches constantly. There is an emptiness, a darkness that taunts me. Especially at night."

"It doesn't have to be like that anymore. I promise you," said Ruth.

Varis rose and knelt next to Mrs. Caulfield's chair. "Would you like us to pray with you?"

The woman looked back and forth between Ruth and Varis. "I can't believe I've blurted all this out."

Varis patted their landlady's arm. "We're glad you did, so we could tell you that God loves you. He wants to be with you."

Mrs. Thigpen bit her lip then said, "I've been away too long."

Ruth shook her head. "It's never too late, Mrs. Caulfield. Varis, can you pray?"

"I'd be happy to. Dear Father God, we are so grateful for Your love, for the way you watch over and care for us. Thank You for Mrs. Caulfield and her friendship and what she means to You. Bless her, Lord. Please give her Your peace that passes all understanding. Thank You for Your presence in our lives. We love You. In the name of Your Son, Jesus, amen."

They opened their eyes, and Mrs. Caulfield gave them a teary smile. Ruth grinned and said, "You feel it, don't you? God has wrapped His arms around your pain, and now it doesn't hurt so much."

"It's like you said. I can't comprehend it."

"Neither can I. I just know it happens. I'm glad for you."

Mrs. Caulfield's lips pursed, and she plucked at her skirt. "Yes, girls, well, I've taken enough of your time."

Varis set down her cup. "Nonsense. We've enjoyed your visit. You have many beautiful items: sculptures, artwork. Where did you get them?"

"My husband was a collector. Not so much for the sake of the art itself, but its value. He picked up items from all over the British Empire. He even sent a couple of items home while he was in Germany during the war."

Ruth shot a look at Varis. "How did he do that?"

Mrs. Caulfield waved a hand. "One item was sent through the postal service, if you can believe it. The box was a bit battered when it arrived, but the statue was unharmed. Maybe you girls have seen it—the tiny sculpture of a shepherd boy that sits on the mantle in the green parlor.

"The other piece was a painting. He sent it with one of his platoon mates who was coming home after being injured." She shook her head. "The poor man died soon after he arrived home. He got some sort of infection."

Ruth's brow wrinkled. "How big was the painting? It must have been difficult to carry."

"Not at all. It had been removed from the frame and rolled up."

"You can do that?"

The woman shrugged. "Apparently. I didn't study it too closely. About a month after it came, I received news of my husband's death. I put the painting in the closet and haven't look at it since."

Ruth chewed the inside of her lip. Dare she ask to look at it? She glanced at Varis who frowned and shook her head.

Mrs. Caulfield stood. "I really must be going. Thank you for your kindness, girls. Ruth, I hope you heal quickly."

Varis rose and escorted her to the door. "Yes, ma'am."

The woman left without a backward glance, and Varis closed the door behind her.

Ruth grinned. "We need to see that painting, Varis."

Chapter Twenty-Seven

Trevor shielded his eyes against the glare of the sun as he squinted at the sign above the stationery shop. It was one of the few places along the street that still had glass in its display window. A bell above the door tinkled as he stepped inside.

The stocky man behind the counter peered at Trevor above—black horn-rimmed glasses, his face inquisitive. A woman sat at a scarred wooden desk in front of a typewriter, her fingers tapping out a rhythmic beat. "May I help you, sir?"

Holding his identification card up for the man's inspection, Trevor said, "I hope so. I am Detective Inspector Trevor Gelson. I'm looking for Millicent Belvedere, and I believe she works here."

"I'm afraid not. We haven't seen her since Christmas. She took some time off to visit family, or so she said. Not a word from her since. A shame, really. She was a good worker."

From the corner of his vision, Trevor saw the woman's hands hesitate above the typewriter. A moment later she resumed her work, her head slightly tilted toward him. He nodded toward her. "Would you mind if I spoke to the young lady? Perhaps she knows something."

The man tossed a glance at the woman and shrugged. He raised his voice above the clacking keys. "Miss Cook, would you stop what you're doing and join us?"

Her eyes widened slightly, and she rose. "Yes, sir."

"Did you know Mrs. Belvedere?" Trevor spoke in a soft voice.

"Yes, we are...were...friends."

"You've known her a long time, then?"

She nodded. "We were schoolmates. She helped me get the job here. One of the other girls had quit, and Millicent gave my name to Mr. Marshall here. That was over twenty years ago."

"So you'd do anything for her, wouldn't you?"

Miss Cook hesitated. "I would."

"And you have, haven't you?"

Her eyes darted from Trevor to Mr. Marshall, and she bit her lower lip, fear etched on her face.

"You have nothing to be afraid of, Miss Cook." Trevor looked at her boss. "Mr. Marshall won't fire you if you've been in contact with Mrs. Belvedere, right?"

Marshall pulled at his collar and smiled. "That's correct. You're not in trouble. Anything you can tell the detective inspector will be quite helpful, I'm sure."

Miss Cook sighed and slumped against the counter. "I hate keeping secrets. I told Millicent she should talk to you, Mr. Marshall. Really, I did. I don't know what's going on, but she asked me to hold her mail." She looked at Trevor. "You see, I'm responsible for sorting our mail when it arrives each day."

Confusion crossed Marshall's face. "I don't understand why she dropped out of sight. Why she didn't talk to me. If she needed time off, I would have given it to her. She's been a good worker, loyal and efficient at her job."

Miss Cook shrugged. "She wouldn't talk to me either. Just asked me to keep her mail and said she'd been in when she could."

The bell jangled again as a pair of gray-haired women, bundled in wool coats, entered the shop. Trevor held up his hand, and Mr. Marshall moved toward the customers. Miss Cook laced her fingers, eyes downcast.

The shopkeeper kept up a running monologue while he assisted the two with their purchases. Trevor studied the display through the glass case, waiting for the women to leave. Had the moment been lost? Would Miss Cook decide she'd said too much and shut down? It sounded like she didn't know anything. Was that an act?

The customers finally exited, and Mr. Marshall flipped the closed sign, locked the door, then rejoined them at the counter.

"Has Mrs. Belvedere received anything?" Trevor resumed the conversation. "Has she been in to check?"

A tear trickled down Miss Cook's face, and she shook her head. "No, I haven't heard from her at all."

"You wouldn't be holding anything back, would you?"

"No! I want to help Millie, if she's in trouble. I thought she might have gone home, so I called there. Spoke to her sister, but they haven't seen her."

"You know her family?"

Miss Cook gave a tremulous smile. "My father was in the foreign service, and my mother would visit him. Because Millicent and I were friends, I would stay with her family. Those were grand times. We did all sorts of lovely things together. Her parents have always been kind to me. Treated me like their own even though their family is much more important than mine. Certainly more wealthy."

Her eyes seemed to gaze into the distance as she continued to reminisce. "We would go to Bexhill for the summer. They owned a cottage. It was quite a production to get there. Lord Davenport insisted on taking his paintings along. It seemed the servants were always packing, either in preparation to go to the beach or return to the big house. Those poor people."

Trevor's brow wrinkled. "He must have gotten rid of the artwork. There weren't that many pieces in the house when I was there."

She shook her head. "He would never do that. They seemed to have personal meaning for him. He probably has them in the vault."

"The vault?"

"Below the house. In fact, Millicent used to drag me down with her to visit the room. I don't think her father knew, but she had somehow managed to discover the combination. She loves art. She visited the room at least once a week. Would sit for hours just looking. Said she wanted her own collection, just like him."

"Where did he get them all, do you suppose?"

"I have no idea. Truth be told, I'm not much of a student of art. I usually took a book to pass the time with her. Sometimes I'd slip away, but she wouldn't notice. It was all about the paintings with her."

Miss Cook bit her lip and looked at Trevor with pain-filled eyes. "Where could she be? Why did she go?"

"That's what I'm trying to discover." Trevor laid his card on the counter. "Please call if you receive any deliveries for her or she contacts you."

———

After crossing a name off her list, Ruth set down the pencil with a sigh. She had been making calls for thirty minutes with no progress. A noise sounded behind her, and she looked down the hall.

One of the other boarders emerged from a room several doors away, bundled in a black wool coat, her strawberry-blonde hair tucked under a wool cap. She waved and hurried toward the stairs.

Ruth turned back to the phone and picked up the receiver. Maybe this would be the call that would give her the information she needed. "Operator, please connect me with the British Museum."

A series of clicks and buzzes emitted from the phone, then a tinny voice announced, "British Museum. Mr. Regan speaking. How may I help you?"

"Good afternoon, Mr. Regan. My name is Ruth Brown. I'm with the AP service and doing an article on German art and the Great War. I wonder if you might be able to answer some questions."

"What kinds of questions?" His voice sounded full of suspicion.

Ruth doodled on the pad in front of her. "I've got reason to believe that art may have been smuggled out of Germany during and after the last war then sold in England. As a museum curator would you know if anything like that ever happened?"

"We are a reputable establishment. Why would I know anything about smuggled art?"

"I'm not accusing you of anything. I'm looking for an expert in the art field and thought perhaps someone who works for a museum might be able to help me."

"It was war, Miss Brown. I realize you Americans are insulated from the rest of the world, but surely even you could figure out that people will find any number of means to circumvent laws—and have been doing so since the beginning of time."

"Yes, yes. I understand all that. But each industry has its own way of doing things. I thought if I understood that the process of transporting pieces, I could determine how they got the art work out of the country."

"How do I know you're not one of them? A smuggler."

Ruth's grip on the phone tightened. Did he honestly think if she were a contrabandist, she would call for advice? "You could contact the bureau chief here in London. He could vouch for me."

"Really, Miss Brown—if that's your name—I don't have time for this. Good day."

"But..." He was gone.

She banged the receiver into the cradle then flushed at the childish gesture. No need to damage the phone or disturb the other girls. Drawing a dark line through the British Museum, she frowned. There were several contacts remaining, but maybe she should consider another way to find the information she needed. She was getting nowhere fast, and time was slipping away.

Tentative footsteps ascended the stairs. In a moment, her landlady appeared. Ruth sighed, "Mrs. Caulfield. How are you today?"

"Fine." The landlady hesitated. "I overheard your conversation. I didn't mean to eavesdrop, but I was passing by the bottom of the stairs. I may be able to help you with the information you seek."

Ruth's smile broadened. Was the answer she needed right under her nose? Mac Tillman would love the irony of that. The old newspaperman back home never did think she was a real reporter. Ruth's overlooking a potential informant would prove him right. She pushed the thought away and stood. "What could you know about smuggling artwork?"

The woman beckoned Ruth to follow her, and they descended to the parlor. They seated themselves on the worn, overstuffed sofas. Ruth waited as Mrs. Caulfield smoothed her hair then laced her fingers in her lap. Ruth's own fingers itched for a notebook and pencil, but if she excused herself to get them, the moment might be lost. She slid her hands under her thighs to keep them still.

"I haven't told you everything about my husband. The reason I have to house boarders is that he was dishonorably discharged. I don't get any government assistance." Her face flushed, and she looked toward the floor. "He was accused of stealing artifacts from a church in some village in France. Along with some of his friends. They were court-martialed, and each spent six months in the penitentiary."

She lifted an embarrassed face to Ruth. "Somehow, word got out about the incident, and when he got home he was ostracized by all his former friends and even some family members. No one would hire him. People crossed the street rather than speak to him. He was humiliated and shunned. He died shortly thereafter."

"I'm so sorry. That must have been terrible for you."

Mrs. Caulfield's voice was flat. "He killed himself. People said that proved his guilt. What do they know? He said he didn't do it, and I believed him. They made him a scapegoat. After the war, stories were rampant about men bringing home items that didn't belong to them, so they just assumed the accusation was true."

Tears trickled down the woman's face, and her lower lip trembled. Ruth's heart constricted. *Help me, Lord. What do I say?* "You don't need to tell me this, you know."

"Yes, I do. Maybe it will help you help someone."

Ruth patted her arm. "All right, but take your time. There's no hurry."

"Thank you, but I need to get it over with."

Ruth's heart quickened. Would this be the key to breaking the case?

"What I told you earlier was true. My husband was an avid collector of art. He was good at purchasing undervalued pieces and selling them at a large profit. He thought he could do the same thing while overseas. No one wanted items from the Germans; they were tainted. But Stanley knew that if enough time passed, they would regain their value. So he set about buying things and sending them home. The people were starving, and they had no money. They sold family heirlooms for any amount they could get."

Her face hardened. "If my husband was guilty of anything, it was taking advantage of their circumstances. But he paid them. He didn't steal. He wasn't that kind of man. It wasn't like that with others. Stanley said that men bragged about pilfering items from empty villages. Looters—that's what they were. Plain and simple. Then they either packed them in footlockers or shipped them home. It was allowed to happen. The company clerks turned a blind eye."

"That's a serious accusation, Mrs. Caulfield. Do you have any proof?"

"There's a man who works for the British Museum. I sold some of our pieces to him after Stanley's death. He can tell you more."

Ruth shook her head. "I've already talked to a Mr. Regan there. He wouldn't tell me anything."

"No, I don't suppose anyone would over the telephone. You should visit them in person. Ask for Robert Stollman. Tell him I sent you."

"Who is he?"

"Stanley's platoon leader."

Chapter Twenty-Eight

Trevor stepped from the police cruiser and buttoned his coat. The murky sunlight was no match for the chilling breeze, which carried the scent of snow. On days like this, he wished he worked in a cozy office. Should have been a solicitor like his uncle, rather than a policeman like his father. Water under the bridge.

He walked up the stairs and used the ornate brass knocker. He had not telephoned Millicent's family to notify them of his impending visit. Better to catch them unawares.

The door swung open, and Millicent's sister stood in front of him, dressed as if on her way to an important appointment. Surprise flitted across her face before a polite mask slid into place.

"Good afternoon, Miss Davenport. May I speak with your father?"

"Do you have news about my sister, Detective Inspector?"

Trevor shook his head. "No, but I do have some additional questions. May I come in?"

She stepped back. "Forgive my manners. Follow me."

They walked through the house to the library. A stone fireplace filled the far wall, and the remaining space was taken with floor-to-ceiling mahogany shelves. A leather chair stood behind the gleaming desk that faced two matching chairs.

"I'll get my father," Miss Davenport said.

Trevor nodded, and she left the room. He barely had time to glance over the book spines when heavy footsteps approached. Lord Davenport entered the room, his hand outstretched. "Detective Inspector, to what do I owe the pleasure of your visit?"

The search warrant rattled as Trevor passed it to the man. "That will explain everything."

The man's eyes widened as he perused the page. He frowned. "This makes it sound as though I'm hiding something. I was quite candid with you when I answered your questions the other day about my art collection."

"We have reason to believe you were less candid about the art you are housing for your daughter, Millicent."

"Millicent? I told you we haven't spoken in years. How could I have something that belongs to her?"

Trevor looked at Victoria who hovered at the doorway. "But your daughter has. Isn't that right, Miss Davenport?"

Millicent's sister glared at him. "That was between you and me, Detective Inspector."

"This is a murder investigation. Secrets are not a luxury we can afford."

Lord Davenport stared at his daughter, his mouth working to form words. "Is this true? You've seen Millicent? You know where she is?"

She slid her mulish gaze to her father. "What do you care? You threw her out and never looked back. What did she do that was so horrible, other than marry for love? Was that so terrible?"

"You don't understand—"

"You're right. I don't understand. You have plenty of money. You shouldn't have tried to force her to marry that decrepit baron in an effort to expand your holdings. It's archaic. Arranged marriages are a thing of the past, Father."

With a shaking finger, Lord Davenport pointed to the door. "We will discuss your deceit later, young lady. I will not have you insult me in front of a caller."

"I'm afraid you can't banish her just yet." Trevor held up a hand. "She needs to answer some questions."

The man crossed his arms and pursed his lips. Trevor turned to Miss Davenport. "Were you aware that the address you gave me was a stationer's? That it wasn't her home?"

Miss Davenport shook her head. "How would I know that?"

"Did you ever go into the city to try to find her?"

"And how would I do that? He owns everything. I can't take the car without permission nor can I simply leave the house on my own."

"When was the last time you corresponded? It's important that you tell the truth about this."

"The middle of November, sometime. I can't recall exactly. But it was before Mother's birthday which falls on the twentieth. I remember that."

"Did Millicent give any indication she was going away?"

Miss Davenport's mouth formed a hard line for a moment. "No, and I don't know why. We've shared everything over the years. She must be in trouble of some sort. She wouldn't leave without telling me."

"Unless she didn't want the authorities to know where she was."

Miss Davenport blanched. "I don't understand. Why wouldn't Millicent want people…the authorities…to know where she is?"

Trevor's grip tightened on his hat. "I'm not at liberty to say, Miss Davenport. Thank you for your cooperation. Now, Lord Davenport, I'm ready to take a look at your vault, then we'll tour the house."

<hr/>

Ruth stood across the street from Devon Smythe's ramshackle house and took a deep breath. Would he speak with her? Would he provide any information she could use? Her story was at a standstill until she could figure out how the art-theft ring had shattered to untangle the puzzle of Ian Belvedere's death.

She straightened her coat and settled the strap of her purse on her shoulder. Too bad Varis had to work. The moral support would have been nice.

Traffic cleared, and Ruth stepped off the curb. Her feet crunched on the pebbled debris as she hurried to the walkway on the other side.

Before she lost her nerve, she jogged up the steps that led to Devon's front door.

What was the worst thing that could happen? Even if he was Ian's killer, he wouldn't kill her in his own home, would he? Ridiculous. Maybe she'd stay on the porch to be on the safe side.

She rapped on the sun-bleached wooden door. The sound of heavy tread vibrated from within the house. Ruth took an involuntary step back as the door swung open. The swarthy man squinted at her, his greasy hair spiked at odd angles and his clothes in disarray. He swiped at his nose. "Who are you, and what do you want?"

Smiling, she tried to ignore her racing heart. "Mr. Smythe? My name is Ruth Brown, and I'm with the Associated Press. I'd like to ask you a few questions, if you don't mind."

"About what?"

"About your son's so-called accident."

He stiffened, his face darkening. "What do you want to know?"

He scowled and held up a hand. "Wait. What story? What do you want to know?"

Ruth tossed a look up and down the street then gave him a pointed stare. He retreated away from the door and swept his arm toward the inside of the house. Against her better judgment, she entered the foyer. He led her to a tidy parlor, and they seated themselves in tired but comfortable chairs. She glanced at her surroundings.

About twelve feet square, the room contained three chairs, a small blue sofa, an oak coffee table, and a stand-up desk covered in stacks of paper and folders. Her eyebrows raised when she noticed several framed paintings on the walls.

She withdrew the dog-eared photograph from her purse. "This is you with your friends, is it not, Mr. Smythe?"

"I thought this was about my son."

"Please answer my question."

He leaned forward to peer at the picture and nodded. "But you already knew that. It's obviously why you're here."

"I needed to be certain. A good reporter checks her facts." She cleared her throat. "I'm sorry for your son's tragic death. Why don't you think it was an accident?"

"You don't believe me either, do you?"

She tapped the photo. "I'm not saying that, but I don't see a connection."

Devon rubbed his forehead but didn't reply.

"Something happened that tied the four of you together." Ruth spoke with urgency. "Something that made it necessary for Ian to die. Then Nigel. Now your son."

His face paled, his belligerence slipping away. "What? Nigel's dead? When? How?"

"Several days ago. He was hit over the head. Surely you read about it in the paper."

"No, I don't read the papers. They're full of the war. I had enough war the first time." His eyes narrowed. "It has to be Hugh. Or that sister of his. Maybe both."

Ruth bolted upright. "Why do you say that?"

"They were always thick as thieves. He's not real smart, and she's been telling him what to do his whole life. It wouldn't surprise me if she talked him into killing the lads."

"Why would she do that?"

"For any number of reasons. Millicent was ruthless. Oh, she loved Ian in her own way. She wouldn't have given up all that money her family had if she didn't, but he never seemed to measure up. She was always pecking at him to buy her things. Not baubles, mind you. Statues, paintings—that sort of thing."

"You think Millicent had Hugh kill Ian because he wasn't buying artwork for her?"

He shrugged. "Petty, I know, but I wouldn't put something like that past her."

"Then why would she want Nigel and your son dead?"

He snatched the photo from her hands and pointed to the statue and the other items surrounding the smiling men. "We *liberated* those items. Do you see the entrance to the mine? The four of us were doing reconnaissance before a big battle at Somme, and we stumbled on that opening. When we looked inside we found dozens of crates, and they were filled with all kinds of stuff: statues, paintings, rare books, wood carvings, even porcelain vases, and what have you. We had struck it lucky. Here was our chance to set ourselves up for life after the war, and Ian could get Millicent off his back. It was Nigel's idea. He was the ringleader. We made a plan to smuggle the stuff out a bit at a time."

Devon passed a trembling hand across his eyes and sighed. "It didn't work out as planned. There was a series of four paintings. I couldn't tell you who the artist was, but Ian insisted they were valuable. We removed the frames so we could roll them up, and we each took one. Later that week, we were able to secure a couple more pieces, but then our unit shipped out, and that was the end of that."

Ruth turned to study the artwork on the walls. "Is it one of these?"

Shaking his head, Devon frowned. "Mine was stolen about three years after I returned from the war. Came home from work one day to an empty frame above the fireplace. I couldn't go to the police. I thought about tracking down the other guys but decided it wasn't worth it. I was actually kind of relieved to have it gone. Before it was stolen, I felt bad every time I looked at the thing. I had a good life, a good job. Devon Junior was about six months old at the time."

"I'm sorry to be so obtuse, Mr. Smythe, but I don't understand how killing your son is a warning to you."

He stared at her with pain-filled eyes. "Don't you see? I don't know. Maybe they're telling me that they can get to me if they want…that I have to keep my mouth shut about what we did."

"Why wouldn't they simply kill you?"

Devon leapt up from the chair. "What have I done? Now that I've told you the story, they'll find out, and they'll come for me. You need to leave. Now."

"But, Devon, Mr. Smythe—"

"Now!"

Chapter Twenty-Nine

Ruth trudged home from the tube. The sun had broken through the clouds, and it warmed her back. There was more to Smythe's story, but how could she get him to speak with her again? He tossed her out. Had the idea to steal the items been Nigel's, as Devon claimed? It was easy to blame a dead man. Maybe Smythe was the ringleader, and his son's accident was a convenient way to throw the light onto one of the others.

A chill swept over her, and she stopped in her tracks. Would he have killed his own son? No, the pain in his eyes was too real, and nothing pointed to that logic. She was grasping at straws.

She resumed walking and reached the house. Varis would be home soon. They could sift through the information—perhaps come up with a viable theory. She went inside and jogged up the stairs. Mrs. Caulfield stood at the open door to their room with arms crossed and a frown on her face. "Miss Brown. It's about time you returned. I have called the police about this."

Ruth hurried forward then froze. Her room was an upheaval of furniture and clothing. The sheets on both beds had been stripped, and the mattresses slashed. Every drawer in the dressers hung open, their contents strewn around the room. She gasped. Scrawled on the full-length mirror in what looked like red lipstick were the words "Find another story, or you're next."

Hand over her mouth, she stifled a scream.

"Ruth!" Varis rushed up the stairs. They clung to each other. "The girls downstairs told me what happened," Varis said. "Are you all right?"

"Yes. I wasn't here. Mrs. Caulfield hasn't had time to tell me what happened."

Their landlady huffed. "What's happening is that you two are moving out. You cannot stay here another night. I will not have the lives of the other girls endangered. Nor mine."

Ruth and Varis stared at the woman with wide eyes. Anger and hurt warred within Ruth. "Mrs. Caulfield, this isn't Varis's fault. You must let her stay."

Varis shook her head. "We're in this together."

"But, Varis—"

"No buts, Ruth. You're obviously getting close to the truth. You can't stop now." Varis turned to Mrs. Caulfield. "We're sorry you feel this way; we'll be out within the hour."

Ruth said, "We can't ask Louise and her husband to take us in again."

"Perhaps not, but for tonight we'll stay at the *Thistle and Rose.* I have some money put aside; we can use that."

The wailing of a police siren grew louder. Ruth sighed. Trevor would be part of the responding officers or close on their heels. Her heart flipped. Varis stroked her back then moved away to upright the chairs. Sinking into one, she gestured to the other. "Ruth, you know this is going to take a while. Why don't you sit down?"

Ruth gave her a resolute smile. "Because I'd rather meet DI Gelson on my feet."

"You don't know that's who is coming."

"It will be Trevor."

———————————◆———————————

Trevor stopped in the doorway of the small room, his hat in hand. Ruth was standing in the midst of the chaos. Somehow he wasn't surprised. The look on her face dared him to reprimand her. She was fearless. Any other woman he knew would be trembling at the vision of her room turned upside down by an unknown culprit. Instead, she seemed to take pride in the situation as if it were a badge of honor. Did she not care that she could be in danger?

Varis spoke first. "DI Gelson. How nice to see you again. Too bad it is in such unfortunate circumstances."

"Indeed. Are you ladies all right?"

"Fine. Neither of us was home when this occurred."

Footsteps sounded behind him, and he moved aside. Two bobbies entered. He could hear Phillips at the bottom of the stairs speaking with the landlady. Her strident voice carried into the room. "What are you going to do about this, young man? We could have been killed in our beds!"

Trevor shook his head. "Is there somewhere we might go to discuss this? It's crowded."

Ruth still had not spoken, but Varis rose and said, "Of course. There is a parlor at the end of the hall. Follow us."

They made their way to the small room. Varis sank onto the sofa. Ruth seemed to weigh the situation as she stood with arms crossed. He eased himself down and set his hat on a nearby table. Uncertainty flitted over her face then the mask settled back in place.

"I'm pleased to see you are unharmed." He started in neutral territory. "It must be unsettling to come home and find your belongings tossed about."

Ruth's arms flailed. "Unsettling? That's the understatement of the year."

Varis patted the cushion beside her. "Ruth, why don't you sit? This could take a while."

Trevor held his counsel as a look passed between the two women. Ruth dropped onto the couch, and Varis patted her shoulder before speaking. "Thank you for coming, DI Gelson. I'm not sure what we can tell you. Fortunately, as we said, we weren't here when this occurred."

"That is a blessing, isn't it? Have you had a chance to see if anything is missing?"

They shook their heads, and Varis continued, "We were discussing the situation with Mrs. Caulfield."

"Discussing, right." Ruth snarled. She was barking at us as if this were our fault. She wants us to move out."

"You must understand, Ruth…erh…Miss Brown. She's afraid. Not everyone is as stalwart as you."

He watched her knead trembling fingers.

"Can we get on with this, DI Gelson?" She scowled. "We promised Mrs. Caulfield we'd be gone shortly."

"We'll have to disappoint her. This will take some time."

Ruth glanced at her watch. "I'd rather it didn't. I'd like to leave and get some dinner."

Trevor cleared his throat. "Perhaps we can prevail upon Mrs. Caulfield to bring us some refreshments."

"Good luck with that. She seems quite put out about this whole thing."

He stood and walked to the door. "Constable Harris!"

One of the bobbies appeared and saluted. "Yes, sir."

"These women have not had their dinner. Get the landlady to prepare something."

Another salute. "Yes, sir."

Trevor returned to the chair and smiled. "It's sometimes useful to be in charge." He pulled out a notebook and pencil. "Let's get started, shall we?"

He turned to Ruth who seemed to be intent upon proving she was unmoved by the incident. He'd play along. "Based on the message left on your mirror, Miss Brown, we can assume this was meant as a warning to you. I know you reporters like to keep things close to yourselves, but it would be helpful if you could tell me what stories you're working on at the moment in addition to the one about Ian Belvedere."

Ruth looked at him, her brows drawn together."

"Ironically, I'm also researching an article on the dearth of housing in London."

Trevor pressed his lips together. She wouldn't appreciate a clever response on his part. He smoothed the page on his notebook and resumed his questions. "Have you made anyone angry during your investigation? A shady landlord? A housing official?"

"No, I've barely begun. This is about the skeleton." She was firm. "We must be close to finding an answer. No one else's room in Mrs. Caulfield's home was disturbed."

"Then I suggest we determine what, if anything, was taken from your room." He rose and stuffed his notebook and pencil in his breast pocket. The girls stood, and the trio made their way back to the ransacked room.

"Officers, please give us a moment." The men filed out the door, and Trevor gestured for Ruth to take inventory. She hesitated then walked to the nightstand, lifted the overturned drawer and slid it back in place. Kneeling, she picked up her Bible and placed it inside. She sifted through the pile of socks and unearthed what appeared to be a journal. Putting it on top of the Bible, she closed the drawer, and stood. She moved to the desk.

Varis touched Trevor's arm with a finger. "DI Gelson, may I...?"

"Absolutely."

A wave of sympathy swept over Trevor as the women worked. This was the hard part—watching victims try to make sense of the violence in their life. Miss Brown surely knew this wasn't personal, but it had to feel like a violation just the same. Her ramrod-straight back and set jaw belied the hurt and confusion he knew coursed through her.

He rubbed his eyes. She could have been here, could have been injured...or worse. The soft curve of her neck was exposed above her collar, and he wondered at the urge to hold her and tell her everything would be all right. Pulling his thoughts back to the crime scene, Trevor moved to the window and cracked it open. Cool air swept in, and he took a deep breath.

Ruth sank into the nearby chair. "They're not here. Every single research note about Ian's story is gone. All the information I collected from Devon Junior's employer. The interviews, sketches of the building, and where Devon had been standing when it happened: all of it."

"You had drawings? Very thorough, Miss Brown."

"Can you recreate any of it?"

She shrugged. "Maybe, but it will take a while and probably won't be as accurate." She closed her eyes and sighed. "There's no way they'll talk to me again."

"This is discouraging, Ruth," Varis said. "But on the other hand, maybe it's a clue for DI Gelson."

He rubbed his hands together. "Indeed. Perhaps. We'll have to consider how it ties to the Belvedere case."

A constable appeared in the doorway carrying a tray filled with cups of tea and plates of sandwiches. "Sir? Where would you like me to put this?"

"End of the hall, Officer. In the parlor. The ladies will join you there."

"Very good, sir."

Trevor turned back to the girls. "You've done enough here. My men need to finish cataloguing the scene, and you should rest. When you've finished eating, I'll have Officer Bengsten escort you to his home. His wife is lovely. She'll fix you up."

Ruth shook her head. "I don't want to stay with some policeman and his family. We need to pack our things and check in to the hotel."

"There will be time enough for that tomorrow. I can't say when my men will finish up here."

"Can't or won't?"

A shout sounded from below them. "Detective Inspector Gelson, we found something!"

Chapter Thirty

Officer Bengsten braked in front of the precinct. Ruth thanked him as she stepped out of the car and cast a worried eye at the overcast sky. Would she have to scour the city in a downpour?

Once inside, she unbuttoned her jacket and marched to the front desk. Officer Brookes smiled as she approached. "Good morning, miss. Sleep well?"

She bit back a retort and nodded. "Is DI Gelson in yet?

"We expect him any—"

The door swung open behind her. DI Gelson shed his hat and shook water from his coat. So the weather hadn't cooperated. He gave her a crooked grin, and her face warmed. Ducking her head, she drew her notepad from her purse and waited as he draped his trench coat over a hook and placed his fedora on top.

"Shall we?" He pointed toward his office door, and they entered the room where they seated themselves. Trevor rose again. "Forgive my manners. Would you like some tea?"

"No, but thank you for asking."

"How was your stay with Officer Bengsten?"

"Fine. You were right. His wife is a lovely woman. She worked hard to make us comfortable."

"Excellent. They'll house you until we catch the killer. I can't have you risking your life any longer."

The tangy aroma of his aftershave wafted toward her as he sat back and crossed his legs. In need of a haircut, his hair curled slightly over his collar. His hands rested in his lap. Ruth's gaze traveled to the shoulders that strained slightly against his suit jacket. She blinked several times. What was she doing? She tapped her notepad. "Ready?"

"You know this is highly irregular. I don't make it a habit to discuss ongoing cases with civilians, especially journalists. Other than a few hiccups, we've partnered well so far. I have to go on recording, saying you can't print anything that will jeopardize the case."

"I understand, and I appreciated what you're doing." She swallowed heavily then gave him her landlady's story and told him that Devon claimed his painting of the four-piece set brought back to the States was stolen. "Then he decided my being there made him a target, so he rather unceremoniously tossed me out." She frowned. "I didn't get to finish questioning him."

Ruth closed the book. "That's all I have."

"Good work. Very thorough." He winked. "You'd make an excellent policewoman, if you could get used to the idea that you wouldn't be allowed to ask all the questions you wanted to."

She raised an eyebrow and grinned. "Which is why I won't be going into police work."

Still smiling, he reached across the desk and picked up a thick folder. Sifting through the pages, he stopped about halfway through the stack and ran a finger along the text as he read.

Ruth waited, the sound of her breathing harsh to her ears. Could he hear that too? She couldn't hold her breath—that would only make the waiting worse. How much longer would he be?

Trevor uncrossed his legs, and Ruth's head pivoted at the sound.

His face held the joy of a boy who had just been given his first puppy. "Sorry for the delay. Anyway, I found what I was looking for. Everyone we've spoken to has mentioned Millicent and her desire for wealth. Valuable paintings have been stolen from Devon and Nigel. Nigel and Ian, and possible Devon's son have been murdered, leaving us Hugh and Millicent."

She bolted from the chair. "Who should we see first?"

Trevor laughed. "Aren't you the anxious one?"

Warmth suffused her. "Aren't you?"

"Yes, I'm as anxious to wrap up this case as you are, but rushing makes for sloppy police work. Let's discuss it before we run headlong into another blind alley. I believe seeing Hugh is the obvious course of action. Neither of us has spoken with him. Hugh may give us a new perspective entirely."

"What if his sister Victoria tipped him off about the investigation?"

"I guarantee she has, but I've seen him watching me. He's well aware of the stakes here. I still think he's our best bet." He held out his elbow. "Shall we, Miss Brown?"

Ruth buttoned her coat and straightened her hat. Tucking her hand in his arm, she said, "We shall, DI Gelson."

They marched from the office to the front desk where Trevor informed Officer Brookes of their intended destination.

"Very good, sir. I'll notify Sergeant Phillips when he arrives. Any other message for him?"

"Yes. Have Brookes meet us out front with a car; we may need the extra help."

"Will do."

They hurried out the door and down the steps. Ruth shivered and tucked her scarf closer to her neck as the wind cut through her. An engine roared, and she turned to see a patrol car pull up to the curb. Trevor released her and opened the back door. She slid onto the seat, and he followed her inside. He slammed the door, and Officer Brookes stomped on the accelerator. The tires chirped as the vehicle shot forward.

⸻ ◆ ⸻

"Slow down, Brookes."

"See that man in the brown suit? The one who pushed past the woman in the red coat? That's Devon Smythe. Follow him. I'm curious as to why his is so close to the Davenport house. This isn't exactly his neighborhood."

His presence could be a coincidence or he could provide us with another clue." He rubbed his hands together. "However, I don't tend to believe in coincidences.

Ruth smiled to herself. Trevor was definitely in the right line of work.

Brookes guided the car through the traffic, slowing enough to keep behind their prey without drawing attention to themselves. Ruth clenched her hands together in her lap and leaned forward while Smythe darted between the pedestrians. Several blocks later, he jogged up the steps of a narrow brownstone, and Brookes passed the building before sliding the car into an empty spot across the street. Once at the door, Smythe looked both ways then pounded on it with a fist.

Trevor and Ruth watched the proceedings through the rear window. Smythe scowled and hammered again. The door remained closed. He flicked his wrist to check his watch and banged one last time. When no one answered, he stomped down the steps and trudged forward.

Without waiting for instructions, Brookes flung a look over his shoulder to check for traffic then pulled out of the parking spot to follow. Two blocks later, Smythe ducked into a pub, and Brookes stopped. Trevor pointed to a call box a short distance away. "Call for a team to come keep an eye on our Mr. Smythe."

"Yes, sir." Brookes got out of the car and trotted to the box.

Ruth blew out a breath and flounced against the seat. "So much for watching him being a potential lead."

"Patience. It's all about patience. If we give Mr. Smythe enough rope, he will hang himself."

"If he's guilty."

Cold air blew into the car as Brookes opened the door and sank behind the wheel. "A couple of boys are on their way, sir. Shall we wait?"

Trevor shook his head. "Unless I miss my guess, Mr. Smythe will be here a while. He'll want to drink away his frustrations at not finding anyone home."

An hour later, the door to the pub opened, and Devon stumbled onto the sidewalk. He bumped into a woman and lifted his hat in apology. He turned south and sauntered along the pavement.

Brookes turned on the car and followed his progress. Unsurprisingly, he stopped in front of the brownstone he'd visited earlier.

Looking resolute, he climbed the stairs and banged on the door. It swung open, and he slipped inside.

Trevor turned to Ruth with a satisfied smile. "Our patience may have paid off. Would you care to join me?"

She rolled her eyes. "What do you think?"

He chuckled and helped her out of the vehicle. They hurried across the street and ascended the stairs. He lifted his hand to thump on the door but hesitated at the sudden sound of heated arguing. Knocking with the side of his fist, he shouted, "Devon Smythe, it's DI Gelson and Miss Brown. We'd like a word with you, please."

The voices broke off followed by scuffling then footsteps approaching. The door swung open, and Smythe looked at them in a mixture of confusion and irritation. "What can I do for you, Detective Inspector? I've told you everything I know." He scowled at Ruth. "And why is she here? She's not with the police."

"I thought you'd be happy to see us. Don't you want to get to the bottom of your son's death?"

His face brightened. "Do you have news?"

"Of a sort. May we come in?"

Smythe cast a furtive eye over his shoulder then back at Trevor. "Now is not a good time. Can you come back later?"

"What could possibly be more important than finding out about your son?"

"Well..."

"Devon! Don't leave the man standing at the door. Let him in."

A woman appeared from behind Smythe. Tall and blonde and well-coiffed. Wearing a dress that had to have cost more than his monthly salary, she gave him a regal smile and held out her hand. "Millicent Belvedere. How nice to finally meet you, Detective Inspector Gelson. Won't you come in?"

Trevor sensed Ruth's body go taut, but he had to give her credit; she didn't say a word. He took in the glance that passed between Smythe and Millicent—Smythe's uncertainty and Millicent's triumph. This would prove interesting. Of that he had no doubt.

Smythe turned on his heel and marched down the hall. Millicent widened the door and gestured for Trevor and Ruth to enter. They followed her behind Smythe and entered a large sitting room. Hugh Davenport lounged in one of the overstuffed chairs, a cigarette in one hand and a drink in the other. The satisfaction on his face reminded Trevor of a cat who had finished a bowl of cream.

Hugh took a deep drag from the cigarette and blew out a series of smoke rings. "How nice to finally meet you. To what do we owe the pleasure of your visit, Detective Inspector? And since when do you bring women as backup?"

Trevor shrugged. "Do I need backup, Mr. Davenport? This is Miss Brown. We came to speak with Mr. Smythe. But seeing you and your sister here has shed another light on the conversation, wouldn't you say?"

Hugh's eyes narrowed. He unfolded himself and stood. He put the glass down with a clink and held out his hand. "Where are my manners? How do you do, Miss Brown?"

Ruth shook his hand. "Confused, Mr. Davenport. As you can imagine. We didn't expect to find you and your sister here."

"Didn't you? DI Gelson isn't surprised. Are you, Gelson?"

Trevor shook his head. "No, but I had hoped to find your husband here, too."

Millicent moved closer to Hugh. Shock was quickly replaced by a sneer. "My husband is dead. You saw the skeleton. He walked out on me, and now he's dead. How dare you make a mockery of it."

"Surely you don't believe me to be that stupid, Mrs. Belvedere. You've been playing the part of the jilted wife for so long, you don't know how to do anything else."

Hugh guffawed and gave Millicent a one-armed hug. "He's got your number, Sis. Apparently our detective inspector has been round the block more than once."

She slid out from under his embrace. "Shut up, Hugh."

He looked petulant. "What? I'm just saying that he's smarter than you gave him credit for."

Millicent stomped her foot, the picture of a spoiled toddler. "And I said keep quiet."

Trevor turned to Devon Smythe. "Do you have anything you'd like to tell me about why you're here to see Mrs. Belvedere, or would you like us to lay it out?"

Smythe hung his head and didn't respond.

"So that's how it's to be? All right." He pulled a folded piece of paper from his coat pocket and handed it to Millicent. "That's a search warrant, Mrs. Belvedere. If you read it, you'll see we're here to look for the paintings you stole from Smythe and Nigel Winchester. A painting that is part of the set your husband and his friends smuggled out of Italy."

Arms crossed, her face held a belligerent stare. "Why give it to me?"

"This is your house."

"Says who?"

"The town registry. After Mr. Smythe came here earlier, we called to determine who owned the place. If you didn't want to be found, you shouldn't have used your real name."

"I've got nothing to hide."

Trevor gestured for the two uniformed bobbies to begin their search, and the men left the room. Thumps and bumps could be heard through the walls. Hugh finished his cigarette and crushed it in the ashtray at his elbow on the table. He swallowed the last of his drink then set the glass down with a bang. Rising, he pulled on his sleeves. "If you won't be needing me, Detective Inspector, I'll be on my way."

"Oh, but we will."

Hugh's smirk faltered then returned. He dropped back into the chair. "Fine."

The silence in the room grew. Millicent's eyes darted from Hugh to Smythe and back to Trevor. She licked her lips then adjusted her skirt and patted her hair. Smythe continued to study the floor as if it were the most interesting thing he had ever seen. Hugh seemed to watch the proceedings with calculated amusement.

Trevor heard Ruth shift behind him. What was he thinking when he brought her? He had allowed his admiration to override his good sense.

There. He had said it. He was taken by her. So much so, that it was clouding his judgment. Would she pay the price?

He turned slightly so he could see her. Catching her eye, he gave her what he hoped was a reassuring smile. Her face relaxed, and he nodded in response. Hugh snickered. Trevor's head whirled to find the man watching them with a mocking expression. That wouldn't do. He needed to regain the upper hand.

"Mr. Davenport. I'm happy to see you enjoying all of this. Then you won't mind a trip downtown, so we can discuss things further."

Hugh's eyes narrowed. "You're bluffing, Detective Inspector."

"I wouldn't be so sure, if I were you."

A muffled shout came from upstairs, and Trevor's glance darted from Hugh to Millicent as she yelped then covered her mouth. Her face was marked with guilt. Booted feet thundered down the stairs and approached. A minute later, one of the bobbies entered carrying three rolls of canvas. He unfurled one and held it up.

Smythe came alive and sputtered. "Hey, that's mine. You said you didn't take it. You liar!" He lunged at Hugh, and Millicent squealed. Trevor stuck out his foot. Smythe tripped over it and landed on the floor with a loud "oomph." Hugh jumped up and pointed at Millicent. "It was all her. I had nothing to do with it."

He reached into his pocket, whipped out a snub-nosed revolver, and waved it at Trevor. "I had nothing to do with the paintings or the murders. I'm not going down for this. She's the one. She's the one who planned the whole thing."

"Shut up!" Millicent's voice came out shrill and harsh. "Just shut up and put the gun away."

Hugh continued to brandish the weapon. "Don't come any closer. I don't want to shoot you, but I will."

Trevor retreated, hands held up in surrender. "Okay. Okay. I won't move. But Millicent's right; you should put down the gun. The situation will go easier on you if you do. We simply want to talk, Hugh. That's all."

"Yeah, right. That's what all you cops say. The next thing I know, I'll be cuffed and carted away in the wagon."

The bobby leaned forward and laid the painting on the end table.

Hugh swiveled toward him, the gun wavering.

Trevor lunged and knocked him to the floor. The gun fell with a clatter and slid toward Ruth who skittered out of its path. She bumped into Millicent who shrieked.

The two men wrestled to gain control of the weapon. Trevor grunted as they struggled. Millicent's playboy brother wasn't as soft as he appeared.

Hugh crawled toward the pistol, his hand straining forward. Inching. Inching. His fingers wrapped around the butt of the gun.

Trevor vaulted onto Hugh's back, but he shook Trevor off with a roar and leapt to his feet. Swinging the weapon around the room, he shouted, "Back off!"

The second bobby rushed into the room, and Hugh fired. The bullet pinged off a lamp, and Millicent screamed.

Hugh whirled and fired again. Millicent fell to the ground with a wail, blood saturating her blouse. Ruth dropped beside her. Devon cried out and covered his head.

Trevor leapt to his feet. "Hugh, you don't want to do this!"

Face red and perspiring freely, Hugh snarled. "How do you know what I want?"

"I know you are desperately afraid of going down for something that may not be your fault."

"May not? May not? It's definitely not my fault. I've been taking the heat for her since we were kids. I'm not doing it this time. I'm not!"

Millicent sobbed and clutched her arm as blood seeped between her fingers.

Trevor held out his hand. "Give me the gun, and we'll talk about this in a civilized manner. We can't do that while you're threatening us, and your sister needs medical attention. What do you say?"

Hugh's face contorted. "I say you're going to let me walk out of here. I'm not part of this. Let me go, and I'll disappear. I won't be a problem for anyone."

"I can't let you do that, Hugh. I need your help. You have information that will bring Ian's killer to justice. Do your brother-in-law one last favor by cooperating with us."

Hugh's head swung back and forth. He gestured with the gun for Trevor and the bobby to move away from the door. Millicent continued to whimper. He spoke through clenched teeth. "You're going to stand in that corner, and I'm going to leave. Don't try to stop me. Now move!" He looked at Devon. A sneer curled his lip. "Get up, you sniveling coward. Get over there with the coppers."

Devon climbed to his feet and edged his way to the corner with Trevor and the bobby.

A grim smile filled Hugh's face. "Much better. I'll just be on my way."

"Hugh, don't leave me," Millicent cried out. "I need you."

"You need someone to take the fall. It's not going to happen. Life's going to change for you, my fair-haired sister. You'll be just like everyone else at Holloway Prison. Should do you some good."

Hugh cast a glance at the door then backed toward it. Trevor gave Ruth a reassuring smile, and Hugh snorted a laugh. "Think you've got everything under control? Trying to let your girlfriend know she'll be safe? Maybe I'll take her with me as my ticket to freedom. How's that sound?"

"Like a bad idea. The charges are stacking up against you. Do you want to add kidnapping?"

"I'll do what I've got to do to save my skin." He pointed the gun at Ruth. "Get up. Millicent can take of herself. You're coming with me."

Ruth rose, hands in the air.

Millicent wailed loudly. "It hurts, Hugh. It hurts so bad."

"Shut up! Help will be here soon enough. A little pain is good for you, sis. You've certainly caused enough for everyone else. Including that poor sap of a husband. Although killing him was probably the best thing you could have done for him—taking him out of his misery of being married to you."

"It was you, Millicent?" Devon said. "How could you do that? He loved you."

Millicent's cries grew louder.

Hugh opened the door, grabbed Ruth, and clutched her in front of him with his left arm. His right hand continued to grip the weapon. "I've had enough of this!"

Trevor clenched his fists. He never should have brought Ruth with him. He had let her talk him into it, and now she was in harm's way. The commissioner would have his badge. "Calm down. We can still discuss this rationally."

"No, we can't!" Spittle flew from Hugh's mouth. He yanked on Ruth, and they stumbled out the door.

Trevor's heart sank. Her safety was out of his hands now.

Millicent continued to weep, and Devon snapped, "Quit your crying, Millicent. He's gone."

A muffled shout met their ears. A shot rang out. Then another.

Chapter Thirty-One

Ruth lifted her water glass. "Congratulations on figuring out who killed Ian. I would imagine Detective Inspector Gelson always gets his man. Or in this case, his woman."

Trevor's dark eyes pierced hers as he grinned. "And I would imagine you always get your story, Ruth." He shook his head and looked grieved. "I shouldn't have let you accompany me. You could have been hurt, or killed. It's a good thing the commissioner has bigger fish to fry, although there will be a report going in my record. I suppose it could be worse."

Ruth frowned. He was a good man; he didn't deserve to have his record besmirched because of her. He was doing his job. What more did they want? She forced a smile on her face and nudged Varis's shoulder. "You should have seen the DI, Varis. He was so calm. I was terrified. He kept things from getting out of hand."

Trevor shook his head. "No, I didn't. He took you as a hostage. Or don't you remember?"

"Hugh wasn't going to shoot me. He was shaking more than me. I knew I'd be all right even though I didn't know you had officers waiting at the door for anyone who came out."

He tugged at his collar. "That's why you're the reporter, and I'm the policeman. I make those arrangements as a matter of course. Remember, a criminal's first instinct is to escape."

Varis picked up her fork and stabbed a chunk of potato. "What I don't understand is why Devon's son was killed."

Trevor drank deeply. "It was an accident. Because of his father's connection to the case, we all thought it might be a warning of some kind. But it really was a coincidence. However, the builders have a lot of explaining to do, because his death was a result of several unsafe situations on the job. And they knew it. That's why they were so hostile when Miss Brown started nosing around. They cut corners, and poor Devon Junior died as a result."

Varis swallowed her food. "But how did Hugh get involved? He wasn't there the night Millicent killed Ian. Like everyone else, he thought Ian had walked out on her."

Ruth laid down her cutlery and sat back. "He lied about being in touch with Millicent. He and their sister both kept ties to her after their parents disowned her. A couple of nights after you discovered the skeleton, she contacted him in a panic and told him everything. When he heard about the paintings, he decided to cash in on them. His plan was to lay the groundwork so we would arrest Millicent, then he could be left with the artwork. What he didn't count on was Nigel's unwillingness to sell his piece, so Hugh killed him. He used the same method Millicent had used to murder Ian, so it would point to the same culprit."

Varis shuddered. "To kill someone over a painting. How cruel and pointless."

Trevor nodded. "Murders always are, but this was about the money, not the painting. The piece was one of a set of four. After the war was over, he could have sold them for a significant amount of money and probably be set for life."

Ruth said, "What happens to them now?"

"We've taken photographs, and the originals are on their way to the British Museum, where they will be guarded for the duration of the war. Then they'll be returned to their rightful owner in Italy."

"It seems a shame that Devon Smythe may have to go to jail. It will be hard on his wife. First to lose her son then her husband."

Trevor wiped his mouth on the linen napkin then tossed it onto his empty plate. "He may not have to serve. He had nothing to do with the murders, and he's proving himself quite cooperative about providing information about the original theft. The courts may go easy on him."

Varis's face relaxed. "I hope so. I know he deserves to be punished, but life will be tough enough without his only son."

The door banged open, and cold air swept into the restaurant. Sergeant Phillips rushed to their table. "Sir, I'm sorry to disturb you. A couple of the boys found the body of a young woman in Bushy Park. She's been strangled."

Trevor stood and waved at their waitress. She hurried over, and he pulled money from his pocket and pressed the coins in her hand. He held out his arm to Ruth, with a grin. "Are you coming, Miss Brown? Your journalistic curiosity might shed an intriguing perspective on the case."

Returning his smile, Ruth jumped up and tucked her hand in the crook of his elbow. Another story. Just what she'd been waiting for. And better yet. Working a case with Trevor. "Where is Bushy Park?"

THE END

What did you think of *Under Ground?*

Thank you so much for purchasing *Under Ground*. You could have selected any number of books to read, but you chose this book.

I hope it added encouragement and exhortation to your life. If so, it would be nice if you could share this book with your family and friends by posting to Facebook (www.facebook.com) and/or Twitter (www.twitter.com).

If you enjoyed this book and found some benefit in reading it, I'd appreciate it if you could take some time to post a review on Amazon, Goodreads, Kobo, GooglePlay, Apple Books, or other book review site of your choice. Your feedback and support will help me to improve my writing craft for future projects and make this book even better.

Thank you again for your purchase.

Blessings,
Linda Shenton Matchett

Read the next installment in the Ruth Brown mystery series:

Available at your favorite online retailer or independent bookstore.

Visit http://www.LindaShentonMatchett.com/p/books.html

Under Cover

Chapter One

A scream pierced the air. Ruth Brown's head jerked up at the sound, halting her rush through London's lunchtime crowds on Old Street.

There was a motion from above. A body hurtled to the ground from the brick building across the street. Her eyes widened, and a wave of nausea swept over her.

She turned toward her best friend, Varis Gladstone, whose blue eyes bulged in her whitened face. Murmurs rose from the throng who pointed to the open window in the building, one of many manufacturing plants that had been converted to war-material production two years ago after Hitler declared war on England. A canvas shade flapped in the breeze.

From amidst the mob, a shout rang out. "Is anyone a doctor? We need a doctor!"

Ruth tugged at Varis's arm. "Come on. They need our help."

Varis pulled away. "No they don't. We're not medical professionals."

"Surely we can do something of value. I'm going over."

Ruth threaded her way through the mass of people. A lanky, dark-haired man bullied his way toward her. His shoulder slammed into hers, and he scowled when she stumbled. She glared at his retreating back then broke through the circle that had formed around the lifeless figure lying on the concrete walkway. Ruth froze at the sight of the familiar face and flowing red hair of her friend Amelia Harrell. A sob sounded from behind her, and Ruth turned. Varis stood with her arms wrapped around her middle, tears streaming down her cheeks.

<hr>

A pair of helmeted bobbies cordoned off the accident scene with wooden barriers while several other officers corralled the surging mob of gawkers. Waiting to be interviewed, Ruth and Varis huddled near one of the police vehicles. Ruth's gaze strayed from the blanket-covered corpse on the ground to the ogling faces behind the barricade. She chewed on her lower lip and trembled when Varis's icy hands grabbed at her arm.

How had Amelia fallen from the building? With her fear of heights, she wouldn't have intentionally stood so close to an open window. Maybe she didn't have a choice. Did anyone inside see it happen? Were there others in the room with her? Ruth's fists tightened, fingernails biting into her palms.

"Varis, this is taking too long. I'm going inside to see what I can find out."

"Must you?"

A sigh slipped from Ruth's lips at the wan expression on Varis's face. "No, I guess I can wait. Do you want to find somewhere to sit down?"

Varis shook her head, silent tears trickling from her eyes. Ruth fumbled into her purse and drew out a handkerchief. She dabbed at the wetness on her friend's face. "We could go home. The police can come see us there. Would you like that?"

"Miss?"

Ruth turned toward the voice, and recognition dawned. "Sergeant Phillips. I haven't seen you since Detective Inspector Gelson and you solved the case about the skeleton found under my house. Has the murderer gone to trial yet?"

A grim smile creased the man's face. "You have a good memory, Miss Brown. I'm afraid the wheels of justice move slowly. The trial hasn't started yet." He looked at Varis. "Nice to see you, Miss Gladstone."

Varis nodded mutely.

"Are you still chasing stories for the Associated Press, Miss Brown?"

"Yes, keep your eye on *The Times.* I submitted an article this morning."

"Good for you." Phillips jerked his head toward the cordoned-off area. "One of the folk I've already interviewed indicated you knew the deceased. Could you answer some questions? Either here or down at the station, if that would be more comfortable."

"Here is fine, and her name was Amelia Harrell," Ruth said.

"Ah, yes, of course. My apologies. How long did you know Miss Harrell?"

Ruth's chin trembled. "About six months, I think. Sometimes it felt much longer. We clicked right away. Seemed to have a lot of the same interests."

Varis broke in with a tremulous grin. "And sense of humor. Amelia was a bit of a prankster, and so are you, Ruth."

"I must admit we did come up with some good ones." Ruth swallowed against the growing lump in her throat.

Phillips pushed his tan fedora back on his head. "Was Miss Harrell married, single? Did she go out much? I'll speak with her employer, but anything you could add would be helpful."

A warm breeze lifted Ruth's curls, and her purse slipped from her shoulder. She tucked her pocketbook under her arm and narrowed her eyes. "I'm not sure what I can tell you. We sort of lived in the moment. You know how it is. You get too close to someone, and the next thing you know they're gone. Lost in a bombing raid."

She scrubbed at her face. "I don't remember where she is...um...was from. Somewhere in the north, near Scotland. She was dating some guy for a while. She talked about him but never brought him around."

Phillips scribbled in the notebook engulfed in his large hand. "She wasn't seeing him currently? Did she ever mention his name?"

"I think they broke up. His name is Owen, but she never gave us a last name."

"Wonder why not."

Varis colored. "A few of her coworkers had a theory, but we thought she simply wanted some privacy."

"A theory?"

Ruth shrugged. "Married. Some of them thought he might be married, but Amelia wasn't like that. She was a good girl, very educated. In fact, she spoke several languages. I think her dad was an ambassador or with the Foreign Service, something like that. She didn't talk about him much. I gathered he was a bit overbearing when she was growing up."

"What was she like?" Phillips asked.

Varis's face lit up. "Kind. Generous. She'd give you the shirt off her back. The life of the party, too. Quite chipper, knew how to make everyone laugh. Didn't seem to ever get upset or depressed. Even with the bombs coming every night like they do."

A frown wrinkled Phillips's forehead. "Then why would she kill herself?"

Ruth's voice rose. "Kill herself?"

Phillips pointed to the gaping window. "She jumped out the window. Perhaps she was distraught over this boyfriend. Or maybe it was her job. Women can't always take the pressure of being in the workforce. Maybe she should have stayed at home."

Ruth drew herself to her full height and met Phillips's eyes with a piercing stare. "And do what, Sergeant? Roll bandages? Knit hats for soldiers? There's real work to be done, and we women are quite capable to doing it. Besides, we just told you she didn't get depressed. To kill herself over a man she had been casually seeing? Her job? No. There are any number of reasons for her death. Maybe it was an accident, although I doubt it. Amelia hated heights and would have stood far from an open window. She wasn't 'distraught.' She liked her job and enjoyed her friends."

Phillips raised an eyebrow. "Okay, so Miss Harrell didn't kill herself. If it was an accident, then she should have been more careful."

"Are you always this callous when interviewing witnesses, Sergeant, or is it just when you're talking to me?" Ruth slung her purse back on her shoulder and crossed her arms.

Phillips reddened. "I'm sorry, Miss Brown. I don't mean to be insensitive."

Ruth's voice faltered. "Amelia Harrell was neither careless nor suicidal. Do you think murder has found me again, Sergeant Phillips?"

Acknowledgments

Although writing a book is a solitary task, it is not a solitary journey. There have been many who have helped and encouraged me along the way.

My parents, Richard and Jean Shenton, who presented me with my first writing tablet and encouraged me to capture my imagination with words. Thanks, Mom and Dad!

Scribes212 – my ACFW online critique group: Valerie Goree, Marcia Lahti, and the late Loretta Boyett (passed on to Glory, but never forgotten). Without your input, my writing would not be nearly as effective.

Eva Marie Everson – my mentor/instructor with Christian Writers' Guild. You took a timid, untrained student and turned her into a writer. Many thanks!

SincNE, and the folks who coordinate the Crimebake Writing Conference. I have attended many writing conferences, but without a doubt, Crimebake is one of the best. The workshops, seminars, panels, critiques, and every tiny aspect are well-executed, professional, and educational.

Special thanks to Hank Phillippi Ryan, Halle Ephron, and Roberta Isleib for your encouragement and spot-on critiques of my work during the early years of my career.

Paula Proofreader (https://paulaproofreader.wixsite.com/home): I'm so glad I found you! My work is cleaner because of your eagle eye. Any mistakes are completely mine.

Much appreciation goes to Kevin J. Duffy, Captain, US Army, Lieutenant, NH State Police (retired), who worked with me at the shooting range and answered myriad questions throughout the course of writing this book. I'm hopeful that his comprehensive knowledge and suggestions made *Under Ground* richer for his assistance. Any errors are my own. Kevin: thank you for your friendship and for your service to our great country.

Thanks to my Book Brigade who provide information, encouragement, and support.

A heartfelt thank you to my brothers, Jack Shenton and Douglas Shenton, and my sister, Susan Shenton Greger for being enthusiastic cheerleaders during my writing journey. Your support means more than you'll know.

My husband, Wes, deserves special kudos for understanding my need to write. Thank you for creating my writing room – it's perfect, and I'm thankful for it every day. Thank you for your willingness to accept a house that's a bit cluttered, laundry that's not always done, and meals on the go. I love you.

And finally, to God be the glory. I thank Him for giving me the gift of writing and the inspiration to tell stories that shine the light on His goodness and mercy.

Other Titles

Romance

Love's Harvest, Wartime Brides, Book 1
Love's Rescue, Wartime Brides, Book 2
Love's Belief, Wartime Brides, Book 3
Love's Allegiance, Wartime Brides, Book 4
Love Found in Sherwood Forest
On the Rails
A Love Not Forgotten (Coming March 2020)
A Doctor in the House (The Hope of Christmas Collection)

Mystery

Under Fire
Under Ground
Under Cover

Murder of Convenience, Women of Courage, Book 1

Non-Fiction

WWII Word Find, Volume 1

Linda Shenton Matchett writes about ordinary people who did extraordinary things in days gone by. She is a volunteer docent and archivist at the Wright Museum of WWII and a trustee for her local public library. Born in Baltimore, Maryland, a stone's throw from Fort McHenry, she has lived in historical places most of her life. Now located in central New Hampshire, Linda's favorite activities include exploring historic sites and immersing herself in the imaginary worlds created by other authors.

Website/blog: http://www.LindaShentonMatchett.com
Facebook: http://www.facebook.com/LindaShentonMatchettAuthor
Pinterest: http://www.pinterest.com/lindasmatchett
Amazon: https://www.amazon.com/Linda-Shenton-Matchett/e/B01DNB54S0
Goodreads: http://www.goodreads.com/author_linda_matchett
Bookbub: http://www.bookbub.com/authors/linda-shenton-matchett